HARD

COPYRIGHT

Cover by Book Cover by Design
Photograph by Eric Battershell
Editing by Editing 4 Indies

ISBN: 9781980787983

Other Books by Donna Alam

Chapter One

PAISLEY

One phrase can sum up my whole move to London.

That didn't go quite as planned.

Even closer on the timeline scale, if someone had said a month ago I'd be sitting in a coffee shop waiting for a well-hung stranger to arrive, I'd have told you to keep taking the medicine. You know, for your kind of crazy.

What's worse, I'm not even waiting for said stranger for myself, but rather because of business. No—not the whoring kind of business. Although, if it weren't for my friend, Chastity, I may well have already begun to sell my body in order to eat. But that's another story. One with an unhappy ending, strangely enough, beginning just two months ago. But I don't have time to let my mind wander down *that* particular memory lane of distaste as the door to the hipster-chic coffee shop opens, and a man steps into the space. His large silhouette is framed by the afternoon light, highlighting the cut of his dark suit and how it fits perfectly to his broad shoulders.

I turn my wrist, glancing down at my watch; on time *and* dressed to impress. He certainly seems to be taking this interview seriously.

From my table in the far corner—chosen so as not to upset the late afternoon crowd with talk of dick and pussy and other such things—I stand and wave. It's weird how quickly I've become desensitised. These days, I can discuss the merits of butt plugs and clitoral stimulation with the best of them. Not that I'd necessarily choose to have these conversations in public, with strangers, but I digress.

The arc of afternoon sunlight cuts out as the door closes behind him, making me wonder why these places are always so dark. No matter as his long legs eat up the space between us, his intense gaze flicking my way. *Wow. He's even more handsome in the flesh.* I add a smile to my greeting, unable to resist glancing down once more at the tablet on the table in front of me. A tablet filled with the black and white stills I've been examining all day.

All. Day.

More than is professionally acceptable, for sure. I tell myself it's nerves—that it's because I've never done this part of the job before. Interviewing potential candidates. But I don't know why I'm bothering to lie to myself because I know I've become a dirty ole perve. It's what happens when your new job includes studying a person's photographic résumé, one that includes pictures of the cut of his jawline, abs, and cock. And then there are one or two on-the-job photos—and I mean *on the job*. A woman bent at the waist over a table, his body bowed, her blonde hair twisted in his hand.

I drag my mind from the images as the man hesitates on the other side of our table for two. Butterflies with wings like vultures beat in my chest cavity. I've never interviewed anyone before, porn star or not.

Imagine him naked, my mind whispers. Wait—that's probably what has me twitterpated in the first place.

Honey brown hair and dark eyes, the man is gorgeous. And dressed as he is, he certainly looks at home in the heart of the city—he has that whole *captain of industry vibe* going on. But on my second look, the tiny display of hesitancy in the jut of his brow immediately sets me at ease.

'Hi, I'm Paisley.' I offer him my hand across the table. 'You're expecting Chastity, I know,' I babble as he presses his large hand against mine. *Large hand. Strong wrist. The tensing of a large bicep beneath his sleeve.* 'But she was called away at the last minute. So you got me!' I make a stupid jazz hands motion as the hottie looks back, bemused? Amused? Probably both those things.

'Chastity,' the low rumble of his voice repeats, sending a shiver of appreciation down my spine. Since I'd moved to London a year ago, accents have become my thing. His accent, I'm going to guess is . . .

'You're Scottish, right?'

He agrees with a slight incline of his head.

'And I know what you're thinking; it's a little oxymoronic for a purveyor of porn to be named Chastity.'

I might snort a little, knowing Chas would kill me for using the P word. *It's the dirty connotations in porn*, I almost hear Chas's cut-glass accent intone. *All that deep throating and banging. It just doesn't do it for the mass female audience.*

'You had me at porn.' Amusement colours his tone as he pulls the chair from under the table, lowering his frame into it. And if I'm not mistaken, he's fighting a smile. Hazel eyes, I realise, golden flecks matching his hair, and a large though lean frame. The camera would eat him up. Given half the chance, I think I'd do the same.

Except for the porn thing.

Hell, what was his name again? I've been perving all day at his stills, but I can't remember his name? *No matter*, I decide, babbling again.

'Okay. What can I tell you?' The hottie looks on expectantly as I begin what Chastity calls *the company spiel*. 'Fast Girl Media produces women and couple-centric erotica with an emphasis on seduction, romance, and sensuality. We provide a highly curated experience from beautiful cinematographic sequences to sensual photographic stills. Also available on the website is an extensive collection of erotic literature for a different kind of stimulation.' I pause, feeling a pinprick of discomfort as the barista suddenly appears, placing a tiny white cup in front of him. At least I wasn't in the middle of mouthing the word cock or dildo. Not that I physically mouth those things for the company, you understand. In fact, I don't *do* anything, other than a little assisting. And a little admin

As the hottie gestures to my cup, it suddenly occurs to me that I didn't see him order his own drink. But as I murmur a *no thanks* and the barista retreats, I inhale and begin again.

'You're a little older than I imagined—'

'Is that so?' His mouth hitches in one corner, and good Lord, the man has dimples. Well, at least one of them.

And that accent? I bet he gives amazing aural. He just exudes poise and a taunting, relaxed kind of confidence. So much so, he's totally making me blush. It's almost as though he knows exactly what I've been looking at. Hell, imagining. These are all good signs, I decide. I want him on the job. I mean, I want to *give* him the job.

And me a vicarious screwing.

'W-what I mean to say is, your age totally works in your favour. And,' I add quickly, 'it does not in any way diminish your attraction.' He already knows this, but the advice Chastity supplied was to pander to their egos. 'Or indeed your suitability.'

'Suitability?' His coffee cup half conceals his sultry smirk as he lifts it to his lips.

'Yes,' I say, making a judgment call I know Chas will get behind. 'We have a shoot coming up next week. It'll be filmed on location—Barcelona, to be exact. So providing you can supply the appropriate paperwork in time and don't have an aversion to anal, I'd like to offer you the gig.'

His response has me squealing a little as I jump up from my seat.

I wipe the coffee explosion from my face as my mind intones once again, *Well, that didn't go at all as planned.*

Chapter Two

KEIR

'Jesus Christ,' I reply, coughing and trying to wipe both the coffee and the smile from my face. 'That's some offer. But I only came in to grab a coffee.' I pass her a paper napkin from the dispenser as her expression falters, the smile quickly slipping from her face.

'You mean you're not . . . ' Her words trail off as she pats her face dry, bending at the waist to swipe the electronic tablet on the table, the action causing the front of her dress to gape. *Full, soft breasts, and a barely there black bra.* I drag my reluctant gaze away but not before I get another eyeful as the tablet lights up.

'Oh, fuck,' she mutters, and somehow, this doesn't sound as harsh in her soft, American accent. She flips the thing upside down, snapping ramrod straight.

'That's not me, and that's definitely not my dick,' I answer, chuckling as she turns suddenly and begins rifling through a bag the size of Sicily hanging on the back of her chair.

And the rear view is as fantastic as the front.

'Antonio Uccello!' she calls in the vein of *eureka! a*s she pulls a battered white envelope from her bag. 'I'm looking for Antonio Uccello.'

'I'd say you were just looking at quite a bit of him.' Even in the low lighting, it's easy to see the two distinct spots of pink colouring her cheeks. Leaning back in my chair, I fold my arms across my chest, feeling a certain satisfaction at her flustered expression. It's been a long time since I've allowed myself to flirt—even this little bit. It feels good. Gratifying. 'And that's not me.'

'Hell,' she breathes out softly. 'Your accent should've been my first clue. You know, with this name.' She waves the envelope as she takes her seat again.

'Not really. I went to school with a lad called Aldo De Luca. And you couldn't find a more Scottish sounding fella.'

'You can never tell a book by its cover, huh?'

'Looking at you? I'd say that's especially true.' I let my eyes deliberately wander over her again. A navy blue dress printed with tiny birds, the kind of dress I've heard Sadie, my mate's wife, describe as *vintage*. 'You don't look like the kind of girl who works for a porn company.' She looks like she might work in an art gallery or something. Then again, one girl's art is another man's porn, I suppose.

'Erotica,' she replies, a touch defensively. 'Visually artistic with an emphasis on seduction, romance, and sensuality.'

'And fucking. I bet there's plenty of that going on.'

I regret my words the second they hit the air. I'm usually much more circumspect around the fairer sex. *Even those who work in porn*. That thought, of course, leads to another. Does *she* do porn? While gorgeous, she doesn't look the type—not just because of a lack of platinum hair, or long fingernails, or silicone rack. Maybe she stars in the girl-next-door type scenes. All startling blue eyes and pink lips . . .

Sir, you want to put that where?

I shake my head, dislodging the inappropriateness again.

'There's nothing wrong with sex,' she says, her spine straightening again. And the front of her dress pulling a little too tight . . .

Unless you're not getting any, I don't say. And I'd know because I'm not. Getting any, that is. And I haven't for a while. *A conscious decision*, I remind myself.

'True,' I answer, uncrossing my arms. 'But I'm not likely to be starring in porn at this time.'

'Yes, well, I'm sorry for the confusion,' she replies as I stand, tilting her head to indicate the offending tablet on the table between us. Next to it is an empty cappuccino cup plus a dainty plate with a dollop of cream and a slice of strawberry abandoned on it. 'Apologies for the, er . . . '

'Full frontal nude?' I supply. She nods her head rapidly, big blue eyes blinking back at me. 'Well, here's to hoping he rocks your world when he does arrive.' At odds with the tightness in my belly, I offer a bawdy wink as I pull myself away.

'What are you smiling about?' Flynn, my assistant, asks as I walk back into the office.

'What? Am I not allowed to smile now?'

'Doesn't happen fucking often,' he says, his Aussie accent as thick as the peanut butter he has spread on his toast.

'What have I told you about that mouth?'

'I'm on my lunch break,' he protests, picking the last square of toast balanced on a tea plate on his chest.

'Remind me why I keep you around again?'

'Because you couldn't find your way out of a lunch sack without me. And also because I know where the bodies are buried.' He kicks his feet down from his desk. 'Come on, what's put that smile on your face? You went out for coffee looking about as happy as a bastard on Father's Day. And anyway, where's my Frappuccino?'

His words piss on my mood immediately, reminding me why I was in a foul mood when I left.

'Who in the hell schedules a business dinner on a Friday night?'

'Ah, there's my little ray of sunshine. Didn't we already establish someone hoping to get you relaxed enough to screw up? Just drunk enough, just sloppy enough, to promise them something you don't want to deliver. Whether it be a signed contract or a night in your bed.'

'Joe's not my type,' I grumble. 'Beer bellies don't do it for me.'

Joe Shelby is in construction, the same as me. I pass a decent amount of work his way. *Mainly subcontracted.* I'm currently trying to buy a disused convent from the local archdiocese, and the sly fucker thinks I haven't realised he's trying to get into bed with me. *Figuratively, at least.* Not so figurative is his daughter, Amelia's, interest. But I only have time for one female in my life, and that's my own child, so neither of those scenarios interest me. But in business, you've got to play it canny.

'The daughter, though? She's hot.'

'Aye, hot like a stolen car. And just as much trouble.'

'I'd still do her.'

'And that, right there, is why I'm the boss and you're the PA.'

'Boss or not, I'd still go for a piece of that.'

'And I wouldn't screw her with your dick, so let's call it a difference of opinion and move the fuck on.'

'You're the boss.' Flynn picks the iPad up from his desk. 'And I am the lowly serf. So you've got the conference call in fifteen, and the plans for the Barclay job are on your desk. The architect for Ullridge is waiting on a callback and . . . '

Flynn's voice suddenly becomes background noise, the afternoon's demands no longer of importance as I notice a tiny coffee stain on the cuff of my white shirt. I can't resist examining it, my mind roaming back to the pretty girl in the coffee shop.

I wonder if she really *does* porn?

It's late in the evening when the cab drops me home. It's been a long day, and I'm in a bastard of a mood, but it's my own fault. I should've said no to dinner. *A dinner that dragged more hours into my workday.* But truthfully, where work is concerned, I find it hard to draw the line. I suppose it's a healthy kind of fear that keeps me powering along, but it's also tiring. While I might now wear a tailored suit to work rather than a hard hat and steel toe-capped boots, my days are no less taxing. The difference is, these days, the things that drive me aren't the basics of an existence; food in my belly or a roof over my head. I won't ever need to worry about where my next meal is coming from, or how I'll pay my bills.

Yet I'm still jogging on that treadmill.

Like tonight. I could've said no—should've said no. And now, I'm pretty pissed off that work has once again eaten into my me time. I know, *me time* sounds a bit gay, but Friday nights are the only time I get to myself.

I spend my days working my arse off—five days a week, often fourteen-hour days. Outside of that, I'm all about Sorcha, my little girl.

The life of a single parent is absolutely rewarding but sometimes hard.

I'm lucky I have Agnes, Sorcha's pseudo granny, to help. Though I pay her well to head up our home, she's really more like family. She's more of a mother to me than my own ever was and loves Sorcha with the fierceness of any grandmother tied to a child through blood. You might say that little girl is the central hub from which the spokes of both of our lives turn.

There's nothing like bringing a child into the world to set your priorities straight, I think as I close the front door with a quiet *click*. And nothing more compelling than being the sole person responsible for that life. As a parent, you'd chop off your right arm for your little one if that was the only path. Forfeit your life for the sake of theirs.

I walk through the darkened house until I reach the kitchen where I pour myself a generous couple of fingers of whisky, before taking the stairs to the first floor at a swift pace.

I'm tired; the bone-aching kind. But it's another kind of bone I'm concentrating on now. After I'd closed my office door this afternoon, I went straight to my computer to Google the names of women-centric porn companies with bases in the London area . . . because I couldn't remember the hot girl's name or who she worked for. I remember it had something to do with bad girls, but of course, I'd remember that. Because bad girls used to be a favourite of mine, B.D. that is. *Before divorce.*

I remember her face as clear as day. Deep blue eyes and discomforted pink cheeks. The way she twisted the strands of her long, dark hair between her pale fingers. And that soft, American accent. But as I was pondering some of her very obvious charms . . . her name came back to me in a blinding flash.

Paisley.

Who calls their kid that? May as well have called her herringbone, or polka dot, or something equally as ridiculous.

And then I found it—Fast Girl Media. *Funny, I used to be fond of fast girls, too.*

So I did what any man shielded by a closed door and a PA would do. I watched a few *highly curated cinematographic images* in search of the lovely Paisley. Or, to put it another way, I spent more time than I had available on my calendar watching high-end women-centric porn.

And what a glorious afternoon it was.

Unfortunately, though—or maybe fortunately— Paisley wasn't in any of the shots. And I paid good attention. She definitely wasn't featured having her pussy licked or *licking* pussy. *Like I said, women-centric. And fucking fine with me.*

But I digress because my *me time* is calling.

I push open the door to my darkened bedroom, toeing off my shoes as I take a mouthful of my drink, relishing the smooth slide of it down my throat. Tomorrow morning, Sorcha has a ballet class, then we have a million other things planned. Sunday, I'll play rugby with the lads, then we'll all go to lunch. So I'd better make this next hour count.

I put down my drink and pull off my tie, flipping the light low before making quick work of the rest of my clothing.

I work bloody hard. Take care of my family. Look after my body. I eat right and drink plenty of water. Go to the gym when I can. Self-care, they call it. I read that in one of those glossy women's magazines in a dentist's waiting room.

But it's the other kind of self-care I have in mind tonight. The kind that has my hand sinking into my boxer briefs as soon as my slacks hit the deck.

I let out a groan, long and low, as I take my cock into my hand, my body relaxing with a distinct bone-melting kind of relief.

Today has been a long day.

Fucking Joe, I think, tightening my grip on my dick. Did he really think bringing his daughter was going to make the difference? And did she really think, as she slid her shiny red fingernails up my thigh, that I'd give in—to either of her suggestions?

Mutually beneficial relationships, my left bollock.

Because I never mix business and pleasure. And Joe is a cock of the first fucking order. And Amelia, his daughter, reminds me too much of my ex-wife. Hard-on killer right there. But I persevere, bringing my semi back with a swift squeeze even though I feel like a deviant.

Joe's daughter isn't the reason I feel conflicted. Nor is it because I have my cock in my hand because come on, I'm a bloke—and a single one at that. A red-blooded, sex-starved, heterosexual fucker.

Self-inflicted sex starved, but still.

Celibate, I almost hear my mate Will spit from behind. But it's not Will I'm thinking about. *My deviancy doesn't swing that way.* I'm not even thinking about the women I've watched on screen today. Because I'm thinking about Paisley. Or rather, thinking about *fucking* Paisley. And I have been since she'd jumped up from her chair when I'd sprayed coffee over her and she'd flashed me more than just her shocked expression.

Shiny black stocking tops. A flash of frilly garter belt.

'*Eungh.*'

I slide my hand over the head of my cock, gripping it a little tighter on the backslide as I imagine flipping that flirty little dress up and over her round arse to find out what kind of knickers she was wearing.

Lacy, I'll bet.

At the thought of my fingertips trailing the peachy crack of her backside, my body bows. One hand falls to the mattress to support myself while the other begins to slowly jack.

Fuck, she looked like she could've been a handful. Enough tits and arse for my hands. As she'd reached for her electronic tablet, her dress had pulled just a little too tight over her breasts, the space between the buttons gaping and flashing a little black bra and a delicious swell of soft flesh.

But fuck, she was too young for me. She only looked about twenty-three.

I'm not usually interested in younger women. Well, not especially.

Okay, so no more than the next straight, celibate bloke with a cock in his hand.

'*Jesus, fuck!*'

My grip is firm as I slide my hand along my length, twisting just the right amount at the head. Lube would help, but I'm too close. *Yes, already*. Besides, I doubt my knees would operate if I took a step towards the nightstand. Instead, I slide the precum from my tip to work against the drag as I imagine her sitting in front of me on the bed. Imagine her there in her dark, gossamer underwear, her hair curled around her shoulders, looking so innocent and pristine.

Innocent. The girl who works for an adult entertainment company.

Fuck, fancy that.

I work myself harder, my hand sliding from root to tip, my knees connecting with the mattress as the point of no return hits me, liquid heat shooting from spine to tip. I close my eyes as Paisley pants, opening her mouth as I prepare to defile her with strands of milky—

'Daddy?'

The door handle rattles, and I almost give myself whiplash as my head snaps in response to the sound.

Big head, little head. Who'll win the battle now?

'Daddy,' Sorcha's voice calls a little louder. 'Why is the door locked?'

'B . . . because I need a moment,' I call back, my voice a touch hoarse.

'What? I mean, pardon?' she asks, correcting herself.

The handle rattles again, and this time, I really do feel like a deviant as, up against the clock, I begin to wank furiously.

'Come on, you fucker,' I mutter.

'Daddy, I can't hear you,' she calls, frustrated. And she's not the only one.

'Go back to bed, darlin'. I'll be out in a minute,' I say louder before going back to muttering again. 'What the fuck happened to the sleepover? Oh, fuck!'

My knees do buckle now as the fire turns white hot, building at the base of my spine this time.

'The handle won't turn,' she whines, 'it's too *hard.*'

Hard and aching and almost ready to blow.

'Go back to bed,' I grate out harshly.

'I can't. Agnes is in my room, and she's snoring. And I have a tummy ache.'

'And I've got fucking ball ache,' I mumble, past the point of rationality—too far past the point of no return.

Or so I'd thought. The image of my scantily clad Paisley evaporates like the dream as reality comes crashing back in.

'Dad-deee-*bleurgggh.*'

Yep, that is the sound of my daughter vomiting.

And the sound of my cock retracting and my balls crawling away from my hand.

'*Daddy,*' comes her pitiful wail.

Me time, I think, dropping my head. Being a parent is so hard sometimes.

Chapter Three

PAISLEY

'Paisley!'

'Oh, somebody's in trou-ble!' Max trills from beside me.

'Not again,' I grumble, pulling myself up from the sofa and wrapping my robe tighter, following Chastity's voice to her gleaming commercial-grade kitchen.

Her golden hair in large rollers, she stands by the open door of the dishwasher as steam billows out.

'Why is my dishwasher full of dildos?' she asks.

'Because you told me to load them in the dishwasher,' I reply, gesturing with an open palm to a job well done even as the realisation dawns that this is somehow mistake number 221 for the week. And I'm suddenly pleased I didn't tell her about the interview yesterday . . .

'I *asked* you, not told,' she corrects with the patience of a teacher dealing with an underachieving child. 'But I didn't think for one minute you'd bring them home.'

'What was I supposed to do with them?' I ask perplexed. 'Is that what the rubber gloves were for?' My face scrunches with distaste because *eww! Hand washing other people's fun from silicone?* 'Please don't say yes because that would be a new low—at a time that already feels like rock bottom.'

'I meant in the studio dishwasher not the dishwasher at home, for fuck's sake.'

I will never get used to the way she sounds when she swears. She looks like she's just tumbled from heaven, all cherubic cheeks, blond ringlets, and doe eyes, and she's just so goddamned posh, both how she looks and sounds, and is at complete odds with what sometimes comes out of her mouth. Especially when we're on set and she's giving out directions.

Milos, darling, if you could pull out of her before you come, we'll get the money shot . . . yes, all over her bottom, if you will. Deena, can you try to deep throat him this time?

Welcome to my life because while Chastity is the owner, director, and producer for Fast Girl Media, I'm her new right-hand girl. That is, if right-hand girls fit like a left-hand glove with the fingers glued into a fist. But I also do on-set makeup, which is what I did in my previous professional life. Only then, I applied it mainly from the neck up . . .

That aside, we're an odd pairing, Chastity and me. Her with her blue blood and me with the Upstate New York hay still stuck in my hair. But I don't know where I'd be without her. *Or her spare room.* Not after the shit my fiancé pulled.

'For the record,' she begins patiently again. 'Toy washing isn't your responsibility. Ever. But these toys? They're new. I'm thinking of stocking them on the website and thought I'd ask the professionals for their opinions. But I say again; they're new—unused. I would never . . . ' Her expression twists indelicately. 'But I appreciate your help, anyway.'

'Even when I get it wrong?'

'Yes, even then.' She pushes the dishwasher door closed with her foot as though it's contaminated.

'For someone who spends her day watching people stick their bits into other people's bits, you're awfully squeamish,' Max, her brother, suddenly gloats from the doorway.

'Leave her alone,' Chas warns.

'I was talking about you,' he responds.

'I'm not talking about this *with* you.'

'No, you won't talk business with me at all,' he complains mulishly.

'I've said it before and I'll say it again; go play porn star somewhere else. I have no issues with you being in the business, but I'm not watching or paying you to fuck.'

'Backing away slowly,' I say, doing just that.

'Good,' Chas retorts. 'Go put on your pretty dress. We've a wedding to attend.'

Dammit. 'But I don't want to go,' I reply on a whine, stamping my slipper-shod foot against the tile. 'It's just plain cruel to make me.'

'But there's a kindness in my cruelty. And I think you know that well.'

'Why don't I just fuck her?' Max pipes up. 'It'd save you a wedding gift. Look, she's already in her dressing gown. And I bet she's wearing a little Agent Provocateur under there.'

'Have you been peeking!' I squeak, grasping the neck of my robe tighter. Neither of us take his suggestion seriously. Max is Chas's *little* brother, though he towers over us both. He's twenty-two, fresh out of university, and has no idea what to do with his life. While he might be interested in the business, he's joking about being in front of the camera. *I think.*

'We all know a suitcase full of Louboutins and fancy underwear was all you brought with you when you walked out,' Max replies. And though his delivery is light-hearted, it still burns because what he's referring to is when I left my fiancé after finding he'd somehow tripped and accidentally inserted his dick into someone else.

I open my mouth to protest, but nothing comes out. My chest feels tight, panicked by a lack of air suddenly.

'And possibly a case of only left feet shoes at that,' he then adds.

'Stay out of her room, pervert,' Chas warns on my behalf, patting his cheek as she passes. 'It's probably him hiding your shoes, darling,' she says, turning back to me.

But it's not Max. My shoes have an awful habit of hiding themselves, and they have done so for most of my life. It's like they can sense when I want to wear a particular pair, then make only one of that pair available to me. It's a curse, I'm sure.

Chas pauses dramatically at the door. 'And while I'm sure Paisley is, no doubt, touched by your generosity, brother mine, go near her, and I'll sell you into sex slavery.'

'Don't look too excited,' I add, following her out of the room. 'She means the gay kind.'

In the first-floor bedroom of her swanky Chelsea pad, I find Chastity slipping on her pale green dress, the silk chiffon floating down her slim frame like a cloud of seafoam.

'I really don't see what difference it'll make,' I say, dropping my oversized makeup bag on her bed. 'I'm not in the mood.'

'I'm aware,' she says, catching my gaze through her dresser mirror as she unfastens the large rollers from her hair. 'But trust me.'

'But I really don't want to go,' I say, throwing myself on her soft, downy bed. 'They were never my friends. Not really. Unless you're counting them by proxy.'

'I hope you're not including me in that assumption.'

'Of course I'm not,' I reply, plucking at the hem of a decorative pillow sham. 'If it wasn't for you, I'd be on a plane for bumfuck nowhere by now.' Or, bumfuck Lamberston in Upstate New York. Population: 3,012. And I'd be the girl who snagged a British singer—someone famous—only to lose him again. Of course, no one would mention how I'd moved out of Lamberston to follow my career to Albany for WTEN, making sure the faces for the *Wake up with 10* show didn't go on air looking like zombies. Or how I'd moved to NYC to de-zombie-ize the stars and guests of *Good Morning America*. Nope. Because like lots of small town folk, the gossip would focus on how I couldn't keep my man and how my fabulous London life was just a bubble that was bound to burst.

I suppress a shiver at the thought of going back. I might not be feeling exactly fabulous right now, but at least I'm not in Lamberston.

'Those kinds of friends you don't need, sweets.' Chas is referring to my supposed London friends who dropped me like a pair of dirty panties when Robin and I split. Though her assumption could equally relate to my thoughts.

'It's a good thing you chose me over him is all I can say.' Chastity is one of the many people I met through Robin, my ex-fiancé. She was one of his friends originally. She also happens to be the only one who hung around after we split. *Hung around. Offered moral support, a kind ear. Then later, a job and a place to live.*

'Like there was even a choice to be made.' Sitting next to me, she takes my hand in hers. 'I, for one, am so very pleased you're still in London. And while I would've preferred you not to have suffered the indignities of finding out your fiancé was cheating on you, it's better you found out now rather than later.'

'Yeah, like after the wedding.' I chuckle, though it sounds as forced as it feels. I'm no longer heartbroken, but I'm still sad. I'm also grateful for Chas, and squeeze her hand as though this could somehow convey just how thankful I am. Without her, I wouldn't be functioning, never mind making a living while I look for something new. Without her, I wouldn't even have a roof over my head.

'And he won't be there today, not that it matters. It's time, darling. Time to move on and show those around you that you've moved on. That they and their fair-weather friendship means nothing to you.'

'But if I'm no longer part of their world, I don't need to go.'

'Good try,' she answers with a sad smile, glancing down at my stained robe. 'But it's time to try harder now.'

'But it's still hard,' I whisper.

'I know it is. But it's the other kind of hard you need. We just need to get you out of that grubby thing and into your dress because that look isn't doing it for anybody.'

'Except for Max.'

'Darling, he'd do my dog. If I had one.'

'Thanks,' I respond, laughing a little.

'For God's sake, put a little of this on,' she says, hefting my makeup bag between us. A bag with a slogan that reads, *contouring is my cardio*.

Makeup is my world. At least, it's what brought me to London in the first place. I met Robin at work. He had a short interview as part of his tour, though, at that point, he was still largely unknown. There I was, working and making faces look a little less *I get out of bed at 4 a.m. for this shit,* when he'd sat in my chair. I'd tucked the tissues into the collar of his shirt, our eyes had met, and the rest, as they say, was history.

The ancient kind of history now. Long dead and crumbling to dust.

'Chas, promise me you'll never fall in love with a rock star.'

'Rock star, my left tit.' She snorts—the kind of snort unbecoming of a lady. 'And I don't give a flying fuck if he hates the label *pop star* because he's not even that. Not that I'd find the label very flattering, either.'

'He's more folksy pop.'

'He's more the grandma crowd, as well as a complete arse wipe.'

Both are sadly true. He does play the kind of music that appeals to families. Middle-of-the-road stuff. Though I would never have said it to him. His ego is . . . delicate. At least, I thought it was. Until I found him screwing Tamara, his assistant. Or his assistant's assistant.

'God, what had my life come to that I'd call Robin's hangers-on my friends?' I find myself asking.

'Exactly.'

'So much I took for granted—so much I thought I knew. I thought I knew him. I thought his songs were about our love! Sung from his heart, standing on the stage with his guitar and his messy, roan hair.'

'Roan,' Chastity scoffs. 'The man is ginger. An ugly carrot-top.'

'With a fiery crotch to match.' I snigger, covering my mouth with my hand.

'The only thing outstanding about the area,' she affirms with a quirk of her brow.

So I might've told her about that over wine. Okay, crying angry tears and drunk off my ass. Let's just say that average, as a description, is an overstatement.

'You deserve better than *is it in yet,* so coming back to the topic of hard . . . You need hard loving, and that's what you get from me. But you also need the other kind of hard. The kind I can't give you.'

'Is that some kind of riddle? Because I don't really—'

'Dick, darling,' she says, cutting in. 'You need a man with a hard dick. An alpha—the absolute opposite of the kind of man you fell for.' While I might suggest she's overstepping, I don't. Because she already did that when she gifted me a dildo.

Patting my hand, she rises from the bed and makes her way back to her dressing table mirror. 'The reason we're going tonight is that a wedding hookup is the perfect scenario. It's practically a singles tradition.'

'You have the weirdest ideas.'

Turning her head over her shoulder with the poise of a debutant, she asks, 'Like starting a porn company?'

'Women-centric adult entertainment, thank you very much. And no, that seems to have been a fantastic idea.' Financially, at least.

'And I'm full of them,' she replies, twirling to face me again. 'And this one is much better than my first.'

'The look on your face has me worried. Should I be worried?'

'Well, my original plan was—and still possibly is, especially if you're absolutely against tonight—that I could set you up with one of the boys.'

'Boys?' I repeat, frowning back at her. 'You mean, with one of the p—adult actors?' I ask, quickly catching my mistake.

'The men who work for me all seem to know what they're doing in that department. And I've seen the way one or two of them look at you.' She shrugs lightly, as though this conversation is nothing. As though she was offering me a selection of bonbons and not men. 'And why wouldn't they?' she asks the room at large. 'You're a total babe even if you have become a bit of a slob.'

'A slob!' I repeat, incredulous.

'Did that hit a nerve?' she asks with a slight wince.

'Well, yes!'

'Good,' she adds in a firmer tone. 'You are a bit of a mess. You used to be obsessed with makeup, and now you barely even moisturise.'

'So you thought you'd ask a porn star to pity fuck me?' I whisper-hiss. I might shout but for the fact that Max is downstairs, and I could do without his input.

'How ridiculous,' she retorts. 'You're being deliberately obtuse. You are gorgeous, makeup or not. I'm just worried you've lost a little *joie de vivre*. Your mojo.'

'I know what *joie de vivre* means!' Sort of. And I'm still not banging a porn star. 'My God, this wedding is looking more and more attractive by the second.'

'Good—perfect, in fact.'

'Going to a wedding doesn't mean I'm agreeing to anything else.'

'Darling, think about it. If you visit a bad restaurant, it doesn't put you off food forever. You just choose another.' Jumping up from her stool, she pulls my reluctant form from the bed and leads me to the seat she just vacated. 'What is it you Americans say? You need to get back on the horse that threw you?'

'Something like that.'

'Well, tonight, you're getting a whole new ride.'

I wonder if I was ever as brave as she is. Ever as sure about anything, I think, as I open my makeup bag when, leaning over my shoulder, Chas swipes the Charlotte Tilbury lipstick out of my hand.

'Bond Girl,' she murmurs, reading from the base of the golden tube. 'There's an idea. Let's give you a pseudonym tonight . . . one with a Bond girl theme. You can be Holly Goodhead. That is, assuming you give good—'

'Really?' Through the mirror, I begin applying a perfectly winged stroke of liner. It's strange how some women have problems applying the stuff, and others have problems keeping men.

'If you're not sure, I can call Sonia from today's shoot. Did you see how she inhaled Nathan's penis like a total champ?'

'Nathan?' I repeat. Chas nods. 'The improbably named Nathan Cox?'

'Yes, why?'

'Not that his name sounds anything like naked cocks or anything?'

'I hadn't thought about it like that. That's rather clever.'

'Yeah, well I'm not sucking any cock, Nathan's or otherwise.'

'If you're not happy being Holly Goodhead, you can always be Pussy Galore. Although that always makes me think of a woman with an overly large vagina.'

'This is one of those times I wish you and I had a safe word,' I reply, holding my head in my hands. 'Boundaries, Chastity.'

'Boundaries are meant to be tested,' she replies, beginning to slick the berry shade of lipstick across her lips. 'Or how else would we discover the true breadth of things we enjoy?'

'Here, do it properly.' I pass her the lip primer and brush, the tools of my old trade.

'Ever the purist,' Chas responds with a smile. 'Is this the long-lasting stuff?'

'Yeah, it's really good,' I begin, animated. The topic of makeup gets me a little excited—makeup is totally my spirit animal. 'It doesn't come off for hours.'

'Unlike my aim for your knickers tonight.'

My shoulders slump as I eye her through the mirror, a sudden thought adding to my torment. 'But what happens if Robin does show up?' I swear I've seen him a couple of times out on the street, not that I'd tell Chas. She already worries about me enough.

'If he does, fuck him. Only don't,' she adds quickly. 'Or I will junk punch you both. Of course, I'll have to find his first,' she adds with a sly wave of the pinkie finger on her right hand.

I smile because, evil reasons. And she's not exactly wrong.

'But I don't want to make a scene,' I answer softly. Weddings might be an easy place to score, but not with your ex in the same room. I just couldn't. And more to the point, I don't really want to. 'I don't get why you're so keen to go yourself.'

She might have been born into the Chelsea set, but she so doesn't ascribe to being seen in the right places or hanging out with the right crowd. Just the opposite—she's the posh girl with the porn company!

'I'm just a little excited, I suppose. It's not every day you get invited to the wedding of someone famous; someone whose picture you had hanging on your bedroom wall.'

'Yet Robin never impressed you.'

'Ginger was never my thing.' She scrunches up her nose. '*Bust Out*, however, was my favourite band, and Chad, their front man, was my high school secret crush.'

'Pity he's getting married then, huh? You won't get to kiss him for realz now.' Chastity slides me a sly look, but she wouldn't . . . would she?

'I do think it's acceptable, indeed appropriate, to kiss the groom congratulations.'

'Depends on the use of tongues,' I answer, askance.

'I'll keep it to a minimum,' she teases. 'Not too much depth unless you don't do as you're told, of course.'

'Yeah, sure. A wedding hookup. I can do that.' There isn't a drop of sincerity in my tone. 'Because I'm so responsive to blackmail. I could totally sue you for harassment in the workplace.'

'I think you probably could, given what happened in Prague last week.'

'I couldn't sue you for that. Not for taking me to such a beautiful historic city. It's not your fault that Sasha sneezed so hard she expelled a dildo from her body, and it nearly knocked me out.'

'Oh, God,' she says, taking a deep, shaky breath. 'Don't make me laugh. I'll pee myself. I want you to know I risked life and limb and went into your room to find you a matching pair of shoes.'

'Are you trying to say I'm a mess?' Of course, she is. My life at the moment is one big mess.

'You're messy, not a mess. And if you're not going to sue me for damages to your mental or physical health, or for harassment in the workplace, there's only one thing left to do.' Chastity picks up her phone as it pings. 'And that's find you a nice young man tonight, one to fill the void in your life. And by that, I mean your—'

'Thank you!' I yell, covering my ears. 'That will do!'

Chapter Four

PAISLEY

'Well, that would've gone worse,' Chastity murmurs, taking her seat at the table next to me.

'Aside from the vows,' I agree. The bride's twenty-minute vow soliloquy was a little much. Twenty minutes of declarations of love and promises to let him sleep on the left side of the bed forever even though that's her favourite side. And to honour her promise to let him *"shag"* Scarlett Johansson should the fantasy become a possible reality because "even celebrities are allowed a celebrity shag". And that's not the dance kind as I came to find out after moving to London.

'Such sacrifices in the name of love,' I say with a wry grin, sliding my fingers around the dainty stem of my champagne glass.

'Love is—'

'A battlefield?'

'I was going to say like anal.'

I almost spray champagne over the pristine white tablecloth. 'Chas, what the hell!'

'Love *is* like anal,' Chastity replies, taking a graceful sip from her own glass. 'At least, like shooting anal. A total pain in the arse.'

'Oh, Lord. What a conversation to have on a day like this.'

'What? You think those two haven't had a little buttseggs.'

'Really? Today, you want to talk about this?' My gaze follows hers to the top table and the gorgeous blonde in the princess dress. Her groom is a little older and a little more relaxed in his demeanour. As the front man of a once-successful band, something tells me this isn't the first time he's been king for a day.

'I'd put money on them both being familiar. She looks like the type to grin and bear it, literally. And he looks like someone completely *au-fait* with a little bum play.'

'I say again . . . on a day like this? In a place like this?'

'Okay,' she replies with a long-suffering sigh. 'Fine. But just because we're in Claridge's.'

Because the venue *is* beautiful. Perfect, in fact, and Claridge's is, well, the epitome of London swank. Chandeliers sparkle, marble floors gleam, and Art Deco mirrors reflect the candlelight splendour of the place. And the food? If the hors d'oeuvres are any indication, it's divine. And even though I'd prefer to be at home in my sweats, or better still, my ratty robe, the champagne has taken the edge off the day.

We eat, we drink, and I pretend to be merry as we chat with our tablemates. Fake it until you make it, right? Fake it until it no longer hurts to remember you paid a deposit to secure your own wedding here.

'You feeling okay?' Chastity asks.

Folding my lips in, I nod. I didn't tell her our wedding planner had brought me here. That I'd imagined myself in a white dress, dancing around this very room. I assume she's asking if I'm okay about Robin being here. Because, yes, he showed up. Just as I knew he would. It's not the first time I've seen him since our split, and though I've always managed to be civil, seeing him always makes my stomach twist with the most painful ache. He's also the reason I no longer listen to the radio.

Hypocrite. Fraud. Unfaithful fuck!

I shudder, tears pricking my eyelids. Sad tears. Angry tears. And everything in between. For the first time since Chastity suggested it, I almost want to screw some random man just as a way of clawing a little something back.

Only, as I look around the ballroom, I think how futile this idea is. These are all his types; the *lovey-darling* showbiz crowd. People whose fondness for vodka breakfasts I used to paint away for morning TV.

God, they're a shitty, shallow bunch. *Maybe I should've stayed off the champagne.*

'Hey, where'd you go?' Chas's forehead creases in a frown.

'It's just so sad that they spoiled a fantastic meal by following it with a trio of fruit desserts.' I frown down at the rectangular plate in front of me.

'Seriously, what's wrong with people? Where's the chocolate? The caramel?'

'You're an odd one,' Chas says, pulling me in to her side.

'It almost makes me wish Robin was sitting at our table. I would've had somewhere to shove this dragon fruit.'

She starts to giggle. 'But darling, they wouldn't dare shove superstar Robin in the back of the room with us.'

Yep, because we're at *that* table. The one you see at every wedding with the mismatched inhabitants—distant relatives and oddballs.

Her giggles stop abruptly, her gaze sliding over my shoulder. 'I want to punch his pudding face so bad.' In truth, it's more of a glare than a look. 'We need a whole barrel of dragon fruit because that skank is here now, too.'

The champagne bubbles turn to acid on my tongue. Chas has met Tamara before, but she must be mistaken. 'It must be someone else,' I reply. 'He's an asshole, but he wouldn't be so cruel . . . ' Because this isn't what grown-ups do.

'If it's not her,' Chastity begins, 'then Satan's freed her doppelgänger dog from hell today. Doppelbanger, maybe. Ow, sweetie, I can't feel my hand.'

I release her fingers, and she shakes her hand repeatedly before snatching a glass of champagne from a passing waitress, swapping it for the empty one threatening to crack in my hand.

'Don't. Don't you dare,' she whispers fiercely. 'If you cry, I'm going to *really* give you something to cry about.'

'Okay, *Mom*.' My words come out on a smiling half-sob as she repeats something every mother everywhere has said. Though for me, it would be something my grandma, long since passed, would've said. *Don't let them see you're upset. Hold that head high.* But these aren't sad tears now. These are angry motherfuckers. Tears of fire and temper. 'That absolute . . . lowlife, lying, stinking . . . *bastard*.'

'Come on, you can do better than that,' Chas says.

'He's a needle-dick butt fucker,' I almost yell, causing the grandmotherly type on the other side of the table to mutter, 'Well, really.' Only in a much fancier accent. *Well, riiiley!* Thankfully, but for her and the even older gentleman sitting by her side—who appears to have nodded off—our other tablemates have vacated the space.

'That was a good one, but I think I'll still go and throat punch a bitch.'

'No.' I put my hand on her arm. 'Not here.' The bride and groom don't need that kind of reminder of their day. I can't help but glance behind me, and this time, I see the bitch's smug-ugly face. *And Robin's arm looped around the back of her chair.*

'That bitch,' I breathe. 'Taking my man is one thing, but she's wearing my fucking dress!'

'What?' Chastity's head whips around. 'But she's—oh my God!' Her eyes sparkle with malicious glee as she sees what I mean. Tamara is wearing the *exact* same gown as I am. 'Did you tell her what you were wearing?'

'When? Before I found her vagina inhaling Robin? No, of course not. But his stylist did. She chose the thing and paid for it with Robin's credit card.'

I suddenly feel very uncomfortable. I'm here wearing a dress he paid for. In fact, during our relationship, he paid for most things. But we were partners—we shared a life. Sure, I was sharing less than him in the monetary stakes, but that was because I had less. I mean, he took care of the bills, but I still paid my way. We were getting married—it was supposed to be a partnership. And if he'd wanted to borrow my Shishido illuminator or my Chanel bronzer, I'd have no problem with that. I would've given him anything.

Like my heart.

And look how careless he was with that.

'So little Miss Opens-Her-Legs was so jealous, she stole not only your man but also your dress. That is so low.'

I shrug because that's all I've got. What the hell am I doing? Two months ago, I was looking at honeymoons in Bora-fucking-Bora, and now I'm more annoyed that she's stolen my dress? It just doesn't make sense.

'She can keep them—both of them. My only regret is that we're in Claridge's. If we were anywhere else, I'd be tempted to whip off the tablecloth to wear like a toga and stuff this piece of designer loveliness in the trash.'

'How about some perfect payback instead?'

'I could go for payback. As long as it's not going to land us in jail for the night.'

'I didn't have anything illegal in mind. Immoral, maybe.' She places her glass down. 'And *I* wasn't planning on doing anything. Well, other than molesting the best man.'

'I thought the groom was your not-so-secret crush?'

'My recently married crush. The best man, however, is single still.'

'And a decade older than you are, at least.'

'Stop changing the subject. I have a dastardly plan to impart! Revenge of the most delicious kind. Well, don't look too excited,' she says with an impatient huff.

'It's hard to be excited when I see that glint in your eye.'

'Have faith. And finish your champagne.'

'Oh, that's not good. If I need alcohol, this plan is—'

'The best kind of revenge. Now, tell me what attracted you to Robin.'

'What the hell! Revenge isn't therapy, Chas.'

'Hear me out,' she demands. 'Come on. What was it about him that attracted you? What set your heart aflame?'

'Well, he was British,' I say with a shrug. 'I loved his accent. Plus, he was sort of unassuming. And sweet. He made me laugh.'

'Yes,' she replies, sort of sniggering. 'That skillset melt a girl's panties *every* time.'

'Look, he was—'

'Excuse me.' From the other side of the table, our elderly tablemate speaks. If I had to guess, I'd say she's aged somewhere in her seventies. Her back is ramrod straight, her silver-grey hair pulled into a neat chignon, and her clothing understated and elegant. She reminds me of a ballet teacher I once had as a child.

'Whilst I didn't mean to eavesdrop,' she says when neither Chas nor I respond, 'it is quite difficult not to. You, my dear,' she says, waving a bony finger at Chastity, 'are rather loud.'

Chas starts to laugh as I begin damage control.

'I'm sorry if we disturbed you, but—'

'Nothing of the kind,' she says, waving one dismissive hand. 'But I do believe I may have something of interest to impart, if you'll allow.' Chastity and I exchange glances—mine wary, hers still full of mirth. 'I believe what you're looking for is standing over there.' One thin hand wrapped around her champagne flute gestures towards either the table housing the wedding party or the dance floor. It's hard to tell. 'If it's virility you're looking for, one need look no further than a man brave enough to wear a skirt.'

'A skirt?' Chas repeats, sounding delighted. I, meanwhile, wonder how much champagne is healthy for a septuagenarian. 'That's such an excellent idea!'

'Yes,' the old lady drawls with an air of *been there, done that*. 'I once thought so myself.'

'She's right,' Chas begins, her words tumbling over themselves in her haste. 'Lack of pants notwithstanding, he's the antithesis of Robin.'

I look back blankly, not able to make sense of the words spilling from her berry-painted mouth.

'Just look at him,' she demands. So I do, and now that I am, it's kind of hard to look away. 'I'll bet you couldn't get skinny jeans to cover those legs. Or arse.' True, the man looks kind of cut. 'And look at that jawline—it has more structure than . . . than your life!'

'A puddle has more structure than my life,' I reply as though on autopilot because there's something about the man standing at the edge of the dance floor dressed in a kilt. Something familiar, I think

'I suggest you make haste,' the old lady pipes up. 'Yours aren't the only eyes following him.'

'Yes, get up there and flirt like crazy with him.'

'I-I . . . ' Can't imagine anything less terrifying at this minute.

'Drive Robin crazy just because you can.'

'That's . . . ' *slightly less terrifying*. And definitely more appealing.

'And then take him upstairs,' she says, feeding the champagne glass back into my hand. 'And let the hot alpha man in a skirt stick his penis in you.'

Now, there is something you'll never read on the front page of Fast Girl's webpage.

Chapter Five

KEIR

In case anyone asks, you picked the Julia Snelling sterling silver and pearl cock ring from the gift registry.

Please tell me you're joking . . .

Would I joke about something as serious as a wedding gift? Or love?

I stare down at my phone, not sure whether to laugh or succumb to an aneurism.

Flynn . . . I type out. *You fucker.*

Keir . . .

Hitting call, I step out into the hallway.

'I asked you to choose something from the registry, pay for it with the credit card, then have it wrapped, delivered, and all that shit. Not for you to wind me up, you arsehole.'

'Who's winding you up?' he replies in a cool tone. 'I did as you asked. I also picked up your shirts from the cleaners, plus the kilt you're wearing. I mowed your lawns, got the electrician in to fix the broken light in the pool, paid for a term of Sorcha's gourmet school lunches . . .'

'You didn't mow the lawn. You just paid the landscape company bill.'

'I pay all your bills. Sort out any maintenance issues in your home—everything. In fact, why don't you shove a broom up my arse, and I can sweep the floor as I'm running around after you?'

'You shouldn't give me ideas,' I half huff, half laugh. 'Come on, man. A cock ring?'

'What can I tell you? It was on the registry.'

'How is it a gift? A his-and-her gift?'

'I dunno. Ask the people who chose it. It's got a pearl,' he then says, apropos of nothing. 'A vibrating pearl.' *Oh. Well then.*

'You're a bastard.' And I'm laughing.

'And this is payback for my birthday.'

'You asked for a stripper,' I reply, trying not to laugh. And mostly winning.

'Not a bloke! And definitely not one as old as my grandad!'

Ah, that was at least one laugh for the day. I can't imagine there'll be many more. The last thing I want to do is spend my Saturday at a wedding—especially at a wedding of someone I have a less than fabulous connection to—when I have a child with chickenpox at home. Yep, the vomiting turned to a mild fever, and a fever into a rash, and a week later, poor wee Sorcha looks like something from a plague painting. So yes, I could think of other places I'd rather be than at the wedding of a girl whose father was intent on driving me insane.

'Keir!' Joe, the man in question, slaps me on the back in one of those manly, magnanimous *I'm so macho* gestures. 'So pleased you could make it.'

Like I had any choice. We still haven't agreed on a price for the parcel of land he owns—land I need. Land he's using to worm his way in on the deal. A daughter he's using to get in on my business.

Not happening, Joe. Not in a million years.

'Wouldn't have missed it for the world,' I say, stretching the truth like an elastic band. Hopefully one that won't ping me in the arse later. Seriously, I'd rather be at home dabbing calamine lotion on Sorcha's scabs. Yep, I'm just *that* excited to be here, and I don't give a fuck if he has "*dropped a hundred and fifty k on the day*".

Claridge's ballroom sparkles in its Art Deco splendour, mirrors lining the walls reflecting the opulence by candlelight. Tables heavy with linens, silverware, and glass stand behind us, a dance floor constructed in front.

'Doesn't she look a picture?' I follow Joe's beady gaze to the top table beyond the dance floor where his elder daughter and her new husband sit.

'Aye, she's a bonny girl. He's a lucky man.' I take a sip from my whisky, washing down the lie. Not that his daughter doesn't make a beautiful bride— she does. But weddings are complete shite as far as I'm concerned.

Love is blind, or so they say. But there's nothing like a divorce to sort your eyesight out.

'He is lucky.' Frowning, Joe pulls the snowy white handkerchief from his top pocket, dabbing the sweat from his shiny forehead. 'He's also pissed—drunk from too much champagne.'

That's not true, and I think we both know that because the groom is off his face. I saw him doing a couple of lines in the toilets not twenty minutes ago.

'These creative types, eh?' he says, almost as though he's read my mind.

Joe might've mentioned once or a hundred times that the groom is the front man for a boy band. Not that he looks very boyish right now, but I suppose a hundred quid a day habit is bound to leave you looking a bit worse for wear.

'But I wasn't talking about the bride,' Joe says quite suddenly. 'I meant Amelia, her sister. It goes without saying the bride is the star of the show, and while both my daughters are stunners, I've always thought Amelia's something special.'

And I've always thought parents weren't supposed to favour one child over the other, I manage not to say.

'Aye, she looks bonny, too.'

'And ripe for the plucking.'

Who the fuck says that about their own daughter? I keep my expression impassive, watching as Joe mentally plays back his words. 'That is,' he blusters, 'what I mean to say was some lucky man will pluck her up soon—snatch her from the marriage market.'

Amelia's gaze catches mine from across the room where she sits to her sister's right. And the look she's giving me? Fucking blatant. And while I wouldn't say it to Joe, I reckon Amelia has been *plucked* plenty.

And as for any kind of snatch . . . yeah, I'm not going there. *Not even remotely,* I think, remembering how at dinner last week, she'd opened her legs wide under the table, sliding me a similar look.

Confidence is one thing, but desperation is never sexy.

Never degrade another man's daughter. Not as a father of a daughter yourself.

I mentally berate myself as Agnes's words fill my head, and I sigh heavily. It's been a while since I degraded any girl. In fact, these days, I'm lucky to get five minutes alone to degrade myself. You'd think in a house the size of mine I'd be able to grab a few minutes alone with my hand, but no.

And as for relationships, divorce definitely has a way of making you think twice. *Hell, twenty times.* And casual is just a myth constructed by people who want to fool themselves. Look at Mac and Will, my best mates. Their religion was a casual fuck and now look at them. Fiancées. Wives. Babies. Not that there's anything wrong with those things. And they've both chosen well. I, on the other hand, must've been dropped on my head as a baby because my choices have not been so stellar. And now that I'm responsible for a whole other person, I'm mindful of my past and how the choices I make in my life impact her life.

Bottom line? Despite Will's assertions that weddings are the perfect pulling ground, half-drunk bridesmaids aren't on my to-do list.

And neither is Amelia.

Realising Joe is still waiting for an answer, I grab at the first thing I notice. 'Cameras at the ready. It looks like it's time for the first dance.'

A vaguely familiar face walks to the edge of the dance floor with an acoustic guitar in hand. Despite the decent cut of his suit, the fella looks in need of a wash and a shave. He'd give Scooby Doo's mate a run for his money on the grooming front.

As the familiar strains of a recent chart-topping song beginning to play, Joe excuses himself, bustling away as a smattering of *oohs* and *ahhs* sound from tables nearby as the bride and groom take to the dance floor.

The ginger begins to sing a soft ballad about love and the passing of time. Of dancing in the night-time. Of growing old together. It's a song I've heard play on the radio—one Sorcha has hummed along to on the way to school. The sentiment is very pretty, the words sugary fake.

'It's a beautiful song, isn't it?' I turn to the husky voice to the right of me. Dark hair, pale skin, and the bluest eyes. I can literally feel the smile creeping across my face.

'Hello, Paisley.'

'Oh, it is you!' She begins to laugh softly, the smile almost immediately slipping from her face. I follow her gaze as she looks over her shoulder to where a cherubic looking blonde holds up both thumbs, her face a rictus of manic grin.

'Friend of yours?' I ask as she turns back.

'Yes.' Her expression twists, her nose scrunched like a wee rabbit. 'And my boss, and she doesn't know about us.'

'Us?' I repeat, the connotations fizzing low in my belly.

'About the other day, I mean.'

'When I caught you looking at cock?' It's not like me to be so crass. I mean, I'm a bloke and probably as crass as the next one, but around women, I'm usually a little better behaved. But she laughs anyway, looping one arm around the front of her waist.

'All in a day's work,' she responds. 'But I meant about interviewing you. By mistake. I didn't tell her.'

'Oh?'

'Yeah. I mean, Antonio showed up not long after you.'

'Mission accomplished, then?' The fizzing turns to a tightening.

'I booked him for Barcelona, if that's what you're asking. But I don't think that's what you are asking.' I give her a very bland non-answer in the guise of a shrug. 'Though I have wondered why you came over to the table? Why you sat down even, Mr . . . ?'

'Keir,' I supply. 'Just Keir.' She's thought about it. Thought about me. I wonder if her interest extended to *me time* masturbation, too. 'And truthfully, I'm not sure. All I can say is an attractive woman waved me over.' I shrug again. 'I followed my feet.' *Or my dick.*

'Your feet, huh?' With a knowing smile, her gaze turns to the happy couple.

'You could almost believe in love,' she says softly. 'Listening to him sing.'

Her tone is even, but something in her posture belies her words. The way her fingers are almost white around the stem of the glass, and the slight shimmer of moisture in her gaze, one I'm sure isn't a reaction to watching the newlyweds shuffle around in front of us.

'What's his name again?' I turn and give her my full attention; for the first time in a long while, my interest is piqued. *As well as other things.*

'H-his name is Robin Reed.'

'Aye, I've heard this one on the radio. It's all right, I suppose. A wee bit like soup.' She coughs a little on her sip of champagne, her blue eyes lifting to mine.

'I beg your pardon?'

'The fella's music is a bit like soup. You know, the stuff you feed people who are ill. People who can't handle anything excitable.'

She brings her hand to her mouth to cover an indelicate snort. When was the last time I made a woman laugh? And more to the point, when was the last time a woman's laughter made me feel like that? Warmed internally. Accompanied by a familiar, though often ignored, tugging in my balls.

'People love his music,' she challenges with a cock of her brow.

'I'm sure some people do,' I reply like a kid seeking an adult's attention. 'Boring people. Soup's not very exciting, hen,' I add, mockingly serious.

'Hen?' She looks down at her outfit—a fitted midnight blue gown, knotted at one shoulder and leaving the other bare. Her dark hair is worn off her neck in a crown of loose braids. There's something a little *sexy milkmaid* about the style, the artfully curled loose strands further giving the impression of her having recently enjoyed a roll in the hay.

Imagine that.

And I do.

Right now, I'd fucking join her.

'That's right.' My gaze joins hers, examining her clothing. Her curves. The full heaviness of her breasts that would be a handful in a large man's hands. Her tiny waist and rounded hips made for holding. I suck in a deep breath of air, shaking my head infinitesimally. Maybe I can blame the whisky for being this barefaced.

'Or are you going to tell me that being called *hen* is too familiar? That I should call you something gender neutral or insist I call you *Ms*?'

Christ on a bike. I sound like a right cock.

'No, not at all.' Her words are a cool relief I don't understand. 'I've just never been called hen before.'

'It's Scots,' I reply. 'And maybe it's because I wouldn't mind rufflin' your feathers.'

'Oh, my God.' Her words are more breath than anything else, her cheeks heating as she fights a smile, giving me her profile again. 'You can't say things like that.'

'Why's that?'

Her eyes dart sideways, then immediately back again. 'We've only just met.'

'That's not true,' I say. 'We had coffee together. Talked about anal and saw dick.'

'You really are the worst,' she says, giggling.

'The worst . . . company?'

'The worst kind of tease,' she qualifies.

I send her a knowing smirk, not trusting myself to speak. I can't reply to her assumption because it would be in a completely different vein. A tease? I'm a fucking tease, all right. The kind who'll have you on your back for hours, licking and sucking every inch of your skin all while you sob for release. Or at least, I used to be.

With a short sigh, I thank the Lord I'd worn a heavy hunting kilt tonight. Because no Scotsman worth his name wears anything under his kilt. Except maybe lipstick, if he's had a lucky night.

'So,' she starts nervously as though she can read minds. Or smiles. 'Bride or groom?' Her eyes return to the stage.

'What? Oh, which side. Bride, I suppose. Not that I know her. I'm in business with her dad. What about you?'

'The groom, I suppose.' I follow the path of her gaze to the ginger singer. Despite singing about the glory that is love, he is scowling. In our direction.

'You'd think he'd have made a bit more effort,' I say cocking my head in his way. 'Famous or no', he looks a bit of a sight.' I'm being kind because he looks like a fuckin' hobo.

The corner of her mouth turns up, her deep blue eyes rising to mine. 'Lots of women like that look,' she answers. 'Or so I'm told.'

'It'll be for the money.' I tip the remains of my whisky down my throat, placing the empty glass on a waiter's passing tray. 'Money does all kinds of funny things to some people's perceptions.'

'And you'd know?'

'Unfortunately, I would. The same as I know a scrote like him wouldn't have a chance with most women outside of his fame.'

'Scrote?' she says on a tinkling laugh. 'Another from the Scots dictionary?'

'The man is about as attractive as a scrotum, you have to admit.'

'Oh, my God.' She covers her mouth with her fingers, her eyes sparkling above nude-coloured nails. I get a flash of something tugging in my gut—the image of me pushing my fingers between her raspberry-coloured lips. One hand between her legs as her nails bite into my shoulder, the fingers of my other hand feeding her tongue her own taste.

'So you think wealth makes a man attractive?'

'Wealth makes anyone attractive, to some.' Reason number twenty-two on my list of *Why I don't Date*.

'No need to ask which side of the fence you're seeing this from,' she says, using her words as an excuse to blatantly check me out. 'But what about you? Do you think your wealth makes you attractive?'

'You think you can tell what I'm worth by my clothes?' I glance down at my bespoke outfit. 'This might be a rental.' I tug on the front of my vest, having discarded the jacket to a chair once the ceremony was over; my shirt now rolled at the sleeves and open at the neck.

'That outfit isn't off the rack,' she says, eyeing me again. Turning to face me, her fingertips brush the fabric covering my thigh. I swallow deeply, the tiniest of touches dialling my senses up to a nine.

Flirting. We're definitely flirting—and she's just upped the ante by touching my thigh. The sad truth is this is the most exciting sexual thing that's happened to me in a long while.

Christ, I need to get out more, I think as the words of Will's earlier texts come floating back to me.

Remember, weddings are excellent for hookups.

I hope you've remembered clean underwear.

And that you've taken your testicles out of the sock drawer.

And unwrapped them from the cellophane.

They need an airing. In some lovely, willing girl's mouth.

So some of the texts weren't exactly sane. But it's easy for him to make me the butt of his jokes because he hasn't suffered the turmoil of divorce. Or been forced to raise his child alone. And that's why I shouldn't be standing here, swaying closer to this gorgeous creature and effectively leading her on.

Because this is going nowhere beyond a little flirting.

When was the last time you got your dick wet?

Even in his texts, Will has no fucking boundaries.

'What kind of fabric or material is this?' she asks softly, examining the kilt at my thigh.

'I can tell you what it's not.' My voice strains from her fingers being so close to my dick. It could be my words or my tone that causes her to raise her head to stare up at me from beneath her endlessly long blue-black lashes.

My heart beats *bah-dum, bah-dum* because flirting or not, I can't not be straight or honest. It's just who I am.

'That material isn't the boyfriend kind.'

She nods her understanding, and I feel the loss of her fingers almost immediately; though as she stares up at me, my head is filled with a million things.

Is she trembling?

Can she tell I am?

Her hair would be soft in my hand.

I bet she'd taste as good as she looks.

'Are you staying in the hotel tonight?' Her long, black lashes blink up at me.

Christ. In suggesting my kilt isn't boyfriend material, I've somehow managed to imply I'm down to fuck. But that doesn't answer why my heart is beating out of my chest. Or why I want more than anything else to say yes.

Chapter Six

PAISLEY

I might have been avoiding Robin's gaze since my interaction with Keir began, but currently, he couldn't be further from my mind as I nervously chew on the inside of my mouth, willing him to reply. Am I reading him wrong? Wishful thinking? Drunk on half a bottle of champagne?

Would you like to come up to my room? I may as well have said. Or more truthful still would be, *Do you like me enough to fuck me?*

It's almost like actual question is hanging in the air between us. And it's been like eleven million minutes since I'd asked it. If he doesn't speak soon, I'm going to start babbling. Or bawling. Or both.

'Seriously, though? What is this material?'

I go to touch his kilt again—the man is wearing an honest to goodness kilt in a look that's sort of rugged and manly. That's not to say he didn't look good in the coffee shop—because he did. But that was a more handsomely urbane look. *Like David Gandy in Dolce Gabbana.* But how he looks tonight? Off the charts hot.

The black boots he wears with thick wrinkled socks give his outfit a manly look, the open neck of his shirt revealing a strong, tan cording of muscles on either side of his neck. His shirt stretches across his broad shoulders and muscular arms, a watch with a dark leather strap banded against one strong wrist. He has such big . . . hands. And feet. But I'm not letting my mind connect those things. Big feet really only guarantee one thing.

Big shoes.

But wow, he is handsome. His eyes look dark in this light; his hair cut short. *Maybe because it has a tendency to curl. It looks that way.* He's just sort of golden in the candlelight.

'I've always wondered what's under one of these things.' Filling the silence, I reach my finger out to brush the soft material again.

'If you get any closer,' he says, his right hand catching mine, 'you'll find out.'

'Oh.'

'Aye, oh indeed.' He's smiling. Swallowing. Tightening his fingers on mine. 'And while it'd be easy to answer yes to your question, I really can't.'

'But . . . ' But I was already imagining it. His hard body against mine, strong arms holding me tight. 'But I only asked if you were staying in the hotel tonight.'

'That's what your mouth said. Your eyes said otherwise.'

My heart sinks like a stone in a jug of cheap bubbly.

I suddenly want the floor to open up and swallow me whole. I want to tip my head to the sky and ask the heavens why. What did I do to deserve this kind of shitty evening? Has tonight not been humiliating enough? Have I not been humiliated enough these past months? Instead, I find myself looking at my toes. Briefly anyway, as one of his thick fingers tilts my chin.

'It's not because I don't want to.' His voice sounds husky. Strained. 'It's just not a good idea.'

'Are you with someone?' I ask softly. I'd already checked for a ring—and didn't he start the whole flirting thing? Maybe even back in the coffee shop because what kind of man in a relationship doesn't correct someone's pornified mistake? A flirting one!

'Not that it matters, but no.'

Oh. Well. That still makes no sense. And though his expression is almost regretful, I don't need his apology, and I sure as heck don't need his pity.

'Really, that's fine.' I smile—probably grimace— through my humiliation with a sort of half shrug, pulling away from his attention and his fingertip. 'As it happens, I'm in the market for making mistakes tonight, so I obviously just need to find someone willing.' I laugh despite myself. 'Because only *I* would find the one man at a wedding who didn't want to fuck.'

'That's not it,' he growls, stepping into me again and taking my face in his hands. 'I'd like nothing more than to take you upstairs and fuck you so solidly, the whole floor would hear you come.'

My eyes widen with shock, his words like sudden fingers thrust between my legs. In response, my core clenches as my cheeks begin to sting. I force myself to giggle—laugh—only it feels strange, almost as though the sound requires more lung capacity than I currently have. Maybe because all the blood in my body has drained to other places. Places that have no business to be pounding like the beat of a drum.

'You think that's funny, do you?'

'A little.' And not at all. *If anyone is being ridiculous, it's me.* 'It's just, I've never done this before. Hooked up, I mean.'

'You've never had a one-night stand.' It's not so much a question as an assertion. One that causes me to straighten my shoulders as I shore up my defences against a second attack.

'No, I haven't. And that's why this has just struck me as ridiculous. You don't know me. How could you? And if you did, you'd know I'm not the kind of girl who screams. Ever.' I sound snarky. Bitchy, probably.

Keir's expression clouds as he attempts to process the verbiage I've just spewed. Or maybe I've needled his manly ego. *His me-go.* I snigger again.

'I'm sorry,' I repeat. 'I really do need to go.'

But I don't get very far, my feet faltering at his next words. The presence of his large body suddenly burning me from behind as he grasps my forearm.

'You know what that tells me? You've never been fucked properly.'

'And that tells me you watch too much porn,' I retort, turning my head over my shoulder.

His sudden burst of deep laughter is startling.

'You know, you might be right on that score. But if I bedded you, you'd whimper, scream, and make every noise in between. I guarantee you that.'

'I guess that's something we'll never find out.'

My heart pounds now in several places as I hold my head high and force myself to stride away without looking back.

At our table at the edge of the room, there's no sign of Chas or the elderly lady and her even more ancient companion. The band has begun playing, I realise, and Robin is no longer serenading the bride and groom. I slip my purse from the velvet seat of my chair and pull out my phone, trying not to listen to the middle-aged couple arguing nearby. It wouldn't be a wedding without at least one argument. As for a wedding without hookups, maybe others will have better luck than me tonight.

The balls of my feet are beginning to ache in my glittery Choos, and I can't wait to pull the pins out of my hair. Strange, but neither of these smart quite as much as Keir's rebuttal. Or the prospect of watching Robin and Tamara on the dance floor.

All seemed to be going well with your sexy Scot, assuming he isn't a half-assed crossdresser and your animated

conversation the result of your joint love of Sephora.

Lifting my head from my phone, I scan the room for Chastity when my phone pings again.

Rest assured, I fed no tongue to the groom, though I have made accommodations elsewhere. Please let me know when you get this and that all is well.

I jot a quick response back. *All good on this end. So I should expect to see you for breakfast?*

Yes, unless Operation Hard Man hasn't happened, she immediately replies. *In which case, I'll be available for room service caviar, champagne, and a pay-per-view movie binge, all on Robin's tab!*

I hadn't told Chastity that the suite has been paid from the partial refund of my own wedding booking deposit. It seemed a bit sad to mention it.

All is going according to plan, I respond. And it is, only not her original plan. Though her second seems pretty fun. A slumber party at Claridge's for one! *Have fun x*

Back at you! comes her final text.

Skirting around the arguing couple and leaving behind my half-drunk glass of lukewarm champagne, I begin to make my way out of the ballroom, then decide to make a detour to the ladies' room first.

This hotel really is the height of sophistication, I think as my heels sound against the marble flooring of the foyer. I rub my lips together, taking a quick peek at my reflection, marvelling at how well my new lipstick has held up. I'm pondering the prospect of a bubble bath over a shower, oblivious to my surroundings, so it comes as a shock when fingers suddenly grip my arm. Something yanks me fiercely, pulling me sideways so quickly, I feel my ankle twist.

'What the fuck do you think that was?' Robin's blue eyes burn, spittle hitting my face as he drags me into the mirror-lined hallway. The same one leading to the restrooms.

'What are you doing?' My voice sounds breathy in my shock. It takes me a moment to register what's happening, but when I do, I bring my free hand to his chest and push. 'Get *off* me!' I grate out, words spat from behind my clenched teeth.

'No, you don't,' he snarls, releasing my forearm only to grasp one wrist and then quickly follow by grabbing the other. My purse clatters to the ground, my sudden shock all consuming. As he twists both my wrists behind my back, I start to panic and thrash. 'Stop fucking about, you bitch.' He shakes me just once, and the back of my head hits the mirror behind me with some force.

Stunned—I fall silent, captive to him and the thundering of my heart as I blink up into his unfamiliar expression. The hate. If it's possible, the venom in his tone and the look on his face is more shocking than the bump I'll no doubt have on my head. And I have no words—nothing to say. No retort. Though my gaze slides left, seeking something, someone. Some kind of help.

'G-get off me,' I finally gasp, beginning once again to struggle against his hold. It's the strangest kind of experience. Never in a million years would I have seen Robin as violent, but more importantly, I would never have seen myself as a victim. Yet here I am, my wrists trapped in his hand, my body compliant to his whims as his free hand grabs my jaw in a piercing hold.

'Did you think you could make me jealous, standing there flirting with that twat in a skirt?'

'What are you talking about? W-we split up.' I'm ashamed to say I cry out as his fingers tighten. 'Please, Robin, you're hurting me,' I whine.

'Do you think I paid for your room tonight so you could fuck someone else in it? Fuck someone in our home?'

Now is maybe not the time to point out the deposit was jointly paid. And honestly? Rationally? Even a little abstract right now? Up until an hour ago, I thought we were still on decent terms. I thought we were dealing with our split like adults. I'd even tried to tell myself he's a fundamentally nice guy—a nice guy who did something wrong.

Now I know all that is untrue. *Especially about him being a good man.*

Yet I still shake my head when he presses me again.

'Did you?' He looms over me; his eyes full of anger and frightening ideas.

'I-I. Let me go, Robin. Please. You don't want to hurt me.'

'Don't I? Can't you see you have me fucking unhinged?'

'I can see that you're angry—' I don't get to finish as he shakes me again.

'It was a mistake—I'm sorry I fucked Tamara. Sorry I hurt you, but you can't do this to me.'

From the corner of my eye, a figure turns into the hallway. As I raise my head, we lock gazes. A woman—someone I've never met. Someone from the wedding . . . someone who looks right through me as she turns back the way she came. Like she hadn't witnessed anything. How? How can someone ignore violence and abuse? What happened to human decency? Sisterly solidarity? Especially as he begins to shake me violently.

'You drive me insane with your hot and your cold. When are you going to make up your mind? Fucking give in. Come back to me!'

Is he drunk? Hot and cold what? We're over. Kaput. Our relationship was dead long before he turned up tonight with Tamara. But I say none of this as his breath blows over my face because it isn't liquor that has him crazy.

'I will. I'll make up my mind'—*have made up my mind; you're a fucking fruitcake*—'just-just let me go.'

'What the fuck?' My head whips around at the low masculine growl, my frightened gaze met by a feral one. 'Get the fuck off her,' Keir growls, striding closer. 'Before I tear your bollocks off and make you eat 'em.'

'This has got nothing to do with you, jock.'

'Oh, that's original.' He looks as agreeable as his sudden tone. Right before he punches Robin in the side of the head.

'Oh!' I cry out, stumbling as Robin releases my wrists.

'I've been insulted better by six-year-olds, you fucker,' Keir grates out, using the tips of his fingers to push Robin farther along the hallway. 'What sort of a man are you, eh? Laying your hands on a woman. Didn't your da ever teach you hitting a woman is the lowest of low?'

'She was going to be my wife!'

'I don't care if she was going to be the fucking queen,' he growls, though I don't miss his gaze sliding to mine with a look of abject *what the fuck*.

'We s-split up two months ago, and he's here with the girl he cheated on me with.' He doesn't reply but for one sardonic brow twitch, which makes me open my mouth and babble. 'I wasn't trying to make him jealous. I swear, it was a serious invitation.'

'Invitation?' Robin shouts. 'What the fuck were you inviting him to?'

'It was an invitation to separate her from her knickers.' Keir's head turns back with precision of a gun turret, pinning the other man with *the* smuggest look. 'And when I've done that, I'm gonna spend the night making her scream my fucking name.'

Robin makes a noise—not actual words—more like a strangled cry as he launches himself at Keir, whose response isn't nearly so manic as he coolly steps into Robin. And with an almost beautiful economy of movement, he headbutts him. The sound of cartilage on bone echoes through the space as Robin reels back

'Argh! You boke my dose!' he yells. 'You ducking well boke my dose!'

'I'll break more than your nose, pal, if you come at me again.'

'I'll ab you! I'll ducking ab you!'

'You reckon?' Keir replies, amused. He turns back to me then, pulling my wrists between our bodies and frowning down at them. 'Has he done this before?' His hazel eyes rise to mine, the fierceness in his gaze startling.

'No,' I answer quietly, tears beginning to gather at the brim. 'I had no idea he could be like this.'

'Ged away brom er!' Robin steps forward as though to intervene.

'You want me to leave her alone? What, so you can bash her again?' I find my wrists in the air, no longer held as Keir begins to move almost as quickly as Robin steps backwards. 'There's a special place in hell for men who hit women.'

'Keir, don't.' Not because I don't want to see him squashed like a bug, but I'd hate for Keir to get into trouble over me. Robin may look like an overgrown student, but he's backed by a powerful machine. Publicity people, and lawyers up the wazoo.

'You want to spare his bruises?' he asks quite unkindly.

I shake my head. 'No, that's not it at all.'

'I'll ab you in courd,' Robin crows. Or at least he tries to.

'See, that's no' to my taste. Corduroy is more for hipster fuck boys like you.'

'I think he means court,' I add, the thought making me sick.

Fingers still at his bloody nose, Robin mistakes my intervention, puffing out his chest. 'Ab you arresded.'

'The police?' Keir looks delighted. 'You must really be sick of your life, pal.' He takes a quick threatening step, causing Robin to almost tip in his haste to stumble back. 'Come on.' Palm up, he curls his fingers in several times. 'Why don't we leave the threats of court and police, and you and me step outside?'

'You're a ducking Neanderdal.'

'And you're gonna need that thing set,' Keir replies, letting his arms drop to his side. He straightens, adding sardonically, 'We wouldn't want to spoil those pretty boy looks.' Then he bursts out laughing. 'Sorry,' he says, wiping a hand down his face as though he could remove his smile. 'But you're a sorry looking fuck. You'd never have a chance with a looker like her,' he says, tilting his head my way. 'Unless you've a dick like a Coke can, but from what she's said, that's not true. Must be your sparkling wit and personality, aye?'

'Duck you,' Robin spits, all bubbling blood and venom. 'An duck her.'

'Now you're talkin',' Keir retorts. 'Come on, darlin',' he says, looping his arm around my waist and pulling me in tight. 'I say we take his advice.'

Chapter Seven

KEIR

'I'm so sorry,' she says for what seems like the hundredth time as we step out of the lift onto her floor. I hear what she says—of course, I do—but the majority of my attention is glued to her arse as she steps out in front. The tight material of her dress hugs her curves like a second skin, leaving me guessing at what she's wearing underneath. I blame the wee peek she blessed me with in the coffee shop; the flash of dark satin and the tiny flowers that seem to have become embedded in my brain.

Seriously, every time I've closed my eyes since, that's what I see.

'You really don't need to walk me back to my room, you know.' Paisley stops dead in her tracks, her hand on my forearm causing my attention to snap up. 'I was thinking maybe I should just head home.' She tips her gaze up to me, all bright blue eyes and trusting face. But she shouldn't trust me. Not with the way I currently feel. I wonder if she can feel my body vibrating under her fingertips?

Fucking and fighting. For me, those two things have always gone hand in hand. From the skinny, scrappy lad who grew up in a shitty flat at the arse end of a working class Scottish town to now; the man with an empire worth hundreds of millions. My fights are less physical these days, but my wins are still the same. On an intellectual level, I get it. Fighting and fucking are both their own kind of stimuli—it's a transference thing. Downstairs, I'd wanted to punch that prick until my arms ached. I couldn't, because adulthood, and now I have this build up, this force inside me needing an outlet. If she slid her hand from my arm to my zipper right now, she'd know. She'd probably recoil from me and quite sensibly so. Because I need to sink my cock deep in her to satiate the ache. Need like I need my next breath.

But I'm good at restraint. Restraint is my thing.

It's so fucked up, I know. I shouldn't be walking her to her room even though it's the right thing to do. Because chivalry might get kicked in the arse when we reach her door. It was easier in the ballroom. Easier to say no. But hyped up and with no outlet for this pent-up energy, I might just throw caution to the wind and throw her up against the wall, then really go to town.

Except I won't. Because I'm not a kid anymore. I'm in charge of my actions, not the other way around. And hasn't it already cost me a fortune in therapy to get to this point?

But still, I'd like to angry fuck some sense into her. It might actually do her some good. *Apart from the pleasure of a good, solid fucking.* Because some women are such shite judges of character when it comes to men. *Like my junkie mother.* I push the thought to the back of my head.

'Keir?'

Fuck. My jaw is rock fucking tight in my effort not to act on how I feel.

'Will there be someone at home?' My tone is rougher than I intended, and I catch myself before I wince at her wide-eyed expression.

'N-no,' she replies, slightly perturbed.

'You can't, then. Men like him don't give up. You can't be alone tonight.' Shite. That didn't sound the way it should've, a thought confirmed as her hand falls away.

'My friend is here in the hotel.'

'Same room?'

She gives a quick shake of her head. 'She's currently . . . otherwise engaged.'

'There's a euphemism if I ever heard one,' I say, taking her arm, our feet finally moving again.

'At least one of us is having fun,' she mumbles.

'Aye, I can think of better ways to spend an evening.' I grit my jaw, wishing I'd pulled the fucker out into the street.

'Again, I'm sorry to have been so much trouble.' She stops again, and while she might not have her hand on one cocked hip, her attitude is the same. I've pissed her off.

'That's not what I mean.' Before my sentient self realises, I've stepped into her, backing her against the door, my hands on the doorframe by her head. 'I meant what I said earlier.'

'And I told you,' she says, raising her chin a fraction higher. 'I don't scream for anyone.'

'You'd scream for me.' Probably from fright if she could see what was running through my head.

'This is me,' she says, producing the key card between us. 'But if you're not coming inside, I guess we'll never find out.'

Against everything I stand for as an adult, and against everything I've been telling myself since we stepped out of the lift, I grasp the card from where it's balanced between her two fingers. It all happens in slow motion.

I lower the key to the reader, her darkened eyes falling closed as I press my hips into her. She feeds her arms around my neck, and the door opens from the momentum of our bodies.

My arm around her waist, my bulk is the counterweight preventing her fall as we stumble into the room, everything speeding up again.

I kick the door closed, dropping the key to fuck knows where as I haul her tighter against me. My mouth commands our kiss, forcing it deeper and wetter until her fingers are pulling my hair and she's moaning into my mouth. And fuck, if that doesn't do it for me, making me frantic. Fills my head with the notion that I could spend an evening devouring her with just my mouth.

And that's a fucking thought. One that makes my whole body physically ache—makes my mouth water for the taste of her. The image of her garter belt and splayed legs heightens my desire, my desperation clear in the tenor of my groans and the wild movement of my hands on her—my lips as I drag them across her jaw, my teeth as I touch them to her neck and the soft swell of her breast. And all the while, I'm moving us farther into the room as she strips me of my jacket, pulling my shirt loose from the waist and dragging it over my head.

It's not a room but a suite, I notice, as we emerge from a dark hallway into the moonlit space. I make out the lounge setting—couches and tables. All kinds of things to bend her over and position her against. Like the back of the console table I push her up against. There's a chair or a couch in front of it, the dark shapes of more furniture gathered around.

If I had half a brain left, I might take her to the bedroom. Make the first time I fuck her count because I know once I crack this seal, once won't be enough. But I can't think of anything beyond her ragged breathing causing her chest to heave under my nose and my desperation to taste her. All of her.

As her backside hits the console table, I frame her tits with my hands, biting her nipples over the fabric and making her exhale a soft curse.

'Bedroom,' she adds huskily as my lips find her neck, the direction and words lost to the night air as she tilts her head back, giving me access to her pale skin. I kiss my way over her bared shoulder, biting the skin where it curves to her neck and causing her to hiss. I lift her knee, dragging it to my hip to grind against her like a teenager.

'I'm so fucking hard for you,' I growl in her ear, watching as she lifts her hand to where her dress is clasped at the shoulder. It falls away from her skin with a stiff kind of reluctance, barely revealing anything as I watch on like a pervert at a peep show.

'Zipper at the side,' she rasps, but I push her hand away as she reaches for it.

'Not so fast.'

'I want to feel you,' she replies, sliding her hand down my chest, causing my abs to tighten in anticipation. She slides it farther between us, pressing her palm to where I'm rock hard under my kilt and tightening her fingers around my girth. For a minute, I wonder if this is what a penitent feels like wearing a hair shirt. As she presses harder, I groan roughly, pulsing into her hand.

'That's so . . . wow,' she whispers, her eyes widening as her gaze flicks to mine. 'You're so big,' she whispers, arching her back. But between her hand, her dress, and my kilt, there's little relief for either of us.

And while it's always good to hear a little appreciation, I try not to smirk as I answer. 'This is all you,' I whisper, pressing my lips to her neck. 'All because of you.'

I lower her leg, placing my palms solidly on the front of her thighs. 'I'm so fucking hard, and I can scarcely think straight for imagining what's waiting for me under this dress.'

With the admission comes the action as I begin to drag the stiff fabric of her dress from her knees up. I don't do it slowly, but with a roughness that absolutely belies my desire. Paisley's breath hitches, and her hand falls from my dick, catching her balance on the table she's leaning against.

'Fuck, yeah.' My eyes are glued to the sheer lace tops of her stockings. Rather than ruffles this time, her garters are sleek and coloured like midnight. 'I'm going to fuck you while you're wearing these.'

'Just . . . please.' The words are exhaled along with a tremulous breath as she tilts her chin, her gaze lifting to the ceiling.

'No, darlin'.' I lift one hand from her thighs momentarily, placing my thumb on her chin. 'You don't want to miss this.'

Her eyes shine dark in the moonlight as she watches my face, not my hands, as I reveal the luminescent skin above her stocking tops. My fingers trail her silky skin, my palms pushing her thighs open.

Her knickers are sheer and almost totally transparent, her femininity on display in the form of a neat strip of curls beneath a smattering of embroidered polka dots.

'I can smell you. Smell your sweet cunt.' Leaning into her, I press two fingers against her crease. Maybe it's the boldness of my words rather than this first touch that has her knees buckling.

Her back arching.

Her whispered curse.

Her body begins to tremble as my finger slides a slow and rhythmic dance, the material dampening against my fingers as she pushes against me.

'Please,' she whispers again.

'Please what?' I answer with an edge of taunt, an edge of tease as I curl my fingers, hooking under the barely there strip of fabric between her legs.

'Please touch me.'

I will. And soon. But for now, I know she's feeling the cool air of the room on her wet pussy, her need building and twisting until she's fit to burst.

'When I get my mouth on you, I know I'll find you shiny and wet. Just for me.'

'God, yes!'

'You still think you won't scream?' She folds her bottom lip between her teeth, trying not to smile. But I don't wait for a definitive answer as I add, 'Get your arse on this table, darlin', because I'm gonna eat you out.'

Fingers at her waist, I make quick work of her zipper and then pull the dress over her head. And then I find myself just staring . . . staring at the perfection of the girl with the milkmaid braids. But there's nothing else simple about this view as she spreads her legs in invitation, baring herself through her gossamer-thin knickers. A bra to match; strapless and straining with the weight of her need.

'You're fucking perfect,' I whisper roughly, my hands spanning her collarbones and then dragging down over her skin. I release her dark nipples from their sheer cups, taking each into my mouth in turn, relishing the tenor of her hiss as I use a threat of teeth. My hands travel farther down, pushing her thighs wider still. The sight and scent of her driving me to the brink of insanity.

I feed my fingers between her legs, pulling the thin strip away from her skin. The material is damp and glistens under the moonlight.

'Look at how wet you are,' I tell her. 'Look at the mess you've made of these.' My gaze travels up her body, the threat in my eyes as well as my words. 'I've a good mind to make you clean them.' Her eyes widen, her breath hitching, and all the while I'm talking, I'm barely brushing her slick skin. 'A good mind to shove them into your mouth as we fuck. But then, how would I hear you scream?'

Christ, I want this pussy. Want this girl. Fighting my urge to pin her down and push myself in, I continue with my tease. As much as I want to press her bones against the table and fuck her solidly, I want to build her need for this. *For us.*

Chapter Eight

PAISLEY

'Look at how wet you are.' His voice is gravelly, his tone more wonder than admonishment as his gaze flicks from my wet panties to my face. 'I've a good mind to shove them into your mouth as we fuck. But then, how would I hear you scream?'

My God, I think I almost came.

With his accent, I knew his aural would be good, but I couldn't have guessed the dirty deliciousness of his words.

'You like the sound of that,' he asserts, staring at my pussy . . . *my cunt*. The word reverberates off the walls of my brain. *And my uterus*. How can I be so turned on by something that would usually make me cringe?

Yes, I know I work for a porn company, but still.

'Fuck, look at that,' he groans, sliding one wet finger against where I'm soaked. I can feel myself pulsing against his finger. Does he see? Can he feel it?

I only need to look at his dark gaze to know the answer.

'You're so fucking sexy,' he rasps, his thumb stroking my hard nipples one at a time. As he bends his head and takes one into his mouth, I buck at the graze of his teeth, welcoming the merging of pleasure and pain. What I'm unprepared for is the deep thrust of his large fingers inside.

I cry out—words of nonsense and need as his teeth tease and the fullness between my legs increases. *Is that two fingers? Three?* Three definitely. Electricity swells beneath my skin; I want to reach out and pull him to me, kiss him, let him taste my need, but I don't want this feeling to end.

Then, in one fluid motion, he drops to his knees and hooks my panties to the side to watch . . . to just stare at my most sensitive of places as he thrusts his fingers inside over and over again, his thumb rubbing my clit.

'That's it, darlin',' he murmurs. 'Ride my fucking hand.'

My fingers grasp the edge of the table as I begin to chant, 'Yes, God, yes! Please, please, please!'

On one deep thrust, Keir leans forward and places a soft kiss on the strip of hair between my legs. Another kiss, then another as he works his way down my pussy. When he reaches my opening, his dark gaze flicks up my body with a look of possession. A look that owns every bit of me. I watch as he parts my lips, stroking his tongue against where I'm most slick. It's barely a touch, but it ignites every nerve ending as he bares my clit. Kisses it. Circles it with his tongue. Engulfs it between his lips.

'Keir, God, yes!'

He grunts— a thoroughly masculine sound, his eyes dropping closed as his tongue licks me, pushing my legs wider, the string of my panties still hooked in his fingers.

'You're so fucking delicious,' he growls against my flesh with almost a sound of awe as he feeds his hands under the cheeks of my ass, pulling me to his face. His tongue strokes, opening me, his whole mouth licking, and sucking, devouring.

I'm not sure how it happens, but one moment, he's in front of me, and the next, I'm sitting on his face. Our position is so dirty, so fucking filthy as his hands find my hips, encouraging me in a sultry rhythm as I ride him. There's no other word for it—I ride his face. Never in my entire life have I felt so sexy. So powerful. So desired as something hot and sleek rushes through my insides.

The noises I make are raw, almost animalistic; my hands are on my breasts, my back arching and my body stiffening as Keir drives me over the edge. I'm panting and crying and chanting his name as I struggle to break free from his face, but he refuses to allow me as he continues to work my tortured flesh with his mouth, coaxing more from my orgasm. Every nerve ending screams for either release or more of his brand of ecstasy, I'm not sure which. It seems impossible that I can feel—or enjoy—more but I do as he groans into the very core of me, drawing out my orgasm.

I'm frayed. Whimpering. Spent.

'I can't . . . I can't.' I can't think. Can't move. Can't articulate what I mean as I fall forward, my palms connecting with the floor as I try to pull away from his large hands anchoring me against him.

'Don't cry, eh?' His tone is deep and smoky, and with a last tormenting lick along my over-sensitized flesh, he pulls away, but not before biting the soft skin of my thigh.

If I wasn't crying out before, I am now, the pounding between my legs only heightened by the press of his teeth.

'Jesus Christ,' he whispers a moment later, 'would you look at that.' But I don't have the wherewithal to move. My head balances on my forearms; my wits are like marbles rolling around the place.

I have never come like that before. Never had someone go down on me, leaving me feeling as limp as overcooked spaghetti noodles. And I sound like I've been running. I hope he doesn't want me to move because I don't think I can. Like, ever again.

I'm brought back to the moment by his large hands on the cheeks of my ass, his thumb hooking my panties farther to one side.

'Someone should paint this view.'

I huff some semblance of a laugh, thinking about the DIY mould kits Chastity considered featuring on the website. Or the MYOPD Max had insisted on. *Mould Your Own Pussy or Dick.*

'I'm serious,' he says, drawing his fingers along my wetness, causing me to whimper a muffled sound. 'Oh, fuck.'

I sense the frustration with his exclamation. Turning my head over my shoulder, I find this moonlit god on his knees behind me, the cut of his jaw and abs not the hardest thing about him right now. Even though his expression is grim, it doesn't stop my insides from fluttering at the sight of my wetness glistening on his lips and chin.

'What is it?' I whisper.

'I don't have a condom.'

'You don't?' Why do I sound so surprised?

'Unless you count the one in my wallet, which was a gag gift.' One shoulder lifts in a slight shrug. One large palm balances on the round of my bottom, and in the other, he holds himself. His dick. Cock. The thing I felt under his kilt but hadn't seen. *The kilt that now lies on the floor behind him*. Not that I'm paying much attention as I stare at him holding himself. Idly touching, stroking the long, thick—

'That condom won't do?' If I sound a little upset, it's because I feel it.

'It's got a picture of Father Christmas on the foil.' He quirks a brow. 'What about in your bag?' I shake my head. I hadn't taken Chastity's plan seriously at all. Not until I saw Keir, at least.

'A call to the concierge it is,' he says, making to move from between my legs.

'No, don't,' I say, reaching behind me and grabbing nothing but air.

'I'm sure they've had stranger requests.'

'No, I mean, I want you. And I can't imagine being tortured another minute while we wait for a prophylactic delivery.'

'Are you complaining?'

'Yes, Mr Smug. I need you to fuck me,' I answer bluntly. More bluntly than I've ever been before. 'I've had a million tests since Rob- . . . since he . . . so if you—'

'You know what they call couples who rely on pulling out?' Before I can answer, his brow tightens further as he grunts, 'Parents.'

'I'm on the pill.'

'That changes things a little,' he says, still scowling. 'Though the last time I fucked without a condom, you were probably still in school.'

'What?' I answer with a little squeak.

But he doesn't reply as he lines himself up, his jaw flexing as he curses again. Then he drives himself inside, expelling a long, throaty groan.

I cry out, still watching over my shoulder as his eyes roll closed. He tilts his head back as though savouring the moment as my insides clench their pleasure around him.

'Keep doin' that,' he says, blowing the words out on a long breath, his thick lashes fluttering as his eyes open once again. 'And this won't last very long.'

'So do it,' I whisper, pushing back against him.

'Do it? You mean fuck you—like this?' He pulls back, pushing back into my pussy deliciously slow. 'Or maybe like this?' My hips in his hands, he drives in fast, skin slapping skin with the impact, once, twice, three times.

'Yes!' I cry out, any of that—all of that.

He alternates his movements between slow thrusts and solid drives until I don't know where my body ends and his begins—until I don't know if I'm crying out his name, or just straight up cursing, or if my words make any sense.

He flicks open my bra, my breasts bouncing free before he slides a hand under me to adjust the tilt of my butt. The change of angle alters the depth of his thrusts, and with it, the tone of my cries as he pushes down on my back.

Keir's tempo changes as he groans, thrusting firmly again and again. His pace is unyielding, and I push my ass back against each of his thrusts as my climax approaches with a frightening speed, the tension twisting and building with the collision of skin.

Higher and higher it spirals, pushing all the air from my chest until I come loudly, my mind fragmenting, my body flexing and arching as it clenches through its release.

With one solid thrust, he grinds against me, and I think that's it—*he's come, too*. But then he pulls out, and covering my body with his, he works his length between the cheeks of my butt.

The experience is . . . I don't have any words. And it doesn't last long as his body lifts from mine. I turn my head again . . . just in time to see him painting my ass and the backs of my stockings with lashings of his cum.

Chapter Nine

KEIR

'That was . . . '

Lying on my back, I can't speak. Can't answer her. It was fucking at its finest. I can barely remember the last time I had a woman in my arms, never mind underneath me. But all I know is, I don't remember any first fuck being as intense and as dirty as that.

The sight of her riding my hand.

The picture of her undulating above me, nipples peeking out from her splayed fingertips.

The way the head of my cock looked sliding between her arse cheeks.

Her silky stockings stained with my cum.

And bare—skin to skin inside of her. *Fuck.*

'That was . . . ' she repeats in an almost breathless tone.

Her face suddenly appears over mine. Her lovely face, her lovely blue eyes and kiss-plumped pink lips. Her dark braids have become loose in a couple of places, but it doesn't detract from how gorgeous she is. I feel a rush of affection for her, frowning as I decide I need to get laid more often before I begin to confuse orgasm in something other than my hand with any kind of warmth of fondness or love.

'Are you dead?' she says, poking me in the ribs.

'*Uff.*' Along with the huffed breath, I may also growl or maybe squeal, '*No!' Growl. Definitely a growl.*

'You're right. Dead people don't frown. And dead people aren't ticklish.'

'I'm not tickl—' The rest of my words are swallowed by a noise that isn't quite laughter, and I squirm as her fingers dig into my ribs. 'Get off me, you mad wench! I'm not ticklish!'

'Then why are you giggling like a girl, huh? *Huh?*'

But then she makes a critical error, sliding her thigh over my body to straddle me. The sight of her wetness spread open in front of me, above me, draws my fingers like a magnet.

'You're so wet.' My words are part wonderment, part groan.

'And whose fault is that?' she whispers back, rocking into my touch.

'Yours. For being so sexy.' I pull her down against me and feel her smile into my kiss, her wetness pressed against me, the shape of her warm body along mine.

'You're not so bad yourself.' She runs her hair through my fingers, toying with the strands.

'So you told me in my interview. I'm glad to hear I measure up,' I say, pulsing up into her.

'Oh, you do,' she purrs. 'You measure up just fine.'

Our lips meet, the tone of this kiss different from before. Our mouths are slow and languid, drawing our kisses into endless moments, our fingers teasing and light in their touch.

'If I ever need a fallback career, you'll put in a good word?'

'I'm sure we could come to some arrangement,' she whispers, the sound and shape of her smile pressed against my lips.

'Why don't we go to the bedroom and discuss the terms. This carpet is embedding itself into my arse.'

'Tell that to my knees.'

'Come on.' I roll onto my side, keeping her tight to my body so she doesn't slip. Also, because naked. Naked girl wins every time. 'I've got some special medicine to remedy that.'

'Is that so?' She sort of giggles, the tone sultry. 'What kind of medicine?'

'It's magical stuff. It works as a liniment, an oral supplement, and even a suppository.'

She sets off giggling again with her head tucked into my chest. The sound of her mirth is almost as intoxicating as her smell—the mixture of her floral perfume and our fucking.

'Come on, up,' I say, sliding my hands down to her round arse.

'What, already?' She giggles. 'I doubt even you're that good.'

'No?'

Lifting her elbow from where it's tucked tight to her chest, Paisley looks down the length of my body. 'Oh.' Her cheeks are pink, and her eyes shining as her gaze snaps back to me.

'You were saying?'

'I think I was saying we should get up from this floor and get into the bedroom,' she replies quickly, scrambling to stand. 'The early bird catches the worm and all that.'

'It's a worm now?' I say, standing myself. 'Funny, I don't remember you crying out, *your worm is so fucking good.*'

'I said no such thing!' she retorts, her cheeks turning bright pink. She still has her garters and stockings on, though the latter are, quite frankly, fucked. 'What are you smiling about?' she chastises, crossing her arms over her ample chest.

'Pretty sure you said something like that.' I try not to smile, the corner of my mouth quirking as I pretend to weigh up my answer. *Pretend not to look at her tits.* 'I remember now. Your cock. Your cock is so fucking good. That was what you said. No worms were mentioned as you came around it, milking it for all its worth.'

'It's worth a lot,' she murmurs, watching as I wrap my fist around my cock. 'Because that is no worm.' It's at home there in my hand. You might say well acquainted, especially during our allotted *me time.* And her watching? I'm A-fucking-okay with that.

'Less worm . . . more like an anaconda.' The second half of her sentence is delivered much later as she watches as I run my hand along my shaft, engulfing the end. 'You still have your boots on,' she whispers.

'I do.'

'You look so hot, with or without the kilt.'

'You like the kilt, eh?'

'It makes me want to get Chastity to make a little *Outlander* porn.'

I'm somewhat familiar with the TV show; romantic tales of *The Rising* and buff Scotsmen in kilts.

'Why ask your friend when you've got the real thing in front of you?'

'Will you let me call you Jamie?' she says, giggling softly.

'I'll think about it,' I reply, kissing her temple before thickening my accent for my next command. 'Wench, get thee to thy bed.' She sets off running, and fuck, if the sight doesn't make my dick twice as hard.

I gather our clothes from the floor and follow her at a more leisurely pace, arriving just in time to see the bathroom door close.

I place our heaped clothing on the bottom of the bed, then switch on the bedside lamp to reveal a room tasteful in creams and pale blues. The Art Deco accents carry on in the form of square lamps and etched mirrors and retro wood. A long, padded bench sits at the end of the bed, and a minimalist chaise sits in front of the large window.

Taking a seat on the bench, I pull my phone from my jacket, feeling a twinge of guilt at the thought of calling home. It's not so late, just a little after nine p.m., but I hope she'll be asleep all the same.

The line rings just once before her wee voice squeals, 'Daddy!

My guilt deepens. How can I not want to hear her wee voice? 'Hiya, darlin'.'

'Why aren't you on the camera?'

'Because, er, there are too many people about.' I mentally kick myself for calling her wee iPod rather than the home phone because we always FaceTime.

'Are you no' in bed yet?' I ask, which is a ridiculous question as far as questions about the obvious go.

'Agnes said I could stay up and see the end of the film we're watching on Netflix. Agnes and me are Netflix and chillin'.' She giggles, though I know she's too young to be winding me up. At her age, she isn't aware of the connotations in that pastime.

'Well, be sure to get yourself to bed afore too long.'

'I want to wait up until you're home,' she says, her tone changing from sweet to petulant.

'No, it'll be too late for you.' My eyes flick to the bathroom door, hoping to get off the phone before Paisley comes out. One-night stands don't need to know the ins and outs of my life. Even one-night stands as lovely as her.

'But I want to,' she asserts. 'And tomorrow is still the weekend.'

'Be that as it may, you're to go to bed once the film is done. Do you hear me?' Sorcha doesn't answer. *She's getting awfully good at dishing out the silent treatment.* I sigh heavily, wondering, not for the first time, if playing mind games is part of her DNA. She hasn't seen her mother since she was tiny, but the older she gets, the more worrying things seem. And what's more, because she's ill, I can't even use tomorrow as bribery; I usually play rugby while she hangs out with Louis, my friend Mac's wee boy. But illness means quarantine, and quarantine is no fun for anyone.

'Well, if you're not going to talk to me, you'd better put Agnes on.' A tiny huff sounds down the line along with an equally huffily muttered, 'Fine.'

'She's crabbit—just miserable,' Agnes says in answer. 'And it's past her bedtime. Pay her no mind.' As usual, Agnes is quick to jump to my daughter's defence.

'I know. Chickenpox is enough to make anyone miserable, I'm sure.'

'You're not to worry. Just you enjoy your night,' she adds, her words pregnant with meaning. See, Will isn't the only one who worries I don't get enough sex, though I'm sure Agnes would argue she only means female companionship.

'I'll be home late,' I say, glancing at the bathroom door again. 'You're okay with that?'

'Aye, aye. Stop your fussing, and I'll see you in the morning. Sorcha,' she then calls in her no-nonsense tone, 'come say good night to your daddy.'

'Good night,' says my daughter, much more contrite.

'Night, darlin'. I'll see you soon.'

I'm staring down at my phone when I sense I'm being watched. When I look up, Paisley stands in the doorway, completely naked now, her hair falling in dark waves around her shoulders.

'You still have your boots on. And you're married.'

'One of those things is true,' I answer wearily. 'And one of them used to be true.'

'So your darling would be . . . ?'

'My daughter.' I move a small way along the bench, patting the cream leather next to me. I don't know when I've seen a lovelier sight as she walks hesitantly towards me. She was gorgeous in the coffee shop. Stunning in her blue dress, decked out for a wedding. Beautiful earlier, semi-naked and ruffled, and under my hands. But right now, unadorned and sort of vulnerable, she looks sublime.

I unlock my phone, opening the photo app, bringing up one of approximately five hundred images of my wee girl.

'This is Sorcha,' I say quietly.

'She looks like you,' Paisley says softly, which surprises me.

'Most people say she looks like her mother.' Shit, why did I say that?

'Does Sorcha live with her mom?'

'Nope.' I feel my mouth twist. 'Her mother has no part in her life. She lives with me and Agnes,' I say, flicking to the next image of many, where I've caught the steel grey-haired woman with a rare smile. It's not that she doesn't smile; she's just a bit serious, I suppose. *And she has no love for cameras.* 'This is Agnes.'

'Sorcha's granny?'

'As good as. Sorcha is the reason I said I couldn't come upstairs wi' you.' On the admission, my accent thickens. 'My life has changed so much since her mother and I split. She is and always will be my world.'

'Of course. That's understandable. But you're saying you don't date?' I shake my head. 'Ever? Not that this is a date or anything,' she's quick to add.

I shake my head. 'The past couple of times, it didn't go too well. Women don't seem to get that she'll always come first.'

'I'm not suggesting this is a date,' she says with that gorgeous tinkling laugh of hers. 'But you don't . . .'

I blow out a breath, rubbing my free hand through my hair. 'Casual fucks. Is there such a thing?'

'Well, I'm no expert,' she begins, tucking her hands between her legs, drawing my gaze to where it shouldn't be. 'But I think there are lots of kinds of sex. Lots of kinds of relationships tied to sex. I mean, in my world, some people get paid to screw, then go out for coffee as nothing but colleagues afterwards. We go on location shoots, and the actors have sex, kiss, and do all manner of things to each other, but that might be the only interaction they have.' Her gaze lifts, and what I see is hope, maybe. Misplaced hope. 'And then there's Max, Chastity's brother. He offers to exorcise me almost daily.'

'Exorcise?' I repeat, the word conjuring up images of the movie, *The Exorcist*.

'Yep, cleanse me of Robin,' she replies a little too enthusiastically as she nods. 'And the thing is, if I were even tempted, I know that'd be it. No strings attached—nothing more than an impersonal exchange of body fluids and then don't let the door hit you where the Good Lord split you.'

'The fella sounds like an opportunist.' It's the nicest description I can muster. The worst isn't fit for feminine ears.

'Quit giving me the side-eye. I'm not sleeping with him,' she says primly.

'I'm wondering if you feel like you still need exorcising?' I ask evenly.

'What? After what happened in there?' she asks a little incredulously, pointing at the other room.

'Aye.'

'Not hardly,' she answers with a cute snort. 'That was a thoroughly . . . thorough exorcism.'

'You're sure about that?'

'Positive.' I cock a brow, tilting my head the tiniest bit to the side. 'Oh. *Oh*. Well, maybe we could, you know, try again. Just to be absolutely sure. And I do think I felt my head spin when you did that thing with your tongue.'

'What thing was that exactly?'

'Maybe if we get into bed, I can demonstrate on you.' My cock jumps between us as she takes my phone from my passive hand. 'But first, so this doesn't get awkward at any point later, I'm going to put my number in your contacts list.' Without looking at me, she types in her number with her thumbs, almost immediately handing it back to me. 'That way, when you leave, you won't feel bad. You know, if I'm sleeping or something.'

'How do you know I'll feel bad?' I try for a little levity in my tone, but I'm not sure if it's a success.

'Because you're a good man. I can tell.'

I could respond in a dozen ways. I could tell her she's wrong. Tell her there's little chance of me calling her after tonight—that I don't deserve her understanding. Maybe remind her of the last man she thought was good. *The same one who frightened her downstairs*. But I don't do any of those things. Instead, I just stare down at my phone.

'Call me,' she says softly. 'Or don't.' Her eyes sparkle with mischief as she stares up at me. 'I might answer anyway.'

Chapter Ten

KEIR

'What are you all doing here?'

'Fine way to greet visitors this lovely Sunday mornin',' Mac replies gruffly, tightening his hold on a wiggling Juno. He steps in through the open door with Louis, his curly dark-haired son, by his side.

'Hang on. You can't come in here. Sorcha's still contagious.'

'That's exactly why we're here, silly,' Ella, his better half, says from behind his bulk.

'We've come to catch Sorcha's disease!' Louis calls, darting under my arm.

'Darling, maybe don't say that to Sorcha,' Ella calls after him.

I stand passively as the whole family shuffles into the house, though Ella pauses, pushing up on her tiptoes to kiss my cheek.

'You look a bit rough. Good wedding, was it?' Her words are heavy with meaning.

'I'm just a wee bit tired,' I answer a touch defensively.

'Hmm, I wonder why.'

'Daddy,' Sorcha says excitedly as I reach the living room. 'Louis has brought me some sweeties and a bottle of Lucozade.'

'That's nice of him.'

'Mummy brings me Lucozade when I'm ill,' he explains. 'It makes my tummy feel all fizzy and better. The sweeties were my idea because sweeties always make me feel happy.'

'Bribery, eh, Sorcha? Seems Auntie Ella wants to swap you goodies for your chickenpox.'

'That's silly!' Sorcha giggles, pulling her skinny legs out from under her Disney blanket to move the stainless-steel salad bowl balanced on her lap to the coffee table. There's no need for her to be hugging the salad bowl except as a means of reminding those around her—namely, me—that she's feeling very sorry for herself. *Like I need reminding.* 'No one wants to feel poorly,' she says brightly. 'Or be all spotty.'

Thankfully—on that front, at least—she seems to have improved overnight. She's still a bit pale and wan looking, but she's stopped itching. But not bitching. She's sick of her own company, and mine. And I can't do anything right after abandoning her to go to a wedding last night. *Like I don't feel guilty enough for the whole fucking evening.*

'It is a little silly,' Ella agrees, 'but also a little bit sensible. See, the younger you are when you contract chickenpox, the easier it is. We thought it might be a good idea for little Juno here to get the illness over with while she's still a baby.'

'She's not a baby!' Louis scorns. 'She's a toddler and getting bigger every day.'

'She's not growing quick enough for his tastes,' Mac adds in an undertone. 'She can'nae play Legos wi' him yet.'

That makes sense.

'And we thought maybe your daddy could go and play rugby this morning while we have—'

'A chicken spots party!'

'Come for the communicable disease, stay for the party?' I ask in a droll tone.

'Well, not a party exactly,' Ella says, her gaze rising to mine. 'Something much more sedate.'

'Movies and popcorn and fun!' Louis adds, throwing his arms wide.

'Din'nae fash,' Mac tells me. 'Seems he helped himself to the whole contents of his own sweetie bag in the car on the way over.'

'Sugar rush?'

'Aye, crash to follow. But we don't have to worry about that,' he says, slapping me on the back. 'We'll be on the field.'

'I feel better already,' Sorcha says. 'Maybe we can all go to rugby, and I can get an ice cream from the park.'

'You can't go to the park with chickenpox,' Agnes cuts in, sliding me a stern glance— a stern glance that says, *grow a pair, man.* She's dressed for Sunday mass but must have popped in through the back door to see to my guests. She lives in a wee bungalow at the back of the house.

'But I want to go outside,' Sorcha says, 'And you promised I could go to the wedding yesterday.'

I cast my eyes to the ceiling, inhaling a deep breath before lowering my gaze again. Big baby blues stare up at me. Eyes just like her mother's.

Jesus, please don't let her turn out like her.

'I know I promised,' I reply evenly. 'But that was before we knew you were going to be ill.'

'But I told you I feel better.'

'You mean, apart from having chickenpox,' I answer wryly.

'Your daddy had to go to the wedding as part of his work,' Agnes cuts in.

Aye, work. Because that's what I was up to last night while my child was ill. Working myself into sexual oblivion over the body of a beautiful and willing girl.

'And,' Agnes continues, 'he needs to go to work to pay for all those trips to that build a wee bear shop you're so fond of. Can I get anyone a coffee?'

'I'll put the kettle on,' Ella's says, scrambling to her feet and leaving us to our domestic.

'But I wanted to wear my new dress.'

Here we go. Sorcha's not a stroppy kid usually, though she does have a hell of a temper. Good job her tantrums are annual these days, though we did suffer through terrible twos, rotten threes, belligerent fours . . . all while I was trying to grow an empire.

'You can wear your lovely frock anytime,' Agnes responds, picking up the salad bowl, no doubt glad of the opportunity to get rid of it. 'Why, isn't your daddy always taking you nice places?'

'Not today he's not,' she replies, whip-sharp. 'And that's just effed in the a.'

Mac snorts, turning it into a cough. But me? My heart sinks, my brows along with it.

'*What* did you just say?'

'Effed in the a,' she repeats, this time with a little less attitude and much less confidence.

'And just where did you learn that wee gem, eh?' I'll bet not in the school I pay a fucking fortune for her to attend. And yes, so I'm a hypocrite. I might swear like a trooper, but I don't fucking well do it around—

'I heard Uncle Will say it,' she says, holding her chin a fraction higher. 'He said it to you. And *you* laughed.'

I'm not laughing now. 'Well, it's not the kind of language you should be using,' I bluster, sounding a bit too much like Agnes. 'Little girls don't say those kinds of things.'

'Why? What does it mean?'

'Never you mind,' Agnes butts in, sliding me a look that says she'll reserve her opinions on this topic for later. 'All you need to know is that it's no' very nice to say and that I'll be giving Uncle Will a piece of my mind when I see him next.' Her narrowed gaze slides back to me. And then Mac.

Tarring us with the same brush is probably sensible even if Mac isn't guilty this time. Just me, the fella who pays her wages, and Will, a peer of the realm. *Lord Travers, you're a very naughty boy*. But then he knows that well enough.

Once upon a time, I'd have instinctively known that in discussing *effing someone in the a*, he'd be recounting a night with a girl. But now that he's settled down and in love, he no longer shares those kinds of tales. Which is just as well as I doubt I'd be able to look Sadie in the eye if he told me he'd been bumming her last night.

There are some things you just don't share.

'Do you want me to stay, darlin'?' I ask softly, causing Agnes's frown to deepen.

'Yes,' Sorcha answers immediately. 'And . . . no.' Her expression and tone conflicting. 'I'm not supposed to say I want you to stay. Even if I do.'

'Why's that, then?'

'Because I'm just jealous. And I don't want to be.'

'That's better now,' Agnes chastises kindly, stroking her hair. 'You're a good girl, and you'll quit your greetin',' she says, referring to the appearance of Sorcha's sudden tears. You don't want to make your daddy feel any worse than he already does.'

'Why should he feel bad?' she complains, pulling her slender legs back under the blanket. 'I'm the one with the spots.'

'Because he's your dad, and your pain is his pain.'

'Well, he can have my chickenpox then.' Swiping the tears away, Sorcha scowls, folding her arms across her Disney nightdress. 'Anyway, I'm too big for Build-A-Bear now.'

'Be that as it may,' Agnes says, straightening the throw over her legs. 'But remember you're not too big for a skelped arse.'

I struggle to hide my smile. Agnes would no more smack her backside than she would mine. But the threat seems just as effective as it was all those years ago when she caught me trying to steal a packet of cigarettes from her corner shop.

She's been looking after me since then. Feeding me. Making sure I'm well.

'But I'm bored,' Sorcha complains.

'Of course, you are, darling,' Ella placates, perching herself on the edge of the sofa and pressing a pink cup into her hand. She brushes Sorcha's golden, though lank, hair from her head. 'As well as sweeties, I've brought a picnic, and Louis has some movies to stream. Do you think you might like to spend the afternoon with us?'

Sorcha nods, all doleful eyes. 'Yes please, Auntie Ella. Daddy can go to rugby, I suppose.'

Jesus Christ, you could sit on that pouty lip.

'Weddings are boring anyway,' asserts Louis, pressing a spouted cup into his little sister's grabby hands. 'It's all stand up, sit down. No talking in the church. Then they take hundreds and hundreds of photographs. Then they talk and talk *and talk!* So boring.'

'How many weddings have you been to?' Sorcha asks suspiciously.

Louis considers for a moment before answering. 'Three. And none of them were fun. Unless you like dancing.'

'Oh, well. I'm glad I didn't go then. Sorry, Daddy,' she adds without an ounce of contrition. 'You can play rugby. But please bring us all ice creams home.'

'Giving out your orders now?' Agnes says.

'Sorry, Auntie Agnes.' For Agnes, at least, she has the sense to look downcast.

'Off you go, then.' Ella masterfully suppresses a chuckle at my expression. 'We'll be here most of the afternoon. Harvesting germs,' she adds in an undertone.

'Aye, away you go,' Agnes says, almost shooing me out of the room. Ella and Mac follow us into the hallway.

'I haven't said I'm going yet. I haven't got my things.'

'We all know you keep your kit in the car,' Mac says, calling me out.

'But I left Sorcha last night,' I say, voicing my guilt. 'And all last week while I worked!'

'And she didn't miss you an ounce.' Agnes confirms something my head already knows. My heart? It doesn't like to admit it. 'That wee girl just delights in giving you a hard time some days.'

'Can we keep Juno at this age?' Mac says, turning to Ella. 'Skip all the painful parts.'

'Painful?' Agnes scoffs. 'Just wait until the teenage years. Boys or girls, they all give you grey hairs.'

'I'd best start saving for hair dye now,' Ella says, chuckling.

'It's to be hoped wee Juno is nothing like you.' I hold my hands up as Agnes points a finger in my direction. She obviously hasn't picked up on how territorial Mac can be. 'The scrapes this one used to get in to.'

'All right, I'm going,' I say, taking the hint. 'But I'm not going for a pint after. I'll come straight home.'

'Bullshit,' Mac grumbles, then, 'Ah, sorry there, Agnes.'

A terse, '*Hmph,*' is Agnes's only response. 'Forgiven. But only if you can get him to give the lassie from last night a call. Maybe he can take her out for coffee or something.'

'You met someone!' Ella almost squeals, before repeating her exclamation in a more even tone. A hopeful tone. 'You met someone. A nice someone?'

'Nice enough to keep him out until the wee hours.' *Jesus, Agnes! Hang me out to dry, why don't you?*

'Oh . . . '

'Stop smiling at me like that,' I say, pointing a finger at Ella.

'Come on,' Mac says, his hand on the door handle. 'Before they squeeze all your secrets out of you.'

'I haven't got any secrets,' I protest. 'I went to a wedding, not an orgy! Am I not allowed any privacy?'

It's a rhetorical question. We all know the answer is *not if they can help it.*

Chapter Eleven

KEIR

'You played shite today.' Taking a deep gulp of his pint, Will places it back on the surface of the sticky bar. 'You weren't your usual killer self.'

'Cheers, fucker.' I raise my own glass. 'There's nothin' like kicking a pal when he's had a tough week.'

'Killer week,' Mac adds, hiding the smile behind his own pint.

'What am I missing?' Will asks, his narrowed gaze flicking back and forth between us. 'You've had sex,' he asserts immediately.

'Fuck off.' I take another sip of my drink, my expression unchanged.

'You have—you've had your balls out of the cellophane!'

'Wanna yell *baws* a bit louder?' Mac grates out. 'I'm sure there's a fucker in the toilets who didn't hear. Jesus wept.' He looks about to lean his folded arms on the bar but then thinks better of it at the last minute, taking in the sticky surface. The pub we're in? Hardly salubrious but it has been our regular hangout for years. 'Why does the conversation always turn to bollix when you're around?'

'It's a talent,' Will replies.

'Must be something to do wi' your blue blood, eh?'

'We're all a bunch of raving knackers,' he agrees.

'So we've had balls, baws, bollix, and knackers. Any other euphemisms for testicles you want to bandy around?' asks an unhappy Mac.

'Just Keir,' Will responds immediately. 'Come on, who's the unlucky girl?'

'Why would she be unlucky?' *Fuck*. 'There is no girl.'

'She'd be unlucky,' Will responds, ignoring my attempt at salvaging the direction of this conversation, 'because you've been storing your testicles in a drawer somewhere—unused for decades.'

'It hasn't been that long.'

'Long enough,' Mac's deep voice cuts in.

'Et tu?'

Mac shrugs. 'I get it. And I don't. How can you go without sex?'

My finger taps furiously against my glass; my lips glued closed to contain all the things I could say. Like how when you put your all into a marriage— love, hope, and faith—only to find you've been taken for a fool, it's enough to put you off any kind of love, including the physical. That in working yourself into the fucking ground to provide for your family only to find you've become the ultimate cliché? It deadens more than just your heart.

Jayne, my wife—*my ex-wife*—decided I wasn't paying her enough attention, so she fucked her personal trainer. Painful? Yes. But nothing a man can't recover from. The rest? That shit stays.

'Have you heard from her lately?' Mac asks, probably reading my expression.

'Not since she wanted money last time.'

The money she wants. Me or my child? Not so much. She hurt me and I thought I'd hurt her back by offering her money in exchange for her claim for custody. I didn't think in a million years she'd agree, but there you go. That right there is hurt enough to make me never want to get involved with anyone. Ever again.

'There are billions of women in the world,' Will begins, but I cut him off.

'You're right, but not one of them will get the chance to screw me over again.' I push off from the bar. 'I need to piss.'

As it happens, I don't need to, but I do need to get away. And by the time I get back to my pint, I've chased the anger away. It's not Will or Mac's fault. They can't understand, and I hope they never do.

'My round?'

'Not at all,' Will says, suddenly looking very pleased with himself. 'Tracey, sweetheart? Another round when you've got a minute.'

'Comin' right up, Willie, love,' she calls back in her heavy *norf*, or north, London accent.

'I'm a man with many names; Doctor, Lord Travers, Will—'

'Arsehole,' adds Mac.

'Sometimes,' Will agrees, 'but Tracey is the only person in the world who gets away with calling me Willie.'

'That must be your porn star name, eh?' I turn my head at Mac's almost non-sequitur. And his strange smile.

'And speaking of porn . . . ' Will begins smugly.

I look down at my phone on the bar, which is currently face down. And not the way I left it before going to the bathroom. If it's possible, the pit of my stomach hits my shoes.

'You fuckers,' I say slowly. I look back and forth between the pair who show not an ounce of contrition. In fact, they seem pretty fucking amused.

'Fast Girl Media, eh? In your browser. Downloaded the app.' Will looks fucking delighted. 'A little too much soft lighting and artsy frames for my taste, but whatever floats your boat. You must've cracked the seal in spectacular style. A toast is in order!' He takes one of the small tumblers of whisky the peroxide-haired Tracey had deposited in front of me.

'To getting your end away,' he declares, raising his glass.

'I'll fucking end you,' I grumble, the tips of my ears beginning to sting.

'Pay him no mind.' Mac slaps my shoulder. 'Y'ken that little things please little minds.'

'That must be why he's always playing with himself,' I retort in a grumble.

'Unlike some people, I don't need to play with myself. That is, unless a certain lady, who shall remain nameless, feels like she wants to watch me take myself in hand.'

'Fuckin' boundaries,' Mac growls. 'I'll need bleach.'

'What for? Your arsehole?'

'Seriously,' I supply. 'This discussion is less fun than putting lotion on wee Sorcha's spots.'

'And speaking of spots . . . ' I know what's coming before he says it, my eyes falling closed as I prepare myself. 'Who, pray tell, is Paisley?'

'What has Paisley got to do with spots?' Mac butts in.

'They're both patterns.' Will shrugs quickly.

'So you thought you'd go through my contacts as well? Is nothing fucking sacred?' I add.

'But no man is an island,' Will says, chuckling. 'Or something. Plus, she was the only one in your contacts with a heart after her name. Sweet boy,' he adds, pinching my cheek.

'Get off.' I push his hand away. 'She put her own name in the thing.'

'Tell us about your second cherry poppin', and we'll leave you alone.'

'You're on your own there,' Mac grumbles to Will. 'I don't need the details.'

'Fucking sweetie wives, the pair of you,' I respond, using the Scots slang for gossip mongers.

'It was the wedding yesterday, wasn't it?' Will says. 'Didn't I tell you it would be the perfect place to hookup? I suppose it also explains why your game was subpar today. It's what happens when you don't clean the pipes out enough.'

I really have no answer for that wee gem, so ignoring Will's assumptions and Mac's continued chuckling, I down my whisky, pleased at least that he didn't order the cheap stuff.

'Get me another would you, Tracey?' I gesture at my glass, and Tracey nods. *I'm not driving, so I may as well.*

'Fine. You don't need to tell us. I mean, we're only your mates—*only* the best mates in the world. Isn't that right, Mac?'

'Your best interests at heart,' he replies, patting his chest where his heart should be. It makes me wonder exactly how much he's had to drink.

'I'm pleased my life is keeping you both entertained.'

'We'd be happier if you told us a little bit about her,' Mac replies evenly. 'It's not all about takin' the piss.'

'Look,' I begin reluctantly and through almost gritted teeth. 'She works for Fast Girl Media, okay?'

'She's in porn?'

'Jesus.' Mac wipes a hand down his face, though I'm not sure if it's a reaction to Will yelling the word "porn" in this spit-and-sawdust pub, or the fact that he now thinks I've fucked a porn star.

'No, she's not in porn,' I almost growl defensively, though whether on behalf of her or me, it's hard to tell. 'At least, not like that.'

'What other way is there to be in porn?' Mac asks. 'Other than starring in it or being into it.'

'Her mate owns the company. As far as I can tell, she does a bit of admin and makeup.'

'Makeup?' they answer in unison.

'Aye. She's a makeup artist by trade.'

'Oh,' Will answers, then, '*Oh!*' This one sounds more like a revelation. 'That answers her text, then.'

'She hasn't sent me a text,' I scoff, swiping my phone from the bar. 'She doesn't have my number.'

'She does now,' answers Mac.

Chapter Twelve

PAISLEY

'Paisley? Could you grab the bounce board for me, sweetie?'

Standing in the kitchen area of the very gorgeous open-plan apartment we're filming in today, I'm in the middle of making myself a cup of tea when Chastity calls me—on location, no less—from fabulous Barcelona. The apartment in the gothic quarter is nothing short of gorgeous—exposed pale stonework and marble floors, the space filled with sunlight spilling in from a pair of ornate French doors. There's even a private balcony, which, I'm told, is rare in this ancient part of the city.

Chastity chose well because privacy is the key. No one filming or being filmed in this afternoon's outdoor sequence wants to draw a crowd. Or be catcalled from nearby windows. Or find themselves the subject of an elderly lady's showering of holy water and cries of *Dios mío!*

I'm told this has happened before.

Grabbing the folding reflector, I make my way into the lounge to where Antonio— yes, *interview Antonio*—has one foot on the floor and his knee on the chair that his partner for the day, Tianka, is kneeling on. It's odd that I take in their positions before actually registering that the pair are naked.

'Great,' Chas says as I hold the silver reflector thingy up. 'If you could just stand there . . . that's it. Up a little bit? It's just to diffuse the light.'

I hold the thing in front of me while he pretends to hump a very bored looking Tia from behind. Chas, meanwhile, takes some technical readings. Something to do with light ratios or something.

'Right. We're just about ready to go. Antonio?' Of course, we all look at him and then at his flaccid member. Because it doesn't look very ready. Or very happy. Though it still looks pretty big.

'I'll be there now, in a minute, beaut,' he replies, his gaze flicking up from his crotch because, in the absence of a fluffer—and I'm not sure that fluffer is a job that really exists—Antonio is currently . . . playing with his man-meat.

I raise the reflector over my face, basically hiding behind it. And so much for thinking Keir couldn't be Antonio Uccello because of his Scots accent because *this* Antonio doesn't sound very Italian, either. Unless there's an Italy in Cardiff. That's Wales, FYI. His accent is sort of singsong-y with peaks and troughs of tone. But not very Italian.

And I don't know how I could've confused Keir for him—Keir's like Ben & Jerry's Karamel Sutra to Antonio's generic vanilla. Not that I suppose being an adult actor is considered vanilla. But there's no comparison.

'That's a proper tidy result, that is.'

Antonio's voice brings me back to the moment. I lower the reflector, unprepared to find him talking about his penis. I quickly raise it again because I'm not sure if he's looking for a congratulations or a round of applause. Also, I need something to hide my giggles behind.

This current moment aside, it's not like I've been present during much filming so far, which means I still struggle to school my expression and remain impassive at the best of times. Sometimes, I feel like someone with Tourette's syndrome, struggling against the impulse to expel words. *I see Dick! Cock! Penis!*

I find myself turning bright red as the actors screw. *Screw in front of me.* Or make an idiot of myself as I tilt my head to the side, wondering how a particular angle works. And then there are the times I just feel ill. The smell of those flavoured lubes turns my stomach some days.

But it's a job, and it both pays my bills plus it helps my friend out. She tells me she likes having me around. The funny thing is, before Robin fucked his assistant's assistant, I'd never even watched porn—if you discount Tumblr—never mind watched real live people get it on. It's not that I'm a prude or anything, but it has been a bit of a culture shock—much more so than when I moved to the UK.

I stifle a yawn as the sound of slapping skin fills the room. I was up late last night. *Or rather, Keir was.* And when I woke this morning, just as I'd expected, he was gone. I didn't feel bad about the evening or the experience—quite the opposite as

I'd sprawled out in the huge bed and the mass of wrinkled sheets like a starfish, relishing the aches he left me with. And I was okay with waking up alone. I think the act of balancing life and a child must be a pretty difficult one.

It's strange that I barely know him, but I can totally see him as a dad. Maybe because he'd stood up to Robin for me, or some other act of chivalry I don't recall. Or maybe I'm just too tired to think straight.

I'm not the only one exhausted, I think as my gaze slides to Chastity. Though she was very close mouthed about her own evening, she'd fallen asleep before our plane had even reached the runway. Also, she has the gait of a woman well tended to in bed. *And isn't that a euphemism unsuitable for a porn set.*

'Oh. *Oooohhh!* Yes! Like that.'

Tianka's moans sound totally legit, somehow making my mind wander to last night. Keir might not make his living with his penis, but he absolutely could. The man had moves women would pay to see. Plus, all those hard muscles and that delicious confidence? He'd be a popular one for sure. Not that I'd suggest it to him. *Not in a million years.*

'Can you move to the sofa, Tia, darling? Yes, on your back.'

I'm pretty sure most porn isn't produced the way Fast Girl Media works. For starters, Chastity has a pretty small crew. None of the usual job descriptions you see at the end of a movie's credits. No gaffer, no grips, no crew. It's all very small scale, but her work is beautiful, obviously so, even to a novice like me.

'Paisley, can you cover the pimple on Antonio's lovely derrière?'

'What?' I'm brought back from my musing, my thoughts coming back to earth with a bump.

'Antonio . . . he has a spot on his bottom.'

Oh, the glamour of my job.

I conceal his pimple, throw away yet another makeup sponge, and make a mental note to order more when we get back to London. Wondering how long we have left with regards to light, I slide my phone from the back pocket of my skinny jeans to check the time and realise I have a text. I swipe the screen, registering the unknown number. Which can only mean . . .

Butterflies take flight in my stomach—and a little farther down—as I open my messages.

What are you doing today, gorgeous?

Smiling widely, I type back a response without thought. **Such glamourous stuff like you wouldn't believe.** Like hiding pimples on places other than faces, I'm not going to say.

Send me something sexy, his immediate response reads.

A sudden blast of ice freezes the butterflies, sending them thudding to the ground. Really. That's what he sends me? After the glorious night we had?

My first instinct is that this isn't from Keir. I mean, I hardly expected him to be in contact so soon, given everything we said. I hoped, of course I did, but I thought he'd have to talk himself into seeing me again. *Which he totally would. The experience was too good not to repeat.*

But when all is said and done, I can't kid myself. The chances of this being a mistake or some random looking for kicks is slim. And, as Occam's razor would demand, the simplest explanation is that Keir has sent me a request for a . . . what? Tit pic? A crotch shot?

That's just . . .

'What's up, sweetie?' Chas enters the kitchen, swiping a bottle of water from the tiled worktop.

'That's just so . . . disappointing!' I huff, handing her my phone.

She looks at it, then me. 'The guy from last night?'

'I thought he was different.'

'On the strength of one evening?'

'On the strength of a lot of things that happened. But yes, on one evening. Does that make me really stupid?' Even I can hear how pitiful I sound.

'Not stupid,' Chas answers, placing my phone on the worktop and cracking the lid on her water. 'Maybe hopeful. Like the rest of us.'

'What is hopeful?' Tianka says, entering the kitchen area next. Thankfully, she's pulled on a white robe. *Adult actors and actresses seem very comfortable in their own skins.*

'Hey, Tia,' I say in greeting. Because, you know, she has clothes on now, so it's totally fine to do so, and this kind of greeting does not incur a furious blush. 'Not what is hopeful, I suppose, but who. And that who would be me.'

Tianka looks on confused, causing Chas to explain.

'She slept with a guy who seemed nice.'

'All men seem nice in the beginning,' Tia scoffs with an air of superiority and a flick of one elegant hand. Tall and milky skinned, Tia has a very improbable shade of red hair. She could totally work regular speaking parts with her smoky voice and a rich Eastern European accent. Not that she's mute during Chastity's movies. No, she's quite, ahem, vocal. Anyway, she's totally got the bad Bond girl thing going on. 'And what has the nice man done to make a mistake?'

'He's just asked me for a picture.' I shrug, a little uncomfortable. 'You know. A naked picture.'

'Like snatch-chat?'

'I think that's Snapchat.'

She waves my response away. 'Bah! Always so juvenile, these men. Take my advice and find an older man. They are more grateful for your time.' Wow. That sounds a little . . . paid for by the hour. Or is it just me? 'Also, they are not so demanding, Viagra or not.'

'Or I could give him the benefit of the doubt?' I suggest aloud . . . much to the amusement of my companions.

'He asked for a dirty picture. I guarantee there'll be a cock shot on your phone within three minutes of you sending him yours.'

'I'm not going to send him a picture of my boobs or anything!'

'Why not?' Tia asks. 'You have nice breasts.' I find myself turning beet red as I bat away her outstretched hand.

'Maybe you should send him a cock shot,' Chastity says suddenly.

'I told you, I'm not sending any dirty pictures. Besides, I don't know whether you've noticed,' I respond, waving my hand in the general area of my crotch, 'but I don't actually *have* one of those.'

'But Chastity has one. Paid in advance, I think.' Tia's head turns to the living room where Antonio sits in a wicker chair, touching his unresponsive penis.

'He'll rub himself raw,' I say to no one in particular.

'He needed a personal break,' Chas says as if that makes perfect sense.

'Antonio,' Tianka calls, catching the man's attention. 'Penis is very unhappy today.'

'I never have this problem, see,' he says, dipping his head to his lap again. It doesn't hide his worried expression. 'I can always get it up.'

'Everyone has moments like these,' Chas placates from beside me. 'Not to worry. You brought pills, yeah?'

'I did, but I don't like to use them,' he answers unhappily in his Welsh singsong tone.

'We don't have much light left, so I'm afraid we might have to.' Pushing off from the worktop, Chas walks back towards the living room. The pair exchange a few low spoken words before she comes back again.

'Here,' she says, handing me back my phone. *The phone I didn't realise she'd taken.* 'Send him this with Antonio's regards.'

I look back at where he sits as naked as a jaybird . . . still with his dick in his hand.

'I'll take one for the team, see,' he calls back, giving me a thumbs-up. 'Even in the movie industry.'

'They call it gay for pay,' Tianka explains. Though I'm not really paying attention as I look down at my phone, swipe the screen, then nearly drop the thing at the image I'm greeted with.

A zoomed in, lubed, though long, flaccid penis.

Chapter Thirteen

KEIR

Send me something sexy.

'You are a cock of the first order,' I say, draining my pint as I shake my head. 'She's going to think I'm a total knob for sending her that.'

'You should never leave your phone unattended around him,' Mac cautions, lifting my phone from the bar to read the text.

'Aye, well, I notice you didn't stop him,' I retort.

'Light-fingered Larry had sent it and was chuckling into his drink before I'd even noticed.'

'Light-fingered?' Will begins, aggrieved. 'Those are some scurrilous accusations. Once upon a time, they'd have landed you in the Tower.'

'You're a lord, not the king,' Mac retorts. 'And you're a thieving one at that.'

'It's in my blood,' Will replies with an amiable shrug. 'What can I say? The landed gentry have been getting away with murder for centuries. Besides, she works for a porn company. I'm sure she'll have heard much worse.'

'Her job has no bearing on this,' I say, pointing my index finger at him. 'Separate Paisley from whatever dirty smut is going on through that cesspit of a mind—'

'Paisley is not a name; it's a tie or a pair of curtains.'

'Grow the fuck up,' I find myself snarling in response.

'*Oooh*, Keir likes a *girl*.' The expression Will's face suddenly adopts is one that could be solved by a punch.

'Leave off,' I growl, turning back to my drink.

'I think it's cute. The unflappable Keir has a crush.'

'I'll crush your head, you total—'

'Now, now, lads,' Mac interjects. 'I'm sure Lord Travers here can grow up a wee bit, if he really tried. Maybe you should leave it to him to apologise.'

'Or maybe you'll apologise to me when you get a little something back via text.' At almost the same time as Will stops speaking, my phone chimes. 'You're welcome, by the way,' he says smugly, lifting his whisky glass.

'And fuck you very much still,' I reply, holding my phone like it's a small incendiary device. Do I want to look? *Of course, I do*. Does that make me as bad as him?

'As charming as that offer is, I'm off the market these days.'

'Christ knows how,' I answer, still staring at the unopened text. Fuck it. It's not like I'm not going to look. She's pretty much all I've thought of since I left her in bed in the wee hours, all tangled hair and sheets, a heady perfume filling the room. *The clean scent of her sweat and sex.*

The recollection is so real; it's like I can almost reach out and touch her. Taste her still. The thought causes my cock to throb, and though I should probably wait until I get home, I'm kidding myself. My impulse control has been shot since I walked her to her hotel room.

I tilt the phone to my chest a little, surreptitiously raising my head a wee bit, though both Mac and Will seem to have purposely turned their attention to the corner of the room where a football match plays out on the large-screen TV.

'Hurry up and have your dirty wee peek,' Will complains without turning his head. 'I don't even like football.'

'Wrong shaped balls,' I murmur.

'That what you get for not shagging for so long.'

'For the love of God,' Mac protests. 'Shut your mouth and give your arse a chance.'

'Agreed,' I add. 'He does talk a load of shite.' As I speak, I unlock my phone, open my texts, and physically recoil.

'Well . . . that's something,' I say, distaste and a morbid sounding chuckle filling my tone.

'Are you done?' Will asks, turning back to face me. I hand him my phone, and like a true bloke, no matter what his heart tells him about being settled and loved up, his brain tells him to *look at the dirty pictures.* And so he does. His face morphs through a myriad of expressions—enquiring surprise, to abhorrent disgust, and everything in between. 'You've shagged a chick with a dick?' His voice echoes through the bar.

'Keep it fuckin' down,' Mac growls.

'This is your fault,' I say, laughing at his abject horror. 'And you're still lookin' at it.'

'It? Why? Why would she send you a picture of a manscaped dick?'

'On account of your stupid first text,' Mac says, snatching the phone out of his hand and plonking it face down in my palm. 'Go sort this out. We'll need to leave soon.' *To get back to Ella and the kids.*

I nod, the stab of guilt resurfacing, though I turn and make my way outside as the call connects. It's begun to rain while we've been in the pub, the grey roads now slick and shiny.

'Hello?' Over the patter of the rain overhead, I hear how her voice brims with laughter even in that one spoken word. The tightness in my chest seems to loosen almost instantly.

'How are you?' Alcohol softens my tone, my enquiry warm.

'I'm as hot as hell.'

'That's maybe a little conceited but also very true.'

'Conceited? This from the man asking me to send intimate images. Via text, no less. Classy, Keir. Real classy.'

'I'm sorry about that.' I blow out the words on a long, regretful breath as I rub my hand against the back of my head. 'But you really showed me, didn't you?'

'I sure showed you something,' she replies, giggling.

'I'm impressed—horrified but impressed.'

'Was it the size of the schlong that did it for you?'

'Ah, no.' I chuckle. 'Though that was also impressive. Horrifyingly impressive.'

'Like you don't compare,' she scoffs.

'I'm not sure what you're suggesting. Maybe a line up? Tape measures at the ready?'

She giggles again, a light, carefree sound. 'I just meant, you know, you have nothing to be shy about.'

'I'll take that as a compliment,' I return, smiling into the rain-washed street. A car passes by with a hiss of wet tires, kicking up moisture into the air.

'You totally should,' she answers, her voice a touch lower now.

'Is it strange that I can still feel you in my hands?' I should regret the admission because I shouldn't be leading her on. But all thoughts of impropriety, guilt, or remorse disappear with her next words.

'I sort of still feel like I'm in your hands.'

'How so?'

'I feel them. Feel your mark all over me.'

My responding chuckle is low, an image from last night reverberating in my head. Paisley, naked and beneath me. Skin sliding against skin. My hands on her. My tongue inside her. My cock . . .

'Are you still there?' she asks softly.

'Yeah. I'm just . . . Can I see you?' The words come from nowhere, but out in the air, I have no wish to take them back.

'If you mean in a text message—' Humour colours her tone, but I cut her off anyway.

'That wasn't me. It was my arsehole mate. Can't leave your phone anywhere, it seems.'

'So define *see me.*'

I rub my lips together to stop the images in my head from turning to spilled words. My wants. My desires. The things I'd like to do to her but didn't get the chance. Sordid things. Fun things. More than fucking in the dark.

'Dinner. Coffee. A walk in the fucking park,' I say instead. 'Whatever tickles your fancy.'

Her laughter warms me from the inside out.

'Oh, I think you've already discovered how my fancy likes to be tickled.'

'Are you suggesting I know how you like to be fucked?'

Her breath hitches as the door to the pub opens, and an old man in a grey cap steps out into the rain. He heard me—heard the uncharacteristic thing I said to Paisley—I know he did. The look that passes between us isn't hard to define. *Life is short. Make hay while the sun shines. Have sex with the lovely girl.*

'Do you want to skip the niceties and go straight to a hotel room?'

Was that an invitation or a trap? I mentally berate myself for the sudden thought. Not all women are like my ex. 'I didn't say that.' But fuck if

I don't want to. 'I'm not easy, Paisley. I'm gonna make you work for it.'

'You're what?' she says, giggling.

'I don't dole out my favours to just anyone.'

'Oh, I believe it,' she replies, still amused.

'This isn't Halloween, and my sexual favours aren't M&M's.'

'So what does a girl have to do to get you into her bed again?'

'I think we should start with dinner on Friday. How are you fixed?'

'Fixed?'

'What's your schedule look like?'

'I get back from Barcelona midweek, so that could work.'

Her *hot as hell* comment suddenly makes more sense—though she absolutely is hot—as I recall our initial *interview*.

'How is Antonio?' My enquiry is not without a touch of chagrin.

'Oh, Antonio's hanging,' she responds airily.

While I'm not overly pleased to imagine her surrounded by swinging dicks, I can't help but be a little confused by what she means.

'You're hanging with Antonio now?' I say, attempting to keep the strain from my voice. *And mostly winning.*

'No.' Static sounds over the phone as though her hair is brushing against the speaker. 'Antonio is *hanging,*' she adds almost in a whisper. 'On the set. Hanging as in the text I sent.'

'Jesus, woman,' I say, chuckling, her meaning becoming suddenly clear. 'Is it not enough that you nearly blinded me in the coffee shop wi' pictures of him!'

'He's not blinding anyone today, let me tell you. At least, not by poking anyone's eye out.' In the distance, someone calls her name. 'I'm sorry,' she says quickly. 'I have to get back. Text me where and I'll see you next week?'

'Sure. I look forward to it.'

With warm goodbyes, we end our call, and I go back into the pub.

'See,' Will says, taking in the splashes of rain on my shirt. 'Even the heavens are weeping with joy because you got your dick wet yesterday.'

'You'll be pleased to know it isn't an unsalvageable mess, no thanks to you.'

'You're going to see her again?' The surprise on his face hits me like a kick in the nuts. Swift and painful.

'That's a grand idea,' Mac says, downing the rest of his drink. 'Are we ready to go?'

Chapter Fourteen

PAISLEY

'Check you out! Where are you off to dressed like that?'

I look down at my outfit, wondering what Chastity means; skinny jeans, heels, and an oversized sweater is hardly worth the look on her face. 'What's wrong with the way I'm dressed?' I ask, looking up again.

'Wrong? Nothing. But I haven't seen you dress up in months.'

'I always try to look nice.' Apart from the weeks post breakup when I wore nothing but stained sweats or my old robe. 'I look nice for work, don't I? Smart—smart casual,' I add, a touch defensive.

'What she means is you look hot.' From his position on the sofa next to Chastity, Max's gaze slides my way—then slides up, then down, taking in my whole outfit. *My whole body.*

'Stop imagining me in my underwear,' I retort, pointing my finger at him. 'It's just jeans and a sweater.'

'And an awful lot of collarbone. And one bared shoulder.' Max smiles, sort of shark-like, plunging his hand into the large bowl of popcorn on Chas's lap, stuffing the contents into his mouth.

'So?' I huff out, a little frustrated. 'It's not like I have a whole lot of T & A on display.'

'You don't have to dress provocatively to look sexy. In fact, the less skin on display, the more sexy a look can be.' Chas then elbows Max sharply in the ribs. 'Not that he's supposed to notice.'

'*Oof!* That's rich coming from the woman who makes her living off people wearing no clothes. And I can't help that I have eyes. Anyone can see she looks like she's off to get boned!'

'Max,' Chas adds in a warning tone. 'Enough.'

'Fine, fine,' he says, sliding his feet from the coffee table. He unfolds his long frame from the chair. 'I can see where I'm not wanted. The movie's finished anyway. You,' he says, clasping my shoulders with his hands, 'look gorgeous.'

'It's still just jeans and a sweater,' I mutter. 'Really.' I want to look nice, and yes, I am off to get boned as Max so charmingly puts it, but I don't want to look obvious. Or desperate.

'Absolutely. And I'm fucking Rihanna.' He bumps the tip of his index finger against my nose. 'Catch you crazy kids later.'

The front door slams as I slide my butt down the sofa arm, facing Chas.

'I'm guessing you're off to meet your hot kilt-wearing stud from the wedding?'

'You guess correct.' Leaning over, I steal a little popcorn from her bowl. 'Keir.'

'What?'

'Keir. That's his name.' Though without the ability to roll my r's, it doesn't sound the same. *Keirrrr. Like roarrrr!*

'What else do we know about this Keir, apart from he wears a kilt, and he sent you an offensive text?'

Ah, so that's what this is about.

'That was a misunderstanding.' Leaning forward, Chastity places the bowl on the table, then turns to face me as she crosses her legs. 'And you already don't like him.'

'It's not for me to like or dislike,' she answers.

'Okay, so you worry about me. You think I'm super naïve.'

She shrugs a little reluctantly. 'You seem to know what you're doing. You just need to decide what you want from this.'

'Fun. I want a little fun. A few dates. Maybe hot sex. Nothing heavy.'

'And that's all well and good, so long as you keep that in mind.'

'Chas, look. I like him. He seems genuine, and he's . . . fun.'

'Genuine doesn't—' she begins, but I cut her off.

'It was a text message sent by his stupid friend!' I say, a little exasperated. I didn't want to worry her, but it looks like I need to go there. 'Look, I didn't tell you, but Robin cornered me and was pretty rough with me the night of the wedding.' She opens her mouth, a million questions written across her expression, but I hold up my hand. 'He grabbed me. In the hotel. Called me a bunch of names and threatened me. Then he sort of shook me a bit, and I banged my head.'

'That little fucker,' she growls. 'I will literally twist off his balls and feed them to him.'

'No need. Keir was there. He headbutted him.'

'Good,' she says, nodding. 'I'm glad. I'm going to get a Robin Reed lookalike and use him as a gimp in one of my films.' I laugh, but it trails off quickly. 'Why are you grimacing?''

'Because I've seen him out on the street. At least, I think I have.'

'You think he's following you? Stalking you?' Her expression darkens, her brow drawing in as her lips thin to one flat line. 'You should go to the police, Paisley.'

'And say what? I think my ex-boyfriend is following me? Only, it might not be him because he can't walk around without a disguise. You know, because he's famous. Famous, and everyone and their grandmother's favourite. Can you hear how mad that sounds?'

'Something is telling you it's him. You should always listen to your intuition, you know. Trust it.'

'My instinct is telling me Keir might be a good distraction.'

'Just a distraction?'

I consider her question for a moment, and it really is only a moment. 'We hooked up at a wedding. That's the extent of our connection.'

'That's it?' she asks doubtfully.

'I mean, I can tell he's a good man. He did squash Robin's nose all over his face on my behalf. And I am mostly the non-violent kind—'

'I'm not,' she almost growls.

'But Robin did make dog food out of my heart, and then had the audacity to tell me I didn't know how to conduct *myself*.'

'And then tried to dish out a different kind of hurting,' Chas replies with a dark look.

'Exactly. Pretty ironic, right?'

'Moronic, more like. But tell me more about this Keir.'

'I think he'll be a good rebound,' I say, nodding. 'He's a little older than I am, is divorced, has a daughter, and doesn't want anything serious.'

'What about you? Do you think you'll be able to stick to those terms?'

'Absolutely,' I reply, standing. 'I've known I've always been a relationship kind of girl, but so much has changed in my life recently. I think Keir will be a good distraction for me. A good reminder. Good for my ego.' Good for now, at least.

'So long as you don't get too attached.'

'I'm a big girl,' I respond, grabbing my bag. 'I know the score. And on that note, don't wait up!'

As Keir had suggested I choose a place to meet tonight, I stick to the Chelsea area, just in case things don't go so well. I've come to love London in the years I've lived here. I no longer look like a tourist and have a pretty good understanding of my surrounds, and I can navigate the underground like a native! But that's not to say I'm familiar with everywhere. London is a big place. So when I'd asked Chastity in a roundabout way where would be a good place to eat—somewhere not too over the top and with a chill vibe—I didn't expect my Uber to pull up to *Perro Morrado*. A Mexican joint? One complete with a *Day of the Dead* theme.

So un-Chastity like, I decide, as a girl dressed for Halloween opens the door. Her dark hair is pulled from her face and pinned in a retro style victory roll, adorned with red flowers, and her face painted in a white skull effect. *Complete with cobwebs dotted with tiny jewels*. This place is very, very un-Chastity like.

I'm led through the bar adorned with South American mosaic tiles and rough-hewn wood, passing a row of brightly coloured woven hammocks to a table at the back. Purple lights hang above, casting my jeans in an eerie glow. I'm early, but that's me. And I am nervous despite the line I'd sold Chas earlier. Of course, I like Keir, and I want him to like me. But I'm under no illusions. We're not looking at long term or to a future that doesn't include clothes discarded to the floor. And that's fine. I'm all about the now, and truthfully? I've never had sex as I'd had with him. *The bone melting, ovary exploding kind*. But I still feel like I need confirmation that the sex was as good as I remember. *I sure hope so*.

And if it does turn out to be as awesome as I recall, I'm might be at risk of developing a little obsession. Except, unlike coke or booze, this kind of addiction takes two for full effect. And there lies the end of that potential problem. It takes two to tango, as my grandma used to say, and something tells me Keir won't be interested in filling up my dance card for too long.

I take my seat on the dark velvet bench, which gives me a view of at least part of the space. I order a drink as the waiter arrives—it seems rude not to—but decide I shouldn't listen to that little voice that suggests something potent to soothe my rattled nerves.

'I'd like a frozen margarita, please,' I tell the waiter as he appears. Much like the female host, his face is also painted a ghostly white, though only above his strongman mustache and a pointed beard. Matching skull motif suspenders and bow tie accompany his white shirt. Even his order pad has a smiling skull motif.

I expect a touch of barely concealed disdain at my choice of beverage—this place is in the heart of Chelsea, and I've just ordered the alcoholic equivalent of a blue raspberry Slurpee. May as well ask them to stick it in a big old thirty-two-ounce plastic cup. It's not like I don't feel "other" enough, sitting alone in a bar the affluent usually frequent. *The high-born and high-cheekboned, by the looks of things.*

My gigantic cocktail arrives on a silver tray as the girls at the table next to me receive glasses of something much more grown-up. I should've ordered a champagne cocktail or something equally as fancy. Nevertheless, I take the plastic straw between my lips for a quick sip to find the drink packs a decent punch. Not that this stops me from lowering my head to the straw again.

'You look like you're enjoying that.' I look up to Keir standing on the other side of the table, his mouth tilted in a half smile. Dark jeans and a white button-down that clings to his muscled chest, a sports jacket, and black boots. Unlike the times before, a sandy rasp of stubble covers his cheeks. He looks good enough to eat.

'Hey.' The word comes out all soft around the edges as I return his smile, partly because he's here—in front of me—so real and so virile. But also because of that accent. The aural he gives.

You're so shiny and wet.

I'm gonna make you scream.

I resist a full-body shudder at the echo of his words, his voice as deep and as cool as the ocean. The rasp around the edge of his need.

He steps closer, navigating the table. One hand on my shoulder, he leans in, placing his lips against my cheek. I restrain the urge to wrap my arms around him, burying my nose into his neck for a comic-sized inhale. He smells so good—spice and cedar—the warmth of his stubbled chin against my cheek doing strange things to my insides.

'Well, are you?' he asks, pulling the wooden chair opposite me out from under the table. *Am I what?* Nerves make me a little ridiculous. Surely, I can come up with more than a gooey *hey. Oh, ha-ay . . .*

'Was I what? Oh, enjoying my drink?' I look down at the oversized glass, more like a fishbowl really, and when I look back up, he's staring at me from under his thick sandy lashes, his hazel eyes darkened by the purple light. I think I like him in jeans almost as much as I do a kilt. Though I think—no, I know—I prefer him dressed in nothing but a sheet. That lean frame and those muscles. The sandy fuzz just under his navel leading to the dick that rocked my world.

'Hey, polka dot?'

When I look up, he's sort of crouching as though to catch my gaze. He also looks on the verge of laughter.

'Paisley,' I correct automatically.

'I know what your name is,' he says, definitely chuckling now. 'Polka dot is probably your sister's name, though, right?'

'Yeah, along with my big brothers Argyle and Plaid.'

As his laughter deepens, he leans back in his chair. Out of the purple glow, the stubble on the scruff of his cheeks now glows gold. *Like someone who looks like him needs further gilding.* And Lord, I know how that stubble feels between my legs. I shake my head a little because this so isn't the time to swoon.

Go on, make it obvious you're easy for him, why don't you?

'You look nice.' His mouth might say *nice,* but the way his gaze devours me says something else. Something that looks more like *utterly fuckable.*

Maybe Max was right. Maybe there is such a thing as too much collarbone because where his gaze touches, my skin feels alive. I spent a while getting ready tonight, not that I'd admit it out loud. A long time pulling my hair into a messy bun that screams *this look took thirty seconds rather than thirty minutes*. I was excited, sure. It's been so long since I've been on a date. But something tells me he's not scanning my clothes. But maybe he's anticipating my underwear.

And I do like underwear.

'Have you been here before?'

'Do I come here often?' I repeat, taking another sip from my glass. 'No, I've never been here. I didn't realise it was so . . . '

'Mad?'

'I was going to say pretentious, but mad works, too.'

The outer corners of his eyes crinkle with mirth as he scans the place; the barman mixing cocktails *at* other tables, the waitress wearing little more than underwear and face paint. The braying laughter of some jackass city types.

'There's something you'd never hear a bloke say in Scotland,' Keir murmurs, turning back to me with a wry smile.

'Why? What did they say?'

'Barman!' Keir begins in a perfect imitation of one of Chastity's uppity friends. 'Bring me a bottle of your best champagne!' Then he claps his hands like a flamenco dancer.

'Scotsmen don't drink champagne?' I ask, trying hard not to laugh.

'Not when they're out on a night with the lads. It's more likely to be pints of beer or shots of whisky. And cries of *g'wan* and *get another round in!*'

I hiccup a little around my straw. My drink is melting rapidly under the purple light, and I'm probably consuming it a little too fast. 'You're good at that, you know. Switching between accents.'

'I must have missed my calling then. Maybe I should've been a thespian?'

'Oh, I know there's a market for it.'

'Thespian porn?' he asks just as the waitress arrives by his side.

'Something like that,' I mumble pink-faced in response.

Flipping open the beverage menu, he frowns down at it, eventually opting for a craft beer.

'Not a Mexican one?' I ask as the slightly overfriendly waitress retreats.

'The kind you have to add fruit to, to make it palatable?' His mouth twists on one side. 'I prefer the kind of beer that needs no adulteration.'

'Naked beer, huh?'

'I like naked,' he responds, his tone low and definitely seductive.

'I'm sorry,' I say, because I am, because I led him there. He's only just sat down! I need to get a hold of my behaviour this evening. Rein it in a little.

'This margarita is making me inappropriate.'
Because I've got naked on the brain.

'Maybe I should get you another one,' he suggests
with a smirk.

'Hold that thought,' I say, sliding my legs out
from under the table. 'I've got to visit the little
girl's room.'

'Take all the time you need.'

Naked came up a little too quickly, I advise
myself once in the confines of the equally strangely
decorated powder room; velvet and street graffiti.
Posters of *Lucha Libre* wrestlers. *The designers
must've dropped acid before tackling this place.*

'Naked might be the name of the game,' I mutter
to my reflection as I wash my hands. 'But there's
such a thing as too soon. Too easy, right?'

My reflection doesn't answer, but the Nordic
looking blonde who exits the cubicle behind me
frowns. *Frowns as she steps around me. Frowns
as she washes her hands. And, yep, she's still
frowning as she leaves.*

'Maybe they're a serious race of people,' I
mumble. As no further answer is provided, I dry
my hands and leave.

The way into the restaurant is blocked by a
couple of drunks—more city jackass types. They're
probably called Giles and Tarquin, or something
equally ridiculous.

'Excuse me.' I tap one shoulder of the swaying
pair. 'I need to get by.'

'Oh, an 'merican,' the heavier of the two says as
he turns, his accent denoting him as someone

Robin would call a *toff*—someone who attended private school and who has more money than brain cells. I roll my eyes in response to they way he's looking at me. 'A girl with attitude. I like it,' he scoffs—a sort of scoff-slur.

'Had an American au pair once,' says the leaner of the two.

'Did you?' the first asks, turning his head to his companion on a wobbling neck.

'Yep. Over the kitchen table. Girlfriend at the time wasn't terribly pleased.'

The pair begin to bray. *Yep, I called it—jackasses.* 'Come on, guys,' I say firmly. 'I need to get past.'

'Say please,' the first replies, reaching out as though to touch my bare shoulder. I step back out of his reach, squaring said shoulders as I wonder which one I'll knee in the balls first. 'Say please and give us a little kiss.'

'I don't kiss frogs.' His friend begins to laugh, so I serve him a share of the stink eye. 'And I don't kiss pond scum, either.' His laughter stops immediately.

'What did you say, bitch?' I open my mouth, a retort balancing on the end of my tongue, but I'm beaten to it.

'What the fuck is going on here?' At Keir's barely suppressed growl, the pair turn.

'This has got nothing to do with you,' Fat Kermit says, drawing himself taller. Taller, but not tall enough. Keir towers over the pair. He's older. Broader. And despite his dapper appearance, he looks a little wilder, too. In the growl from his lips and the razor-sharp focus of his gaze, he makes the two of them look like schoolboys searching for a fight; inexperienced and ineffectual.

'I suggest you leave the lady alone and get yourselves back to your champagne.' His words drip with disdain.

'Do you know who I am?' Fat Kermit says indignantly.

'Nope. Nor do I give a flyin' fuck. Just do yourself a favour and step away from the girl.'

'Or what?' He puffs up his chest. Maybe he's a toad, not a frog.

'Or I'll break your face.'

'I could have you arrested.'

'Aye, but not a'fore I break your face,' he answers reasonably.

'Come on, Tristan,' Pond Scum mutters, pulling on his friend's arm. 'It's not worth it.'

Tristan seems to weigh up his friend's words, eventually answering, 'You're right. She's not worth it at all.'

'You wouldn't know what to do with a woman like this,' Keir growls as the pair shuffle away. 'Discretion is the better part of valour, eh lads?' He watches them leave the bar before turning to me. 'Why're people always threatening me with arrest when I'm around you?'

When I don't answer, the smile slips from his face. I don't get the sense that he's worried about my lack of words, but rather it's like a temporary mask that's slipped away. His eyes scan my body as though assessing me for signs of handling or fingerprints. *Fierce. Possessive. Like he'd punish me for their attention.*

The last thought sets off a lightbulb in my head. He likes hard, angry fucking. Like a chain reaction, my heartrate trips, setting off a deep fluttering in my belly because maybe I like that, too.

'Paisley,' he says urgently, taking me in his hands. *Not his arms.* 'Did those fuckers frighten you?'

I wet my suddenly parched lips; his eyes follow the motion, though I feel he does so almost reluctantly. My voice sounds scratchy when I finally speak, my pulse tripping so hard in my neck I can actually feel it. 'I want to leave.'

'You want me to take you home?' His words are even, completely void of inflection, the mask back in place again.

'No. I don't want to sit here and pretend this isn't happening tonight. I want to leave right now. With you.'

He doesn't answer, and he doesn't move his gaze from mine. But he eventually takes my hand and leads me out of the narrow hallway. After tossing a few bills down on the table next to his barely touched drink and my half-empty glass, he leads me out into the crisp autumn evening.

We take twenty or thirty hurried steps then turn a corner, our mouths crashing together as Keir pushes me up against a brick wall. In the twilight, cars rush past the opening of the alleyway as we kiss with a ferocity that melts me to the bone. A Ferocity that makes Keir groan into my mouth.

'I couldn't wait.' His growly tone seeps fire into my bloodstream, his lips finding my neck. 'I want you so bad,' he whispers ferverently, licking and kissing his way up my neck. I want him to bite—to mark me. I want to feel the weight of his need against my skin. 'Why me?'

'Because you fuck like a champ,' I answer hoarsely, ignoring the smug lift of his lips against my skin.

'So you're using me for sex?'

'Not right now, I'm not.' I stifle a sigh as his teeth graze my earlobe. 'And I guess you're on the clock.'

'Are you suggesting I'm in a hurry, or that I rush things?'

'I'm down for a little hustle,' I rasp as his large hand draws down my arm.

'You make it sound so sordid.'

'And you make it sound like it turns you on.' My whole body reacts as one of his hands finds my hips, his thumb rubbing in small circles.

'Dirty fucking is underrated,' he answers, 'but I wonder if you think you know me that well or if you recognise the same things in yourself?'

'Why don't you find out?'

'That sounds like a dare.' His mouth finds my neck again, his tongue licking the column of my neck.

'You did say I was trouble.'

My heart beats with a thousand anticipations as his hands lift from my hips, his fingers clasping mine. My feet work on delay, along with the rest of my body and brain as he begins to lead me away.

'Filthy alleyways aren't the kind of sordid I enjoy. And you deserve better,' he says, tugging on my reluctant hand. 'Always remember that.'

Our footsteps echo against the sidewalk, the minutes that pass thick with anticipation. Then we come to a hotel; the kind with an expensive façade and a uniformed doorman out front. We make our way to the reception where Keir lets go of my hand to pull out his wallet.

'Checking in, sir?' asks the twenty-something receptionist. Her hair pulled into a chignon, her expression is a perfectly professional yet blank mask.

'One night, no reservation,' Keir answers succinctly, handing over a dark coloured credit card to secure the room as he wraps his arm around my waist.

The receptionist slides a form across the desk, his arms briefly leaving my body as he fills it in, leaving much of the information blank. *No car registration needed. A company name for an address.* Transaction complete, the tips of her ears turn red as he tells her we don't need help with our luggage . . . as we don't have any.

'That was a little unnecessary,' I whisper as we reach the elevator.

'What?'

'Telling her we have no luggage.'

'What would you have had me say?' He smirks, chin tipped as he watches the old-fashioned numbers above the doors light up as the elevator passes each floor.

'I don't know. Maybe our bags haven't arrived from our flight.'

'And your shoulder is red from what?' His amused gaze slides to my shoulder. 'The strap of your handbag?'

The elevator *dings* as it opens, my grip tightening on the clutch purse pressed between my arm and body as my free hand drifts to my shoulder. *Did he bite me there?* As we step inside the mirrored elevator, I see exactly what he means.

'Hickeys? Are you kidding me?' Three sucking marks adorn my right shoulder.

'It was the only flesh available to me.' His eyes flick my way, lingering on my shoulder before moving down. 'Don't worry. The next lot aren't going to be so visible.'

'Oh yeah?' Less challenge and more an enquiry as he steps into me, his hand drifting to between my legs. *But barely touching.*

'I'm gonna decorate the silky skin of your inner thighs. Suck. Bite. Lick.'

The words bloom between my legs like the most delicious surprise. 'I'm down for that.' I try to appear unaffected, hoping to conceal the shake in my voice. I feel so desperate for him to touch me. Frantic for the sensations of his fingertips. *His teeth.*

'What else are you *down for*?'

God, his voice. He could read the phone book and make it sound sexy. Suddenly, the echo of Chastity's words floats into my consciousness.

'Boundaries are meant to be tested,' I hear myself repeat.

Above me, Keir's eyes light up like Christmas has arrived early.

Chapter Fifteen

PAISLEY

The door closes, the sound of my heart the only noise in the room. Keir walks farther into the space, placing his wallet and the spare key on the dresser as he passes, walking to the wall of windows before turning to face me.

'It's not quite Claridge's,' he says quietly, taking in the king-size bed, the pair of chairs set against the window, the dresser, and upholstered chair. I can't help but wonder if he's considering their uses for *all* the wicked things. 'But it'll do.'

He's right; this isn't a suite in Claridge's, but it will do. The room is warm after the crisp chill of the autumn night and rich with tactile fabrics in shades of grey and plum. Not that it matters. Especially as I consider I might have gone to at least third base in that grimy alleyway.

I place my clutch down next to his wallet and lean against the dresser. I'm not shy, I don't think, but I'm not exactly forward. Even when my body literally hums with need.

'It's nice.'

'Nice?' Keir gives in to the smile he's fighting. 'Is nice what you came here for?'

'I'm not really sure why I'm here.' I stretch my legs out, crossing them at the ankles, clasping my hands together in front. *To stop them from shaking. To hide how I ache for his touch.*

'Tell the truth and shame the devil.'

'What?' My word bubbles with laughter.

'It's just another way of sayin' I don't believe you, hen. You know why you're here. Same as me. Because you couldn't stop thinking of the last time we fucked.'

'Maybe I just need a little direction.'

A deep burst of laughter breaks free from his chest. 'Well, aren't you just the perfect girl.'

Hands still between my legs, I shrug as though unaffected even as his words warm my insides. 'I try.'

Keir's eyes roam over me, and just when I think he's going to tell me to strip, he stalks towards me. His fingers are warm and a little calloused as he takes my hand, encouraging me to stand.

'I don't know what I did to deserve seconds,' he says when we're toe to toe and he's twirling a curl that hangs almost to my shoulder. 'But I'll admit I'm greedy for it. Greedy for you.'

When he reaches behind me, my eyes fall closed, my every nerve ending alive in anticipation of his first touch. His fingertips brush against the nape of my neck, eliciting a shiver before he begins to expertly pull the pins loose from my hair.

'You've done this before,' I whisper, my eyes opening to the tilt of his lips.

'I might've,' he says as he pulls my ponytail holder free without causing me pain. 'At least once or twice.' It's silly, but I don't want to think about that. At least, not until he says, 'I can also plait a mean braid.'

A man who learned to braid for his child? Now *that* must be something to appreciate. Something to swoon a little over even. And a man who can loosen a girl's updo pain free, only to gather the strands in his fist oh-so gently? Also totally swoon worthy.

He pulls my hair to tilt my head, allowing him access to my neck and collarbone. Each press of his lips, each swipe of his tongue unravels me a little further until my whole body is shaking, and I know that he's aware.

'Kiss me,' he whispers, his mouth hovering just over mine. I try, but it's hard to do with his grip on my hair. 'What are you waiting for?' he whispers, his mouth just a breath from mine.

I wet my lips and, struck by a sudden thought, run my palm down the front of his jeans—along the hard outline of him. He lets out a sharp hiss but doesn't release me. Instead, he brings his mouth to my ear to whisper, 'Cheat.'

'I'd nod my head in agreement if I could.' I smile as his lips and tongue trail their way across my neck

'And I'd tie you up if I could. How do you think your boundaries would feel about that?'

'Oh.' That one breathy sound isn't an adequate response. My real response to being tied up isn't happening in the vicinity of my mouth but much farther down. I'd be embarrassed to admit that if he cupped between my legs, he might find what he's looking for in more ways than one.

'Well, trouble, do we have a definitive answer?'

'We could try,' I suggest.

'You'll put yourself in my hands.' I nod as best as I can. 'Trust me with your body,' he whispers, kissing the soft skin at the base of my neck.

'*Uh-huh.*'

'Let me tie and tether you.' I nod again. His mouth at my shoulder now, he sucks hard, pulling the purple of his previous sucking bites farther to the surface, no doubt. Probably deepening them. My knees almost give out, my insides pulsing with each suck—throbbing as he pulls his mouth away. 'Let me eat you out until you're squirming all over my face.'

'Yes.' *God, yes.*

'Fuck you so hard you won't remember your name.'

My eyes flutter open as his free hand lands on the curve of my hip and he says my name.

'W-what?'

'I asked if you're down for that.'

Was my melting, throbbing response not enough for him? Can't he see I've almost turned to a puddle of need?

'I've got all night.' There's an edge of warning in his voice but also something else. Despite the ferocity of his gaze, I think I get what he's saying.

He's not going to fuck me, then run off. He's got time, and he wants my permission to take it.

'Yes.' My voice sounds thick when I eventually speak. 'Yes, please. Take your time.' Do whatever to me.

Keir's gaze never moves from mine. My hair still in his fist, he watches me intently as though weighing my sincerity. *Or looking for cracks in my resolve.* But I like how he holds me—like the strength of his gaze. Like the feel of his fingers against my hip. Relish the tethering hold of my hair in his hand. I delight in how he takes up the whole of my vision, revel in how consumed my thoughts are with what he might do.

What he will do.

He kisses me then, each press of his lips against mine is a little deeper, a little more desperate, until he's feeding me his tongue and I'm moaning for him. But just as quickly as it starts, he pulls away, his hands falling from my hair, the base of my skull pulsing in beats as blood flow returns.

He feeds his hand into his jacket pocket, pulling out a navy coloured neck tie.

'One you prepared earlier?' I aim for a little tease but end up sounding sultry.

'More like a pleasant coincidence,' he answers, wrapping the blue silk around his fist. I can't help but watch him, thinking about my hair in his fist and what it felt like to be vulnerable to him. How wet it made me. How wet I feel now.

In the still of the room, Keir slides his jacket from his shoulders, dropping it onto a chrome and wood suitcase stand. Then he returns to the window; though, this time, he sits on one of a pair of silver-coloured velvet armless chairs.

'Take off your clothes.' He's not even looking at me as he speaks, but rather unfolding his tie and spreading it across his thigh. 'Leave your underwear on.' His head rises, and this time, his eyes do find mine. His deep voice and attention like a sudden shot of hard liquor straight to the vein. 'Well?'

My clothes. I cross my arms at the edge of my sweater and pull it over my head as the cloud of my hair settles around my shoulders and back, an added layer of sensation I really don't need. I slip off my shoes as he watches, then unzip my jeans and push the tight denim over my thighs, then off my feet.

Standing in only my cream lace underwear, I watch as his eyes roam over me, taking in the triangle of my panties and the slight ruffle at the edge of my strapless bra.

'No polka dots tonight?' He half smiles, pushing his long legs out in front with a sigh. 'Do you know how lovely you are,' he asks, beckoning me over.

Tiny shivers of anticipation run down my spine at his words. But I don't move. Not yet. I give myself this moment to revel a little. To appreciate the size of him. The breadth of him. My desire for him.

But it would be counterproductive to wait too long. In several steps, he's taking my hand to pull me to straddle his legs. My hands fall naturally to his shoulders, his own finding my hips where he settles me against him. *Against the hardness of his lap.* Closer now, I can smell the minty freshness of toothpaste over the scent of his aftershave as I run my fingers through his hair. 'So lovely,' he repeats. 'And I know you taste as good as you look.'

'You're a sweet-talking man.' Sweet talking and deceptively devilish.

'Am I now?' I nod. 'Let's see if you still think so when you're begging me to let you come.' I fold my lips together so as not to react to his words. All in vain as he speaks again. 'When you're begging me to make it stop.'

I groan a whispered *yes*, rocking my centre against him, desperate for some kind of relief. 'That's right. You work that pussy. That's where your only power lies tonight.'

He takes my hands in his, pressing them together, prayer like, before wrapping the navy blue silk twice around my wrists. Then, feeding one end under the wrapping, he ties the loose ends in a knot. And all the while I watch. Who knew a necktie and a little anticipation could make you feel like this?

'I get the feeling you've done this before.'

'Surely, you wouldn't allow someone with no experience to tie you. I only wish I had something a little longer,' he says, almost as though to himself. 'Something with a few more options. Maybe next time,' he adds, his fiery gaze meeting mine.

'Maybe,' I demur, biting back an excited grin, but whether at the mention of a next time or the rabbit hole he's suggesting hop down, it's hard to tell.

Finally, he lifts my hands between us, feeding them over my head. Sitting on his lap with my legs over his and my breasts pushed out? It feels kind of thrilling. Kind of exposing. Even though I'm technically covered by my underwear. Maybe it's the way he's looking at me. The way he's devouring without touching.

Keir presses his large hand to my breastbone, dragging it down and gripping the middle of my bra. When I think he might pull, he instead slides his fingers into one cup, lifting the weight of my breast out to balance it against the fabric and underwiring. One then the other. My nipples, already pebbled, ache for his touch.

He runs a calloused finger in a small circle around my nipple, tightening the flesh farther still. 'Do you like this?'

Does he mean being tied or his touch? Before I can form an answer, he pinches the tight bud.

'*Yes!*' I hiss out in answer—to his words *and* his touch.

My chest heaves between us as he bends his head to lap and soothe with his tongue. I moan a helpless and hungered sound.

'I can't wait to have you squirming all over me, desperate for my cock.'

'Please,' I whisper, rocking against him, my insides clenching emptily. 'I already am.'

'No, trouble. Not yet. You only think you are.'

It takes him a million years to loosen the buttons of his shirt and a million more to take off my bra. To take my breasts fully in his hands and to love them a little more. To cup them. To thumb my nipples. To pass swipes of teasing tongue and the threat of teeth.

'Oh, God.' I throw back my head, pushing myself farther into him.

'That's it, darlin',' he growls. 'You ride me. You've got me so hard for you. So fuckin' wild.'

'Show me,' I beg. 'Show me what I do to you. I need you, Keir, please.'

With a smile wicked enough for the devil, Keir slides his hands under my bottom. Picking me up as he stands, he deposits me on the bed so that my knees are bent over the edge.

'Still on the pill?' he asks as he loosens the button fly of his jeans. I nod, words unavailable to my parched throat as he slides his jeans down the strong muscles of his thighs. Boxers follow, then he takes himself in his hand, the ladder of his abdominals rippling.

'You want this.'

I don't answer but squirm against the bed like a cat in her first heat. I think I might also make the same sounds as I lift my tied hands above my head.

'Fuck, that is sexy,' he growls, watching as I spread my legs and arch upwards.

I've never touched myself in front of a man. Never gotten myself off while a boyfriend—a man—watched, but I know I'd be doing so now if my hands weren't tied. But then, maybe that's the point. Maybe restriction of movement heightens everything.

Whatever the reason, and I suspect the reason is purely Keir, my skin feels tight enough to burst. Like with one touch from him, I'll detonate.

One minute, he's holding himself, and the next, he's crawling over me, bending his head to my chest and licking my nipples until they're taut and wet and shining in the lamplight. Heavy and aching.

'Please, Keir,' I whisper, sliding my hands over his head to pull him to me. 'I need you.'

With a chuckle, he straddles my body, admiring the sight of me before he slides down, pulling my panties down my legs. His nostrils flare as though he can smell me—smell my need—his eyes darkening, anticipating the taste of me.

Placing one hand on my inner thigh, he spreads my legs wider.

'You're so wet, and I haven't even touched you.'

I don't have any reply beyond a soft sigh as his breath blows between my legs. I feed my tethered hands under my head now, raising my vantage point to watch his wicked gaze, to watch as he bows his sandy head.

My body tingles with anticipation of his touch which comes unexpectedly at the soft inside of my thigh. *But he did say he'd bite me there next*. What he didn't say was how hard.

'*Oh! Ow . . .*' My cry draws off as his teeth stop pressing quite so hard, releasing the flesh to a dark and delicious kind of sting. '*Oh, fuck.*' I attempt to squirm away from him as he lowers his head again, this time placing his tongue against the bite mark. The position oddly soothes, more so as he begins alternating sweet kisses and short licks until my body relaxes, no longer tense against the bed . . . when he spreads me wider still and bites my other thigh.

This time, I can feel the line of his teeth against my skin, the sensation resonating at the apex of my legs where my pussy begins to throb with need. Each bite deepens the sensation, each kiss and lick—each brush of his stubbled cheek—pushing me closer to a feeling of delirium—each set of indentations drawing closer to where I need him the most.

When it's clear there's no place else to go, my whole body quivers in anticipation. Quivers in need and in fear. I want the wet slide of his tongue and the threat of his teeth, but is that what he has planned? My mind is awash with questions, each one turning anticipation into a pleasurable yet angsty stew.

Will he bite me there?

Will I survive it?

Will it hurt as I come between his teeth?

What about when he fucks me?

'Please, I want this,' I pant hoarsely, not sure exactly what experience it is I think I'm asking for. 'I just want it,' I plead. 'Please.'

'Look at you,' Keir growls, his desire coupled with the deep timbre of his voice tightening my insides. 'Just fucking look at you,' he says again, right before he pushes his mouth into my very centre.

With one swipe of his tongue, I'm crying out. His hands push my thighs impossibly wide, his thumbs pressuring the crisscross of bites until they throb. It's the best kind of torture. A wicked kind of divine. My insides pulse and heat, the bites throbbing alongside the feeling and twisting my orgasm into something else. Something hot and frantic. Something wet and wild.

He said he'd make me scream last time, and I thought I did, but that experience has nothing on this. Not as he spears me with his fingers, not as his mouth envelops my clit. I am dead. Officially spent. And if I had a voice, I might tell him so as he climbs my body, pressing kisses against my skin, before rolling onto his back and taking me with him.

'I can't,' I moan, even as I push against him. 'Please.'

'Of course, you can. You're the Amazing Paisley. You can do anything.'

Propped against the mountain of pillows, he pulls me over to where he holds himself in his hand. It seems to take forever to feel him ease into me—too long. I want to slam myself down, fill myself with him, but at the first push, he grabs my hips to better position me.

'Look,' he whispers, his fingers tightening on my hips. 'Look at how you take me so beautifully.'

I glance down at where we join. At where my skin parts, at where my wetness spreads around him. At where I envelop him.

'Look at my marks,' he whispers, rubbing his thumb over the indents in my skin. My insides begin to pulse again, the sound of his deep groan almost hypnotic. 'You're gonna make me come so hard.' The pulse in his throat throbs deeply as he tips back his head.

'Yes. I want that.' I want all of that—all of him inside me, hard and wild. And I don't think I've ever wanted anything as bad. 'Please, let me,' I whine, trying to lower myself, trying to take a little more of him inside.

'All in good time,' Keir whispers, holding me wide and pushing up a little farther into me. And that's how it goes with each slide. Glacial. Slow. Excruciating. Until he's seated deep inside me. 'Put your hands behind your head.'

I do so, flushed and shaking, every inch of my body screaming with the need of this release. But he barely moves, just whispering to me—words of how good I am. How he can feel every inch of me. How he can't wait to see his cum dripping from me.

My thighs sting from the strain of keeping upright and from the rigidity in his pose. My arms ache as sweat trickles down my spine and between my breasts. But it all changes as Keir feeds his hand up my back to grab my shoulders, pulling me farther onto him.

I slide my legs wider than I ever thought possible, almost as though my body would envelop the whole of his. I'm hungered, so wet and filled, but it's still not enough. Each time he pushes up into me, my clit brushes his skin, and it's torturous. His movements make me beg and chant for release.

Please. Please. Please. Let me come.

The bite marks on my legs ache from the abrasion of the coarse hairs on his legs and the brush of his skin—the friction he sits higher, starting to buck and fuck up into me. His hands pull on the tie tethering my wrists, bowing my back and offering my breasts to his mouth.

My whole body jerks as his lips find my nipple. He hisses out a half curse as I pulse deeply around him. Pinned, he works me with his hips, spearing me again and again until I'm bucking and thrashing and losing my goddamned mind.

'Yes!' he hisses out. 'I can feel you coming—oh, fuck! That's . . . that's . . .'

If he says anything else, I don't hear it. I think I might go blind as well as deaf. I don't see stars. There's no white noise. There is nothing but his hands holding me down and the explosion of pleasure between my legs.

Chapter Sixteen

KEIR

Collapsed against me with her tethered arms now around my neck, Paisley's tears wet my skin. I know I didn't hurt her—no more than she wanted me to. No more than she could stand, at least. But fuck me, I don't remember it ever being this intense.

'Sweetheart, are you okay?' I gather her dark hair, pushing it across her shoulders. 'Say something.'

She shakes her head, nuzzling closer when I really need to see her face. I'm officially beginning to panic when she kisses my jawline, then presses her lips against my pulse point.

'I thought I'd lost you for a moment there.'

'I thought I'd lost my mind.' Her voice is a hoarse—kind of twenty-a-day hoarse—her body moving against my deep chuckle.

'Come on. Give me your hands.'

'I don't want be cut loose,' she half whines, though cooperative as I lift her hands from behind my head.

Truthfully, I don't really feel like moving her. *Bareback fucking is sublime.* My dick has softened inside her and the results of our fucking is dripping from between her legs. Part of me wants to look—to lay her down against the comforter and spread her legs. *Part of me*. The dirty part who doesn't get out much these days.

Her hands between us, I begin to wish I'd thought to bring scissors, but even I'm not that fucking clever. The fact that the tie was in my pocket was surprise enough.

'It's a nice tie,' Paisley mumbles, attempting to use her shoulder to move her hair. I brush it from her face, running my fingers along the dark silky strands and her back. This woman. She's . . . stunning.

'Even with the racoon eyes I must be sporting.'

I huff out a laugh, surprised I'd spoken my thoughts. 'Especially because of your panda eyes. Pandas are cute.'

'I like the way you say cute.'

'How do I say it?' I ask, returning to the tightened knot. *I'm going to look like a proper tool if I can't get it loose.*

'Like it has a *Q*. And an extra syllable.'

'You're somethin' else.'

'Trouble, you said. About this tie. How attached to it are you?'

'Attached? Not much. It was a Christmas gift from my PA.'

'Silk? You must pay her well.'

'I do pay him very well. Though he doesn't know that I know he charged it to the company credit card.'

'Wow!' The word comes out in a giggle.

'Aye, he's a cheeky fucker. But that's Aussies for you.'

'How about we call reception and ask to borrow scissors?' she says, right at the moment I lower my head and begin biting the knot to loosen it. 'You're good with your teeth,' she says softly. Teeth tearing into the silk knot, I look up at her. 'I really liked it.'

Something twists deep in the pit of my gut at the same moment the knot begins to slacken, thankfully, because I'm about to start probing the meaning behind those words. Does she like it because I do? Is she messing with me?

'All done.' My voice rumbles as I unravel it from her wrists. The silk has left marks. And fuck if they don't look good.

'You like that,' she asserts. Running her fingers across her wrists, she flicks her gaze alternately between the marks and my guarded expression. 'You like looking at your handiwork.'

No point in hiding it, I decide. Not when she doesn't appear to be judging. *Unlike someone I once knew.* Fuck it. I'm acting like a schoolgirl. What's next? Sending her a note with a request to mark the truth?

You like being tied ✓ X

You don't   ✓X

'Come on. Let's go get cleaned up and I'll tell you whatever you want to know.'

'Clean? I think we'll need bleach and a scrub brush.'

'That's just charming.' I chuckle, taking in her expression.

'I'm serious! Do you know how many people have had sex on this comforter?'

'Strangely enough, I don't.'

'That's the point,' she answers all animated now. 'We'd need a black light and a forensic team to be able to tell! I'm serious,' she says as I laugh, dragging her closer to my chest. 'We'll be lucky to get away without some kind of skeeve.'

'Skeeve, you say?' Using my lower body, I buck up into her, the momentum moving her off my lap.

'Hey!'

'There's only one thing for it. A bath.'

'How come you're free the whole evening?'

The water sloshes up the side of the large bath as Paisley lifts her hand to move a few damp strands of her hair. Pressed skin to skin—her back to my front—we're slick from the heat of the water.

'Sorcha has Brownies on Fridays, then she goes to her grandparents for the evening. I won't see her until I pick her up from her ballet class.'

'So not Agnes—her other grandparents.'

Though I don't need to navigate these waters, I decide I will. 'Agnes isn't my mother. At least, not by blood. My own mother was a bit of a fuckup in the parenting department.' As well as a whore. 'Agnes was a local shopkeeper—she and her husband. Anyway, she kept me right. Kept me fed. Made sure I was safe.' As safe as anyone can be when they live with a crack whore. 'When things got really bad, she and Alf, her husband, took me in.'

'Wow.' She tries to turn, but I'm not ready to let her see my face, so I tighten the band of my arms across her chest, then bury my nose in her hair. How the fuck does she smell like the summer anyway? 'Agnes and Alf must be very special people.'

'They are—were. Alf died before I finished university. When Sorcha was born, Agnes said she'd come to London to help.' I inhale deeply. 'She never went back.'

'But she's like a grandmother to Sorcha. You can absolutely see that in the photographs you showed me on your phone.'

Strange that she would see that, yet at the poncy school I pay for Sorcha to go to, the other parents treat her like the hired help. I mean, I do pay her, but mainly to ease at least a little of my guilt. But Agnes doesn't give a flying fuck what anyone thinks, least of all a bunch of stuck-up snobs. And so long as she's got a few pound notes in her wee purse—which she assures me she always has—and her "party money" put aside in her bank account— that's money she's put away for her funeral, the morbid bugger—she says she's just fine.

'So that must mean Sorcha is with her *other* grandparents.'

'You could be the new Sherlock Holmes.'

At least my ex's parents want to maintain contact. We have a prickly relationship, and we don't often see eye to eye. Although we do have a consensus when it comes to their daughter: we've all washed our hands of her. I think a lot of the issues between us stem from their pain. How could they have raised a daughter who was willing to abandon her own child? But I'm sure they also blame me for offering her money in the first place. In my defence, I was hurting—I never in a million years thought she would accept my offer. Friday sleepovers are a relatively new thing. For all of us.

'I'd look good in one of those funny hats—you know—like Sherlock Holmes?'

'A deerstalker?' She nods. 'You'd look good in a sack.'

'And you are a sweet-talking man.'

'With a gorgeous wet girl in his hands.'

'If wrinkled and prune-y does it for you.'

'*You* do it for me,' I reply, tightening my hands. But fuck if that wasn't a little too much—too much truth. Too heartfelt.

'That was an awfully big sigh.'

'Aye?' Loosening my hold, I wipe a hand down my damp face. 'It's just, I suppose you think you've grown—moved on. Think that the universe has no more lessons to give. No more surprises around the corner. Then it throws you curves like this.' Like magnets, my hands move to the heaviness of her teardrop-shaped tits, and despite my suddenly dour mood, my cock flickers back to life.

'I want to be straight with you.' I tip my head against the edge of the bath, speaking my truth into the damp air. 'I know we've only met twice, but I haven't felt like this about anyone in a long time.' She makes to move again, inhaling as though to speak. 'But I can't be with you. Not like you deserve a man to be.'

'That last bit? I think that's my line,' she says, sort of laughing. 'You know, I think I get to decide what's best for me. Did you forget I just got out of a relationship? We were together three long years. I'm not looking for that right now.'

'Two years? You must've been about twenty when you met him.'

'Again with the sweet-talking! I was twenty-six,' she says. 'And I'm plenty old enough to decide what's right for me.'

'Aye, but—'

'But nothing. I like you. And I want to be with you, but not in the way that *you're* thinking. Not in the way you're afraid of.'

'Who says I'm afraid?' The thought of another relationship is fucking terrifying; not that I need to say it out loud.

'Come on, Keir. Don't make this any harder than it already is.' Her hand snakes between us, her fingers giving my cock a swift tug. 'I like you, you like me, and together, we're a dynamite fuck.'

I grunt, pushing up into her hand. Dragging my hands down her body, I push them to the inside of her thighs. 'I don't want to hurt you.'

'That's not what you said earlier.' Her voice is a soft tease as, from behind, I slide my hands between her thighs. She moans so beautifully, the sound echoing off the tiled walls. There's such sweet agony in her tone as I press my fingers against the purpling marks of my teeth.

'Do they hurt?' My voice is hoarse, and the need to hear her answer consuming as I hook my legs around hers to pull them farther apart.

Her damp hair tickles my chest as she nods. 'Like the best kind of hurt.'

'Think you'd like me to tie you up again?'

'Uh-huh.' Her arms come up out of the water, looping around the back of my head. Thrusting her tits out, she raises her pussy to my touch. Everything drops away as she begins to pant gently as my finger applies pressure to her clit.

I block everything else out—my fear and feelings and how my base reactions are so wrapped up in this woman I feel like I'm bleeding out. In the heat of the moment and the steam of the room, I somehow convince myself that I can make this work without either of us getting hurt.

Chapter Seventeen

PAISLEY

As much as I didn't want to, I left Keir that Saturday morning before he awoke even though my body longed for a few more hours of sleep next to him. But he'd made his position more than clear, and I understood. Even though his words stung, they were also a good reminder. Something I needed to hear.

Since then, there have been other Fridays. Some which have led to lazy hotel Saturday mornings, and others which have ended with one of us creeping out before the morning fully comes to life.

Like this morning.

We ate a rare dinner together last night—we usually feed our more pressing hunger before satiating the other much later from the room service menu. But not yesterday. We ate together. Broke bread, drank wine. Talked about everything and nothing *before* this time. Then later, I watched him sleep. Watched as the dawn peeped through a chink in the heavy drapes, gilding his golden-brown head. Then I dressed in the semi-darkness and crept like a thief from the room.

Fridays have become my favourite, though they do leave me feeling like I've experienced a punishing yoga class come Saturday morning. *Just like now*. In Chas's kitchen, I stretch my legs out along the window seat, relishing the aches, each one tied to a sensation or memory from yesterday.

His dark gaze as I'd peeled him from his jeans.

His carnal groan as I'd taken his cock between my lips.

The way he looked as I'd cried when I came the second time.

In some ways, it seems we were made for the other. Yet I know we can never be more than we are on Fridays, and I'm okay with that. *Mostly*. Sometimes life is just too hard to force in the direction you most want it to go. It is what it is, and I remind myself of this daily.

My dad used to say that people came into your life for either a reason, a season, or a lifetime.

Robin was a learning curve. And in my time with him, I learned. *Boy, did I*. I moved from one side of the world to the other. Moved from what was familiar to what was almost alien. In the process, I came out of my shell a whole lot. Made what I thought were friends. And I flourished for a while. Later, I learned how resilient I truly am. Learned how my heart had the capacity to heal itself.

Chastity is in my life for the long haul whether she knows it or not! That girl picked me up, gave me a place to heal, and then a place to live. And later, a reason to get out of bed. I hope I'll never need to return the favour because I don't want her ever to go through what I did. Also, I can't imagine I'd have much to offer her if the tables were turned. Support? Sure. A safe place to fall? Definitely. A swanky pad in Chelsea? Not unless I win lotto. A job? I suppose she could hold my makeup brushes . . .

But seriously, I'll always be there for her in whatever capacity she needs.

And that leaves Keir. He's my season. One I'd like to think I'll look back on in fifty years when I'm sitting on my front porch and rocking in my chair. My children will have grown, my grandchildren with them. My husband will no doubt be dead because come on, after birthing and raising our brood of four, I'll deserve to be the last woman standing. Maybe I'll be a little like Blanche from the *Golden Girls*—a little man hungry. Or maybe I'll be more like sweet like Rose. But whatever kind of senior citizen I turn out to be, I'll always have my dirty memories.

'You've pulled all the strawberries out again?'

'Hmm?' I turn from the window and the greying clouds that I wasn't really seeing. 'I did what?' I hug my cereal bowl closer to my chest, dropping my feet to the ground as I stretch, then notice the little red lumps rolling from my thigh onto the floor. 'Damn. Who puts strawberries in granola, anyway? Strawberries are bad enough, but dried?' The spoon *chinks* against the china as I push the offensive crumbs into a pile with my foot.

'You're an odd thing,' Chas says, sitting next to me. 'If you don't like fruit, buy granola with nuts or something.'

'I was trying to be virtuous.'

'That dreamy look on your face tells me you spent last night being anything but.'

My cheeks heat immediately. 'Yesterday was Friday.'

'Just call you Captain Obvious, yeah?' Her mouth twists into a worried little pout. 'Are you sure he doesn't have a wife?'

An arched brow is my only response because, really? Just because my boyfriend cheated on me doesn't mean I'm a complete idiot. I mean, not that I can know for certain, but—*fuck it*! Now I'm worrying even though I know—just know—that's not who Keir is. As I glance from the clouds to Chas, she suddenly looks a little contrite.

'Fridays are his day,' I answer with a short shrug. 'It keeps things on track. Transparent. It works for me.' Even though I sometimes long to see him more. Sometimes to the point where I ache for him. Even though we text almost constantly. Check in each morning and last thing at night.

'What happens if you meet someone else? Someone you want to date, not just fuck?'

'Then I'll date.'

'And so you should. You've been seeing Keir for months with no sign of moving on.'

'Six weeks. And I'm hardly throwing my life away.'

'Good, because I've got someone I'd like you to meet. Someone *you'd* like to meet.'

'I think we already agreed no adult entertainers.' Not that I have anything against those who work in the sex industry. But there is jealousy. I'm prone to it, so I don't think I could have a meaningful relationship with someone who screws for a living. Nor with any man who goes gay for pay. 'Chas, you really should be saving your efforts for your own love life. How can you nag me when you don't have a boyfriend yourself?'

'I don't think I could look after a boyfriend,' she replies. 'I'm too busy creating a business. Plus, I don't think I'm ready for the responsibility. I mean, how often do you need to walk a boyfriend? Feed him? That kind of stuff?'

'Har-har.'

'On the other hand, this guy I met—Troy? He's perfect for you.'

'Troy? His parents named him after a movie?'

'Actually, the name Troy predates Brad Pit. Troy is more ancient. Think of the Iliad.'

'I was teasing you.' Mostly. *Wasn't there a much older film, too?* 'Tell me, does he at least look like Brad Pitt?'

'Better.' Her answer is a little too excited. 'Brad's heading for his pension while Troy is only thirty, tall, dark, and pretty buff. Plus, he's got this whole Clark Kent thing going on.'

My heart sinks. I thought she wasn't truly serious—that maybe she'd been window shopping at best. But as she begins to animatedly recount a meeting at her bank, I realise how serious she is about this. She's never met Keir—why would she? Our boundaries dictate that we don't get involved in each other's lives. But maybe if she had met him, she'd know why I'm still hanging onto Friday evenings. Because Keir is fun and decent and good. Plus, the filthiest individual I've ever met. Seriously. He should be the one running a porn company.

'You're not even listening, are you?'

'No—I am.' I duck my head to granola and yoghurt mess. 'I totally am.' When she doesn't speak, I look up. 'What?'

'You might be fooling him. You might even be fooling yourself. But sweets, you're not fooling me. This . . . this whole thing is unhealthy.' She stands, her hands slapping her thighs as she shrugs in a motion of futility. 'I worry about you. You're going to get hurt, I just know it. And if he's as decent as you say he is, you aren't going to be the only one. So soon after Robin, too.'

'This isn't the same,' I say, unable to hold her gaze. 'Robin and I had a past spanning years. Keir and I . . . well, I suppose what we have at best is a temporary contract.' Without a guarantee.

Chas's brow creases, her eyes moving to the gloomy morning beyond the kitchen window. *A morning that started so promising.*

'Speaking of Robin. Have you heard from him at all?'

'Nothing.' And no news is good news, as far as I'm concerned.

'Doesn't that strike you as strange? He chased you for weeks after you left. Flowers, gifts, phone calls. The man was obsessed.'

'I guess having his nose broken was enough to make him stay away. Or maybe the fact that I spent the night with another man was enough to turn him completely off.'

'It's still strange. It's like there's been no closure, don't you think?'

'I got closure enough when I saw him poke his needle dick in some other chick.'

'I wasn't meaning for you—that's a given. I just think it's strange how he stopped bothering *you* all of a sudden.'

On occasion, I get the odd feeling that I'm being watched, but I keep that to myself because voicing those feelings makes me sound like a nut. Besides, I've seen evidence of his moving on. Pictures of him coming out of the places we used to frequent. A different girl on his arm as he attends music events.

'Don't you have a shoot to get ready for? I'm not supposed to be on set today. I'd intended to treat myself to a coffee and maybe mooch around some of the expensive Chelsea boutiques.

'I'm really not looking forward to today.'

'Do you want me to tag along? I don't mind.'

'You wouldn't?' she asks a little cautiously. 'Only, I've booked a couple of rooms at the Bawdy House Hotel. We're doing this whole bordello scene, and Jackson is only in the UK for a few more days.'

'Sure.' I don't have concrete plans. 'What time are we going?'

'Could you meet me there? Say, around three? There are enough bodies for a hotel room as it is, but it would be really great if you could be there at the end.'

'I can do that,' I answer, glad that I can help her in some way. 'I've heard their rooms are something else.'

'More four poster beds than you can tie an orgy to.'

'Then why aren't you more excited? At least the staging won't be a lot of work.' As well as her PA and pimple hider, chief toy washer, and lube holder, I'm also sometimes called to help move furniture, wipe clean mirrors, and throw scatter cushions around. *All in the name of setting the sexy stage.*

'I know. But there's been an uptick in the search engine requests for anal. So that's on the cards for today.'

'At least it's not your butthole that's being pounded.'

'Really?' Chastity says, screwing up her cherub-like face. 'I haven't even eaten breakfast yet.'

'And if you were today's lucky starlet, you definitely wouldn't be eating breakfast.'

'I know. Just inhaling more laxatives than a retirement village.'

0123456

Chapter Eighteen

KEIR

'How come you're free this morning?' Will peers at me over his newspaper cup. 'Aren't you usually dashing around ballet recitals, playgrounds, and Brownie meets?'

'I'm not free. I've already been into the office this morning.'

Sorcha is with her grandparents. They suggested they take her to ballet today, freeing up my day for more work. And that's partly why I'm here with him. Since Will's dad passed and he gained the houses, lands, and title of Lord Travers, among others, I've been helping him with his property issues. Travers Hall is now under the guardianship of The National Trust, and no longer a rotting albatross of a carcass hanging around his neck. Which leaves the castle in Scotland. It's a dreary old place, but it's undergoing a wee bit of a transformation. Bookings are beginning to trickle in for corporate weekends, and I'm pretty sure I've found Will the right team to branch out into functions.

Who doesn't want to get married in an ancient castle? Well, apart from me.

'Saturday morning in the office,' Will crows, flattening his broadsheet newspaper and leaning his long frame back in the oxblood leather club chair. 'I bet Flynn just loved that,' he says, mentioning my assistant. Will has met him a few times in our recent dealings and witnessed our odd working relationship. *The shit he gives me, and the shit I dish back.*

'I believe Flynn's sentiments were somewhat along the lines of *fuck off* and *fuck no*. But he made it in on time anyway.' Carrying coffee, no less.

'Of course, he did. He's Pippa to your Tony Stark.'

'Except we're not fucking.' In his typically crude and laconic way, Flynn slides himself into the spare seat around our small table.

'The pair of you do act like you're married,' Will mocks. Reaching for his coffee cup, he gestures to the waitress for another round.

'Aye, especially when you're buying yourself things on my credit card,' I grumble.

'The company credit card,' Flynn corrects. 'And one of us needs to treat me nice. You know, especially when you're dragging me out of the warm arms of a woman,' he says, making a gesture that speaks of large breasts, not warm arms. 'And just to come hold your . . . notebook.'

In answer, I just laugh as I turn to Will. 'That's his way of telling us he scored last night. He's still thinks he's Jack the Lad.' In a mock whisper, I add, 'We're supposed to pretend to be impressed.'

'Ignore him,' Will says, slapping the arm of Flynn's chair. 'Keir's just jealous on account of his life being one long dry spell.'

'That's where you're wrong, mate,' begins Flynn. 'He's getting plenty of action with his girl Friday.'

Friday evening are almost sacred these days, my *me time* now *our time*—a time I don't want to share or discuss with anyone else.

'Isn't there a nondisclosure clause in your contract?' Despite the mildness of my tone, my whole body is suddenly taut, my gaze seeking to convey the things I don't want to voice aloud. Not that it matters. Flynn is too fucking busy eyeing up the waitress filling our coffee cups.

'Girl Friday?' Will's head turns to me and I just know he's about to fire shit my way. 'You're a dark horse.'

'And you're a nosy arsehole, but sadly, there's fuck all I can do about that.'

'So who is she?' His attentions turn to Flynn, who holds up his hands.

'Don't ask me, mate. I just book the hotels.'

'Ah, hotel sex,' Will says on a reminiscent sigh. 'Do you know what the fastest car in the world is, Flynn?'

'Nah. I'm not much of a rev-head myself,' he says, pushing the thick black frame of his glasses farther up his nose. I think he wears them for effect, not sight issues. Nothing would surprise me. He probably read in some men's magazine that *chicks dig specs*.

'Guess,' Will encourages.

'Bugatti?' he offers with a careless shrug.

'Nope, a rental.' I keep my mouth shut because I've an idea where this is going.

'A rental?' Flynn repeats with more than a note of disbelief. 'Even a compact?'

Will nods. 'Because it's not yours, so it doesn't matter how careless you are—how hard you ride the arse off it on the highway. Same as hotel sex. That arse doesn't belong to you for long, so you can ride it any way you like without fear of consequences.'

'You're a nasty, nasty man, Lord Travers.'

'Says the man having sordid rendezvous. In hotels, no less. Without confiding in his friends. Besides,' he adds, folding his arms, 'I'm a reformed man these days.'

'I'm sure Sadie will be overjoyed to hear.'

'My love knows me as a paragon of virtue. And she knows every saint has a past. And lucky for you, every sinner has a future.'

'Why d'you have to be such a bawheid?'

'Me?' Will asks, pointing his index finger at his own chest. 'I'm the bawheid? I'm only pleased you're not gonna be a claw baws all your life!' I secretly love it when I can get The Right Honourable Will, aka Lord Travers, to drop into the Scots vernacular. *Love it*.

'Fuck it,' complains Flynn. 'I hate it when you start talking in that foreign fucking language.'

'Says the immigrant,' I retort.

'Lemme get this straight,' he says, waving me off. 'You just called him'—he points at Will—'a bawheid. That's like saying he's got testicles for brains? Like he's stupid?'

'Aye.'

'And he called you claw baws. Which is like saying you're always touching yourself.'

'That's enough,' I grumble. 'Keep your translations to yourself.'

Will then sends me an arrogant smirk, one that neither befits his rank or station, but definitely his personality. He's not done with his interrogation, or so he thinks. But me? My thoughts are on another plane as something catches my eye on the other side of the room.

A cherubic blonde. Petite, pink cheeked, and pale hair that curls around her ears. She looks a little agitated, a little uneasy, but more than that, the dark-haired girl with her back to me seems to be very annoyed.

Maybe it's her annoyance that throws me off because it takes me a while to realise the girl with her back to me is Paisley. It's not even as if I recognise her first. It's her arse I recognise. Excuse me for going all Neanderthal for a minute, but fuck, that arse. You could stick a frame around it and hang it in the *Louvre*. On second thoughts, I don't fancy the world and his wife staring at her derrière, even if it doesn't belong to me.

It. Doesn't. Belong. To. Me.

It's a loaner, so to speak.

I'm considering getting my mind out of the crazy gutter when a man arrives at the table. A big fucker—maybe as tall as me but slim built. Dark slicked back hair, he looks like Clark Kent's skinnier cousin and has clearly read the same magazine as Flynn, given the style of his eyewear. My stomach curls like my fists—like my hand around the coffee cup—as the blonde stands, kisses the big fucker's cheek, then hightails it out of the place.

Perfect. Just fucking perfect. She's on a date. She doesn't look like she's on a date—that's not to say she doesn't look gorgeous. She just doesn't currently look like she does when she meets me. *She looks like someone's hot PA.*

A date. *Why did I not see that coming?* And more to the point, why the fuck does it hurt? We've made no promises, and she's a stunningly attractive woman, so why would she be holding out for Fridays with me?

'Oi? Are you paying attention?' Flynn asks, tapping a Mont Blanc on the small table between us. *My Mont Blanc.*

'I was thinking.' I scowl in his direction, though not because he's "appropriated" my pen. 'Stop dickin' about.'

'I'd wondered what that burning smell was,' interjects Will. 'Who pissed on your lollipop all of a sudden?'

'I've just got shit to do. That's all.'

'Oh, right. And I haven't got the tax man breathing down my neck, demanding my firstborn.'

'Aye, so. Come on. Let's move this thing along.' And so we do, though I keep an eye on Paisley and the prat. And I manage. Mostly. At least until she's drank half of her wine, when I decide to send her an unfair text.

What's on the cards for trouble today, Trouble?

I watch as she turns over her phone, reads the text with a worried expression, then places it back down again.

I did *not* see that coming. I turn my attention away from the pair, feeling like I've been poked in the chest with one of Agnes's knitting needles. I can't look at her. I feel . . . angry. Betrayed. Hurt. Dismissed. Pissed off. Territorial and irrational. I feel like I could tear off some fucker's head!

Then, through the red haze, the phone in my hand chimes.

No ballet classes and ice cream afternoons for this girl. I've stopped by to help Chastity. With work.

How? How is that work? Unless—maybe she's taking a meeting for her pal. Though his skinny arse can't be on the top of many women's fantasies. *Unless he's like a tripod.*

I look up again; he's touching her arm. I am not overly enthused by her interview technique.

'Ya, fuckin' bastard,' I growl, beginning to type on my phone again.

'What?' asks Flynn.

'Nothin'. Just the sports results.' They return to their meeting, ignoring me and my sudden sour mood.

You're working on a Saturday? I type. 'Better not be under him.'

People have been known to have sex on a Saturday. Some might suggest they do their best work on the weekends.

Is she talking about her or about him? My mind begins to reel as my thumbs go into overdrive.

Is that so? I thought Friday nights were perfect. Certainly enough to see you through, given the way you looked when you left the hotel this morning. 'This fuckin' morning,' I grumble, my thumbs striking my phone.

I'm not having sex today, comes her reply. ***Just pointing out the industry I work in.***

The bastard gets up from his chair as I hit send on another text. And another. And another. Okay, I bombard her with fucking series of them.

You're sure you're working?

You're not, say, sat in a hotel bar?

Drinking wine

Talking to some nerd

In a pink sweater

A nerd who wouldn't know the first fucking thing to do with you

It's not what it looks like, she responds.

Look at me, I demand. *Turn around and look at me.*

And she does turn, though slowly. Her expression? I can't make it out.

Your date is on his way back to the table, and the man who's fucking you wants to know what the hell is going on

Please understand, this isn't what it looks like, comes her reply. *Give me five minutes.*

Within four, she's gathering her large purse, her cardigan, and her phone, all without looking at me. She straightens and turns, walking into the reception of the hotel, not the door that leads out into the street.

'I've got shite to do,' I say, pushing my chair back. If either of my companions have questions, they aren't asking them.

As I walk toward her, her stiff posture and my mood pulling all kind of reactions from me. Still, I can't help but stare at her arse, my mind filled with inappropriate filth. And it's *beautiful. My thoughts. Her arse. All of it*. I want to bite it. Spank it. Spread the cheeks apart and slam myself home.

She reaches the bottom of the grand staircase, and without turning to see if I'm following, she begins climbing the stairs. I come up behind her at the same sedate pace, my feet placed where her feet have been, my hands trailing up the banister.

From several steps behind her, I watch how her tight pencil skirt hugs her in all the right places. Over the twin rounds of her arse and her hips, it slides over her firm thighs, opening in a small split at the back of her knee. The high heels of her shoes tauten the muscles of her calves, and with each step she takes, I get the flash of a red sole.

I'm gonna make her keep her shoes on next time. My dick inside her, I'll prop her foot against my shoulder and my teeth against her ankle. Because there will be a next time. I need to lock this shit down.

At the top of the staircase, she turns, but this time, she can't resist looking back. Her countenance is flushed. She looks excited. And then over her shoulder, she smiles.

Game fucking on.

Chapter Nineteen

PAISLEY

What's on the cards for trouble today, Trouble? It's past four o'clock, and I'm at the hotel when my phone dings with Keir's text.

No ballet classes and ice cream afternoons for this girl, I type out, referencing his plans for the day. *I've stopped by to help Chastity. With work.*

It's definitely a statement that wouldn't stand up in court. I may have shown up at the hotel under the impression Chastity needed my help, but the reality turned out to be something else.

'Have you lived in the UK for very long?' Troy asks. Yes, *that* Troy. In the flesh. Not in the movie or even Iliad Troy, but the one Chas mentioned just this morning. *Just* this morning. The sly beast. She didn't even have the decency to look embarrassed about railroading me into meeting him. Just introduced us at the bar before turning tail and getting the hell out of the place.

And I have a lot to say about that. But in the meantime, it looks like I'm having a drink. With Troy. While talking to Keir via text.

'I've lived over here for more than two years.'

'You're from Upstate New York Chastity said?'

I nod and take a sip of my wine. It's cold but kind of vinegary. Or maybe that's just my mood. It's not Troy's fault—and he seems like a decent guy. But he's not *my* guy. Not that I'm suggesting Keir is mine, but I can only concentrate on one man at a time. Hard enough trying to talk and text two men.

You're working on a Saturday?

People have been known to have sex on a Saturday, I type back, giving Troy an apologetic smile. No doubt he thinks I'm talking to Chas. Under normal circumstances, I might be. But it's hard to convey anger via text satisfactorily. *Some might suggest they do their best work on the weekends.*

Really? comes his immediate response. *I thought Friday nights were perfect. Certainly enough to see you through, given the way you looked when you left the hotel this morning.*

I bite back a smile. I thought he was sleeping. *He wasn't, and he still let you go*. A niggling voice echoes inside my head even as much lower pulses with remembrance of the evening. I looked well and truly fucked. Because I had been—right into the early hours. But at least I'd taken clean clothes. *I've learned since our first Friday together*. I might leave looking well rode, but I'm also usually well dressed. *Matching shoes and everything.*

I'm not having sex today, just pointing out the industry I work in.

Troy engages me once more in conversation, asking polite questions which I try to concentrate on. But as my phone burns a hole in my skirt with its incessant buzzing, I'm finding it hard. Keir really is going to town with his texts.

When Troy excuses himself to visit the bathroom, I quickly unlock my phone. My heart sinks.

You're sure you're working?

You're not, say, sat at a hotel bar?

Talking to some nerd

In a sweater

A nerd who wouldn't know the first fucking thing to do with you

My heart beats like hooves pounding in my chest, my shoulders rolling inward as though their shadow could deny the evidence of his words. I almost don't want to look behind me for fear of what I'll find. But I know I don't have much time before Troy comes back. He doesn't deserve this. Neither does Keir. Neither do I!

Chastity. What the hell have you done?

It's not what it looks like, I text without turning.

Look at me, comes his response. ***Turn around and look at me.***

I turn slowly in my seat. He's easy to spot, sitting ramrod straight, his expression so fucked off, his eyes burning bright. *And not in a good way.*

My phone dings again.

Your date is on his way back to the table, and the man who's fucking you wants to know what the hell is going on

Please understand, this isn't what it looks like, I type back. *Give me five minutes.*

I don't look at my phone as it chimes again.

'Troy, I'm so sorry. I've got to go. I-I've just had a text from Chastity. She has'—*a death wish*—'some kind of emergency.'

'How awful.' As I stand and gather my jacket and bag, Troy also stands. 'Let me walk you to—'

'No!' In a much saner tone, I add, 'There really is no need. Thank you for the wine. I-I'll be in touch.' *Sometime never.*

I don't shake his hand or do the European two-cheeked kissing thing that Londoners are so fond of. In fact, I'm pretty sure I must look like the hounds of hell are chasing me as I hightail it out of the bar and into the hotel reception.

Keir follows. I don't know how I know, but I do. *Or maybe it's just wishful thinking at this point.*

The Bawdy House isn't a large venue. More a boutique kind of hotel. There's no marble reception or high-powered elevator, but rather the space looks like it could have been lifted from a BBC period drama. A grand sweeping staircase dominates the reception, the walls lined walled with oil paintings ranging from portraits of severe faced matrons to those a touch more erotic. I pause as the toe of my shoe touches the worn Oriental carpet at the base of the staircase, realising I still have the keys to the rooms Chastity booked.

Then I spot him. Keir. Maybe a dozen steps behind me as I turn to the staircase. A mixture of anticipation and excitement and, yes, fear fill my chest cavity as I place my feet one after another to climb.

What if he doesn't follow me?

What if he does?

He looked so angry. So hurt.

At the third floor, I turn left and walk the length of the corridor, taking a sly glance at the open staircase and rolling my lips inward to hide my wide smile of relief. *He's following. But what next?*

No modern key card at this hotel. Rather, a large ornate key on a large red tassel matches the plaque with the name of the room. *Lillith.* I push the door open, glad the room was left in some semblance of order, and ignoring the faint scent of lube in the air, I step inside and leave the door ajar.

Leaning against the frame of the wrought-iron four poster bed, I close my eyes a moment before the door creaks open.

I breathe in. Breathe out. Try to ignore the hammer of my pulse as I feel him drawing closer. Hear his footsteps. Feel his eyes on me.

I wet my lips as his words wind their way around my ear as his fingers brush a lock of hair from my cheek.

'You. Are. *Trouble.*'

I open my eyes to his impassive expression. His strong arms crossed over his chest. Flecks of green and gold glow in his hazel gaze; his lips relaxed, but his jaw tense.

'It's not what it looks like.'

'What did it look like?' his low voice almost growls.

'Like I was on a date.'

'Drinking wine. In a hotel. With a man trying to impress you.'

'He wasn't—'

'Trouble *and* oblivious. And a liar?'

'I am not.'

'But you like him?'

I wet my lips and roll them together. Neither answer works here. If I say yes, I'm a conniving bitch. If I say no, I'm a liar. Could I see myself dating Troy? Yeah. Before Keir, I actually could. Now? I can't see anything but the man in front of me.

'You wet for him?'

My heart begins to thud. He has no right to ask me something like that, and I don't have to answer him . . . even as I find myself widening my stance.

Keir sighs, conflicted. At least, that's what it looks like as he takes my hands in his and encourages me to grasp the hem of my skirt. I wriggle it upwards until it's gathered at my waist— it's so tight it stays there. But I don't have time to feel even slightly ridiculous as he takes my hand, slides it down my stomach, and tucks my fingers under the pale pink silk of my panties.

'You show me,' he demands, covering my hand with his.

I don't know whether to concentrate on his gaze or the path of my fingers right now. They're both equally as unravelling. *Equally as demanding.*

'Spread your legs wider.' The heat in his gaze is unhinging; the low, seductive bass of his tone as tempting as the devil himself. 'What are you waiting for?'

'If I touch myself and I'm wet, you'll think I'm into him.'

'Will I? Or maybe I'll just get off on watching you touch yourself. Come on, trouble. You brought me up here for a reason.'

Did I? An unconscious decision to be with him. 'It's not even Friday,' I whisper, tilting my hips, my fingers toying with the thin strip of ribbon above the silk.

'I'm good with that,' he murmurs, toying with a lock of my hair. Flicking the ends across my skin, he then pushes it from my shoulder. 'Touch yourself. For me.' A shiver shimmers across my skin, desire jumping between us like the dance of electricity as he watches me wet my parched lips, his eyes falling instinctively to where my hand slips under the ribbon adorned waistband.

At the first brush of my own clit, my legs begin to shake, and I whimper from the sensation. Keir presses his lips against mine, whispering a soft *hush* into my mouth.

'I left the door open. Unless you want an audience . . . '

'My eyes flick to the door, which is barely ajar, but the threat of discovery is there. And the threat of discovery seems to heighten things. Exponentially.

Who is this girl I've become?

I push up into my hand, sliding two fingers along my wetness, whimpering as I bring them back to my clit again.

And he watches. Watches my fingers. Watches my face. Bites his lip as though he's dying for a taste.

'You're so fuckin' gorgeous,' his voice rumbles. 'I have never wanted you more than I do right now.'

I cry out softly, his words unravelling me, his gaze intoxicating me more than any liquor or drug could. I've never done this—never gotten myself off for someone else's enjoyment. And it's a powerful feeling to know that your touches are turning someone on. *Someone other than you.*

I begin petting and moving two fingers in a well-practised rhythm of small circles against my clit. But I want more. How can I not when he's standing in front of me, his eyes dark, his muscled arms flexing under the soft cotton of his Henley as his fists clench and unclench as though he's dying to touch me himself.

I arch against the bedpost, pushing harder into my hand, wanting more pressure, more everything.

'Show me. Show me how wet you are for me.' His daring demands have me arching my back against hand.

'Touch me,' I beg. 'Fuck me. I want to feel you.'

'Show me what's mine,' he demands. 'Show me what's mine, and I'll make it so good.'

I pull my fingers from my panties to hook my thumbs into the sides, shimmying them part way down my thighs. The material of my skirt bunched around my waist, I scissor the wetness between my two fingers.

'Fuck me, you're dripping.' Keir's eyes dart from my glistening fingers to my exposed pussy.

In a heartbeat, he grasps my wrist, his eyes falling closed as he sucks my fingers into his mouth. If I wasn't turned on before, you can bet I am now. His tongue works those two digits like his tongue is a stripper and my fingers the pole. And the noises he makes? It's like I'm pure gourmet.

Outside in the corridor, a door slams, and I jump, trying to take back my hand. To no avail as, with one last flick, he pulls my fingers free and jams them between my legs. I cry out long and loud.

'You're gonna make yourself come,' he growls, 'and I'm gonna help.'

I don't register much else as he slides my fingers back to my clit, replacing them with his own. He works me roughly—deeply—his fingers spearing sharply before curling inside.

'You can do better than that.'

My legs turn to liquid as I begin to apply pressure to the tight bundle of nerves as his fingers thrust and scissor, curl and torment. And all the while, he's whispering the sweetest of filth.

Of how he knows what I need.

How he'll fill me.

Stick his fingers inside me.

His cock.

How when he's done with me, I won't know my own name.

'Jesus Christ, I need to fuck you.'

'Yes!'

'You're gonna come all over my fingers, then you're gonna lick them clean.' I nod again. 'Then you're gonna come home with me and sit on my face.'

'Yes!'

'That's no' very polite.'

'Yes, please.' I'm rocking up into both our hands now, the images his words conjure pushing me closer to the edge. I'm gasping—whimpering— chanting his name. And I'm coming hard, exploding in a burst of blinding heat and pure ecstasy.

And then I'm coming down, down onto his hand. Down into his kiss. And I don't care if I never move again. That is, until he whispers those magic words,

'Sweetheart, come home with me.'

Chapter Twenty

KEIR

I think I could love her.

Seriously. How mad is that? And it's not because of my reaction to seeing her with another man—I'm not a complete meathead. Okay, maybe I'm a little bit of a meathead. But at least I didn't want to hit her over the head with my caveman club and drag her back to my lair. *Much*. So I wanted to do some of that. Grab her by the hair, though not for dragging purposes. Holding her hostage by it, maybe. All right, I'll admit it—definitely. It makes me rock fucking hard. But the club across the head I'll save for Mr Sexy Specs. He was lucky I didn't wallop him as I passed.

'What are you staring at?'

Bright sunlight fills the grey interior of my bedroom, and I suddenly realise how fucking dreary the room is. Dark heavy furniture so dreary compared to the brilliant blue of those eyes peeking above the quilt she's pulled up over her nose. She blinks up at me and everything stops; my thoughts no longer like a great rush of water tumbling over rocks.

'Clearly,' she says, pulling the bedding to under her chin. 'You're stunned how you got such a gorgeous creature into your bed.'

'Aye, that's exactly right.' My mouth tugs into a reluctant smile. 'I'm staring at you, wondering how on earth a creature as lovely as you came to be here.'

'I *came* by invitation', she purrs. 'And it was fan-*tastic.*'

We did have an awesome night, and my bed certainly bears the evidence of it. Pillows on the floor, the sheet creased like yesterday's newspaper as it curls away from the edge of the mattress. Know what else bears the evidence of it? My abs. I feel like I've had the best workout ever.

'The pleasure was all mine.'

'Oh, I'm not sure about that.' We use the moment to stare at each other, all goofy smiles—it seems like an endless, joyful moment. Or a perfect ruse as I whip the quilt from her grip, rendering her completely naked. 'Hey!' she squeals.

In the morning light, she looks fantastic. All mussed up, messy hair, so soft and warm. Her cheeks are flushed, her mouth pulled into a soft vowel sound. You know the one; not *a*, not *e*, not *i* . . .

'*Oh* . . . '

I insinuate myself between her legs, spreading my hands on her inner thighs to spread her open.

'Fuck me, you are so pretty.'

'Is that a compliment to—'

I slide my finger through her soft pink ribbon of flesh, and she rises to my touch immediately, her words lost in the experience. Without thought, I'm above her, leaning on one arm. Gripping my cock, I slide it through her wetness.

'You're here. In my bed.' My words are rough, my control tenuous, even as she takes my face in her hands.

'That does appear to be the case. And I'm as surprised as you are, quite frankly.'

What can I say? I don't have a definitive answer for her. I can't explain it either. The last woman I had in this bed . . . There hasn't been any women in this bed. Period.

'Were you trying to assuage your conscience?'

I dip my hips, bringing my cock to line perfectly against her pussy. Framed by her sweet lips. 'I heard *sausage* and *conscience*. You want me to sausage your conscience? By Christ, you're into some filthy shit.'

'I learned everything I know from a certain Scotsman. One with golden brown hair,' she whispers, threading her fingers into my hair.

Beneath me, her hardened nipples rub my chest, her body rocking up against me for the purpose of a little friction.

"I'm so glad you said yes,' I whisper, pressing my mouth against hers. Small, exploratory kisses become deeper and wetter, each press of our lips a little more desperate, each slip of tongue a little more real, until our tongues are tangling, our fingers grasping, and she's moaning into my mouth.

'How long have we got?'

'About ten inches.'

Paisley giggles, and it's the *best* sound—the best fucking sound. Second only to Sorcha's mirth.

'You're nuts, you know that?'

'I'm aware,' I growl into the soft skin of her neck. Licking, teasing, bringing her hands above her head. 'I must be nuts not to have had you here before. Fucked you here in my bed.'

'Is that so?' She stretches out like a content cat.

'Aye. This might be the first time, but it isn't the last.' My head is filled with filthy images, causing me to grind my hips into her. But my words? They're the truth. Fridays aren't enough and never will be again. I'm not sure how or why, but I need more of her. More of this—more fucking. More skin. More kisses and cuddles. More getting to know her. 'I'm going to fuck you here in my bed. Then maybe in the shower. Maybe in the pool.'

'I hope it's not outdoors,' she muses.

'Then the kitchen. I'll push your palms flat on the table, then I'll stand between your legs and finger you until you're dripping.'

'Fingering is so underrated,' she agrees all breathily, following the path of my gaze down our joined bodies. 'Oh, my. That is so hot,' she says, staring at the wet head of my cock, the rest of me nestled between her perfect pink lips.

'It is, isn't it?' I can't help my grin. The sight of me between her legs. The way her eyes have darkened. The way she doesn't move her hands. 'It's all perfect. Picture fucking perfect. It makes me wish I had my phone.'

'Do it,' she whispers urgently. 'Do it.' It takes me a moment to realise she's answering my lust-spilled words. 'Use my phone, only don't stop talking. Keep saying dirty things to me.'

This girl. This girl right here? She's fucking perfect.

Her nightstand is nearer—it wasn't hers before, but it is now—and her phone lies there encased in a glittery pink case. I feel the loss of her immediately as I reach for it, snagging it from the nightstand, and repositioning myself.

'You really should have a passcode on this,' I tell her as I open her phone.

'Later. Now talk—we were in the kitchen.'

'So we were.'

Click. I take a photo of the length of my cock framed by her slick lips.

'I'll finger you until we can both hear how wet you are.' I spread her thighs impossibly wide, lining myself up against her pussy.

Click. My head, wet and glistening, balanced against her wetness.

'Yes! How much I need you.'

Click. Paisley's hands on her tits, rosy nipples peeking between splayed fingertips.

'Your pussy slippery and wet, your thighs coated in your own cum, I'll shove my cock inside you so hard the table will be shunted across the room.'

Click. Her body accepting me as I slide myself home.

'Oh, God!'

The phone abandoned to the mattress, her feet locked around my backs of my thighs, her long lashes closed and almost caressing her cheekbones. *How did I not notice how long her lashes were?* I rock into her, my muscles locked tight, my body's instinctual responses screaming in my need to rut. To fuck. But this moment is different. More somehow. I don't want it to end. This girl in my bed? Right now, she's all I can think of. It's like an obsession or a mania—and then it hits me: I'm infatuated. I can accept this. *With some relief.*

I begin to move, to rock into her with tiny flexes of my hips. It's slow and it's torturous—for us both. The best kind of agony, and the best kind of ecstasy as I tease us with a rolling advance and retreat.

'You feel so fucking good.' I'm not sure if she hears me; my words are barely more than an exhale as I drive myself inside her body hard. 'Oh, fuck.' She clenches around me, lifting her hips to greet me.

I slide my hand to the back of her knee, lifting her leg and bringing it to my shoulder. The change of depth is immediate; pleasure crawls along my spine and tightens my balls, causing me to grunt. And though she might not be wearing her fuck me heels, that's okay. I bite her ankle anyway. She cries out. I thrust a little harder in response, unravelling us both a little more.

'You feel so good.' Her hands lift from her breasts, fingertips running up the ladder of my abs, then my ribs. 'So hard inside me.'

Compliments. They're always good, but from her, they're a little unhinging.

'I want to eat your pussy. See my cum dripping from your lips.' A long, raspy groan accompanies my stream of filthy consciousness when she clenches around my dick, her short nails running over my nipples. The sensation resonates through me, my whole body seeming to ripple in response.

I can't think, and I can't speak as her lush lips pull me like a magnet. She moans into my mouth, and I'm done for as she accepts me at both ends. Her leg falls from my shoulder, wrapping around me as things suddenly become frantic—everything growing in size—in magnitude—in sensation and consciousness. My heart feels like it could burst; our lips smash together as though I want her to inhale me. Accept all of me. Her fingers pull at my hair, and we can't catch our breaths as I rock against her. Pace goes out of the window, replaced by nature and need. With each flex of my hips, our moans become louder and a little more desperate, her tits rubbing against me so deliciously it's hard to hold back. My muscles ache and my pulse pounds as, my body covering hers, I alternate between deep, punishing thrusts and small punches of my hips, the kind of movement that rubs her clit.

From her cries, Paisley loves it. Loves it all.

My hands slide under her arse, pulling her to me, our joining an experience like nothing else.

'I can't, I can't,' she begins to chant. '*I need*.'

'That fuckin' accent,' I growl into the soft skin of her neck, 'drives me fuckin' wild.'

'I-I like you wild.'

'And I like you fine. Just. Fuckin'. Fine.'

Her arse in my big palms, I punctuate my words with my thrusts. My hips begin to jab and flex as I fuck her harder, my fingertips punishing against her flesh.

'I can feel you,' I rasp into the soft skin of her neck. 'I can feel you coming around me.'

As my words and my cock drive her to the edge, her whole body rocks against me, milking me, as she repeats my name again and again. At this moment, I'm aware of nothing else in this world. The sun could fall from the sky, or a supernova could swallow the earth, and I don't think I would realise as Paisley cries out one last time, then falls apart in my arms.

Chapter Twenty-One

KEIR

'God, I'm hungry.' Splayed out across my chest, Paisley's dark mane fans out to under my chin. We're still in bed, which is perfect, with my head propped on the lone pillow left on the bed. Her body lies width ways across the mattress, her toes dangling over the edge.

'I thought you were dead.' My voice sounds raspy and feels sort of hoarse. And I've lost count of the times and ways we've fucked.

'You killed me, but my ravenous appetite brought me back.'

'I'll say you're ravenous.'

'Only for you, babe.' And doesn't that tiny term of endearment hit me like a poke to the chest. A good kind of poke. The kind that leaves me smiling, at least.

'Come on.' Her face is above mine suddenly, her teardrop tits swaying closer as she kisses my nose. 'Feed me.'

As she moves away, I push up onto my elbows, sending thanks heavenward as she bends over, blessing me with the sight of her bare arse. It's short lived as she steps into her knickers and begins sliding them over her knees.

'I wasn't joking.' She turns her head over her shoulder, then resumes looking for her bra, I think. 'I need food.'

'Come over here. I'll feed you.'

'I need sustenance,' she says, laughing. 'Real food. Bread. Cheese. I'd even go for fruit at this point.'

'You don't like fruit?'

'I like bread, cheese, nuts. Crackers. Fruit is like . . . I don't know. Something I push off the top of my cheesecake.'

'I remember,' I say suddenly, pushing myself up to sit at the edge of the bed. 'That day in the coffee shop. You left the strawberry on your plate.'

'You noticed that, huh?' She smiles with a delighted kind of shyness.

'I notice lots of things. Like how when you're creeping out of the hotel room, you can never seem to find one of your shoes.'

'I know!' she agrees, animatedly. 'I think someone put a hex on me years ago! I can literally *never* find a pair of shoes when I need them! Even in a hotel room where I only have two of the damn things. And now, it seems, I can't find my bra.'

'That must be Keir magic,' I reply with a wink. She bites back her smile as I continue to speak. 'Because I know you're the kind of girl who always wears matching underwear.'

'Maybe I only wear matching when I know I'm meeting you?'

'Not true, trouble.' I hold out my hand, and she comes to me, straddling my legs, settling herself lower and purposely rubbing her pussy against me.

'This I need to hear.' Her tone teases. 'Come on, baby. Psychoanalyse me.'

'You're always put together gorgeously. And the very first day we met, I was the lucky recipient of a flash of your underwear.' And then yesterday . . . not even gonna think about yesterday right now. *About Troy. About matching underwear. Because that's not what that was.* I'm also gonna keep my eyes on her face, no matter what it takes. 'I reckon you've got a deep-seated fear of being knocked over by a bus. What would the paramedics think if you were a mess of polka dots and flowers?'

'You're so silly,' she says, running her fingers through my hair. Her cheeks heat as though remembering something dirty. And yep, I still manage to keep my gaze above her neck.

This girl. This bloody girl.

'Your underwear matches your outerwear. You're always pulled together. Co-ordinating shoes and outfit. Perfectly applied makeup. Deliciously matched underwear. And your insides,' I say, placing my palm over her heart, 'are as darling as your looks.' To stop myself from embarrassing us both, I give her lips a quick peck, and as I stand, I slide her feet to the floor. 'Come on, trouble. Let me show you some fruit you'll love.'

In the kitchen, Paisley takes a seat at the breakfast bar, eyeing the large dish of well-polished fruit between us.

'It all looks plastic.' She grasps a shining red apple, turning it in fingers. 'Or painted.'

'It's organic fruit, but Agnes still likes to wash the fuck out of it once it's delivered. She used to seem content to let me pick the apples straight from her garden when I was a lad, but woe betide anyone who feed Sorcha an unwashed pear.' Come to think of it, she used to let me steal the apples because I wasn't getting enough food at home.

'She must love Sorcha very much.' Paisley's voice pulls me from my dark thoughts.

'Aye, she does that.'

'So where are they today that you can walk around your house, flashing your hotness around while tempting random passing girls?'

I can barely recall the last time I walked around in the semi-buff. And I definitely can't remember the last time a girl wore one of my shirts. *And very little else.* Sleeves rolled, the hem hits mid-thigh, so it's not super revealing. But there's just something about seeing a hot girl wearing your things. Whether it's a territorial thing, or maybe because it signifies we've already had our clothes *off*, I don't know. All I can say is that it's as sexy as fuck.

'I'm only interested in tempting one girl. She's trouble enough.' I send her a flirty wink. 'And today is one of those very rare Saturdays. I'm sure Agnes will be in her wee cottage at the back of the house, and I don't have to pick up Sorcha until this afternoon. We've got hours and hours yet.'

'You make it sound like you have plans.'

'Oh, I do, trouble. Lots and lots of plan. Starting with your fruit education.'

Her shoulders slump. 'The other F-word.'

'Come on.' I curl my fingers, beckoning her into the kitchen. When she's in front of me, I back her up against one of the countertops, leaving her momentarily to open the freezer.

'If it's the ice cream kind of fruit, I'm down with that. Especially if it's, say, fudge brownie or chocolate.'

'There must be some very peculiar fruit and veg shops in the US.' From the corner of my eye, I can see Paisley straining to view the contents of the dish I pull from the deep freeze. It's pretty pointless. The thing has a lid, and I'm all about the surprise right now.

'Fruit *and* veg? Those are some strange words you're throwing about.'

'Don't tell me you refuse to eat vegetables, too.' I stop in front of her, placing my hand on her shoulder. 'Do you have something to tell me? Are you eight years old?'

'Cute,' she says. 'I eat vegetables. I just don't like fruit.'

'You're gonna like this fruit.' The cold bowl chinks as I place it on the countertop, just behind her. 'Trust me.'

'That right there is a very wolfish smile. What are you up to?'

'Do you trust me?'

She moves her head to one side, then the other as though contemplating before answering with a simple, 'Yes.'

So I get to work, loosening the buttons of my shirt from the bottom up.

'It might be a good time to point out that, a, I haven't showered and, b, that I'm a little sore at his point.'

I bite back the beginnings of a smile as I spread the sides of the white cotton, drinking in the sight of her pale pink knickers and bare skin. I place my palm over her breastbone, the tanned skin of my hand a sharp contrast to the pale colour of her skin and in my shirt. Her heart beats steadily, her eyes darkening as though a little drugged. A little lust drunk.

'Slide down your knickers.' Without a word of protest, she slips her thumbs into the sides, slipping them partway down her thighs. 'That's enough.' If she takes them off, this might not go the way I plan.

I inhale deeply because I can smell her. Smell the remains of her lingering floral perfume. Smell the evidence of our night.

'Do you have any idea how you look right now?'

She laughs huskily. 'Probably pretty ridiculous.'

'Wrong, trouble. So wrong,' I say, taking her hands and curling them around the edge of the countertop. 'Now, close your eyes and don't let go.' As she does as I ask, I lean behind her and take the top off the bowl, lifting out a piece of frozen ruby red fruit. 'No peeking,' I whisper, rolling the frozen grape over her nipple.

'That's . . . ' Her whole body stiffens. 'That's so cold.' Without a reply, I roll the grape over her other nipple, taking the first hardened bud into my mouth.

'Keir!' Her whole demeanour is conflicted. Hot and wet, cold and a little torturous, she doesn't know how to react, though I sense she's about to lift her hands.

'No cheating. No peeking and no moving your hands.' I pop the grape between my teeth, reaching around her and grabbing another from the bowl. This time, I press the coldness against both nipples at the same time. Paisley hums her appreciation— pants a little as I ghost my mouth over hers.

'Want a taste?' She nods, and I burst the grape with my teeth, kissing her, feeding her the cold sweetness from my tongue. . . . as I swap the warmed grape in my hand for a colder one.

'That's not too bad.' Eyes still closed, Paisley smiles to herself as she chews, and all I can think is how beautiful this all is. This time, we're getting together. The things we're discovering. The unexpected joy in each moment.

As I trail the new frozen grape the length of her body, she whimpers a little.

Moans as I trail it over her pussy.

Gasps as I part her lips.

Cries out as I press it to her clit.

Rub. Glide. Slide.

I press my mouth to hers. Kiss her. Suck her tongue. Lick the sweetness from the seam of her lips. Trail my cold fingers all over her heated skin.

'More,' she whispers as I pull my fingers away.

'Greedy.' Chastisement or delight? Definitely the latter, but she's sore. So I won't do what I want to do. *What I long to do.*

'Touch me,' she says, rocking against my fingers and the cool grape. When I don't answer, her eyes flutter open. 'Please.'

I don't trust myself to speak, so I pull the grape from between her legs. Her breath halts as I paint her arousal over her lips. She's smiling a lazy half smile, her lips shiny and wet. I want to devour her—bend her over the worktop and make her beg. But this morning is more than that. *She's* more than that, I think, as I pop the grape into my mouth, splitting it between my molars to feed her again. She whimpers so beautifully; her chest heaves between us, and the sound of her need echoes through the room. I can almost taste it, and it's such a sweet agony.

I press my lips to hers in a passionate kiss. The earthy salt of her and the sweetness of the grape, her soft cries and how she tries to press her body against me are satisfactions of the sweetest kind. My heart swells, my cock like a pole between us, rock hard for my little deviant.

'Here endeth the fruit lesson.' I pull her panties back up her thighs, unable to conceal my smirk as I pull away, reminding myself that I'm trying to be good. *Even if she isn't.*

'Fruit lessons, huh?' Before I can answer, she has the bowl gripped to her chest and is flicking the little frozen cannonballs at my head.

'Oh! Fuck! You'll put someone's eye out!'

'I know something else that'd put someone's eye out,' she taunts, her gaze on my dick, tenting in the soft cotton of my shorts. 'But *nooo*,' she taunts. 'Instead, someone's being a big. Fat. Tease!'

She punctuates her words with grapes pinging off my thighs. Gives a whole new meaning to grapeshot. And, 'Fuck!' her aim is good, and her tits bounce so perfectly as she moves. 'Ow, watch out!' I round the breakfast bar as she continues to hammer me with grapes.

'You're running scared!' She giggles delightedly, following me to the other side of the room.

'I most certainly am. I might never father a child again—not if you catch me wi' one or two well-aimed grapes.'

'You can see yourself having more kids?' she asks, suddenly halting and momentarily lowering the bowl.

'I could,' I answer, realising this is absolutely true. I don't think the thought ever occurred to me before now but, 'Yeah.' Which can only mean . . .

I lunge and grab the bowl from her hand, grapes rolling everywhere.

'Not so brave now.' For each step she takes back, I take one forward, the threat in my words and my smile wickedly wide.

'Oh, no.' Her eyes widen comically. 'Whatever will I do?'

'Well, I was trying to be nice, given you're a wee bit sore. But now? Now you've had it.'

'Not yet, I haven't.' She squeals, feigning left, then dashing in the direction of the laundry room. 'Stop with the maniacal laughter.' She giggles over her shoulder.

As I round the corner behind her, she realises her error.

'Damn. You caught me. I surrender.' Her words are husky and honeyed, her eyes burning bright. And never were sweeter words spoken as I push her against the dryer, hook my hand under her knee to slide her thigh over my hip, before kissing her for all I'm worth.

'Keir. Keir, listen.'

But I don't want to, lost to her lips, grinding up against her like a kid with his first hard-on. Until I hear the pitter-pat of skipping feet.

'Daddy? What are you doing in the laundry room?'

I freeze—turn to stone. Sorcha's never seen me with a woman. Not in the romantic sense and certainly not like this—half undressed and rubbing up against one another.

We spring apart, Paisley hurriedly working the buttons of my shirt closed. Meanwhile, I grab a bath towel from the pile on the worktop and wrap it around my waist.

'She's not supposed to be here,' I whisper-hiss; my panic-stricken expression reflected in Paisley's gaze. She looks kind of worried, too. Until I start to frantically look around me as though I could hide her somewhere.

'There's no way you're getting me to climb into the dryer,' she says with a chuckle. 'And I'm pretty sure that's the start of a cult horror movie.'

'What's a cult?' says a little voice from behind. 'Who are you?'

'That's not how you're supposed to introduce yourself.' I'm surprised when my tone sounds completely even. Normal, in fact.

I turn to Paisley as she rolls her lips inward, and I know what she's thinking; it's probably not the height of manners to be half dressed for a first meeting, either. With a comic widening of her eyes, she steps around me, holding out her hand to my daughter.

'Hi, Sorcha. I'm Paisley. Your dad and I are friends. He's told me so much about you.'

Over Paisley's shoulder, I watch Sorcha's gaze travel up then down, her face scrunched a wee bit as she tries to work out what's going on. 'Okay.'

'Daddy, what were you doing?'

'Well, I was . . . I was . . . ' Chasing Paisley through the house with the intention of fucking her everywhere is *not* the answer.

'What are you doing in the laundry room? Agnes says you didn't even know we had one.' Paisley laughs, smothering it quickly. 'Have you been having a sleepover?' Before I can deny it, she bulldozes on. 'I went upstairs to look for you first. There were lady's clothes on the floor.'

I try to read what she's saying between the lines but can't find any hidden meaning there. Hair band in her hand—they usually spend more time there than on her head—her long wavy hair falls from her shoulders, shining bright in the light. At least as bright as the sequins on her t-shirt. *Sequined seahorses.* That's the latest fashion statement. A denim skirt, thick grey tights and pink boots that Agnes says look like she should be working on a building site.

'Clothes?' I begin. 'Aye, well, they would be—'

'Mine,' Paisley interjects. 'They would be mine. Because . . . because it was too late to get the bus home.'

A look passes over my daughter's expression. One that says, *I'm a child, not daft.*

'Tiger Blossom from school, her mum and dad are getting a divorce. She says her daddy has lots of sleepovers with ladies. Her daddy is a singer in one of the old-fashioned rock bands'—*of course, he is. From all the way back in 2010, I'll bet*—'and his assistant quit because she said it wasn't in her job description to clean up the condoms.' Sorcha doesn't even come up for breath. 'Condoms are things that stop people from having babies. But Tiger says her daddy can't be using them right 'cause her mum just told her she's pregnant.'

I don't have an answer. Probably something to do with the fact that my jaw has unhinged and hit the floor. I pay a fortune for her to go to that school, and this is the stuff she's learning? That's just . . . effed in the a, to coin an expression.

'So what are you doing in the laundry room?' she asks, her cool blue gaze flicking back and forth between us.

'The . . . here?' I point at the tiled floor, stalling for time. 'What are *you* doing in the laundry room?' Yes, I know. I sound about twelve years old. I can tell as, beside me, Paisley smothers a smile.

'Ballet was cancelled, so Agnes came to collect me. Also, I was looking for you. Also, I was looking for the cat food.'

'But we don't have a cat.' I feel my brows lower. 'So we shouldn't have any cat food. Anywhere.'

'I've been buying cat things with my pocket money,' Sorcha answers sheepishly, pulling open the cupboard under the sink. As she does so, it seems as though an entire pet shop falls out. 'Damn and buggery.'

'Hey. That's not the kind of language we use in this house.'

'No, it's not,' she agrees straightening. 'I've heard you say much worse things.'

'When?' I can't believe I'm arguing with her. In the laundry. About . . . swearing? Standing in the laundry . . . with a half naked Paisley.

'On the phone to Uncle Mac. Or Uncle Will. Sometimes to Flynn.'

And I can't believe I'm being played. She's guilting me about swearing to distract me from—

'A cat. Darlin'. We've had this discussion before. We've no time for a cat. It wouldn't be fair on the thing. You and I are out working or at school all day, and it's not right for us to expect Agnes to take care of one more thing.'

'But Agnes is okay with it, Daddy. She even suggested we go to the cat home on our way here. She said if there was ever a day to get a kitty and for you to be a-peas about it, though I think she meant happy, because how could you be peas?' she asks, hands in the air. 'Anyway, she said today would be the day.'

Should have kept the blinds closed. God knows what Agnes has seen—obviously enough incriminating evidence to get Sorcha a kitten.

Or maybe there's method in this madness . . . maybe the kitten is an epic distraction? And Agnes a fucking genius? These are thoughts that are solidified as, grasping a small pouch of kitten food, my daughter smiles as she holds out her free hand to Paisley.

'Come and meet my Princess kitty,' she says.

Chapter Twenty-Two

PAISLEY

'You're looking delightfully chipper.'

Damn. I thought maybe she wasn't home. I take two steps backwards along the hall and turn and face Chastity through her open home office door. Sitting in front of her supersized chrome screen, she has one of her skin flix playing out silently. Ridiculously, I feel my cheeks heat as I think of my own dirty images—or the photos stored on my phone. I can't believe I did such a thing. *Or how I can't wait to look at them.*

'And I notice you're wearing yesterday's clothes.' She peers over the dark frames sitting on the end of her nose.

'Would you believe it's laundry day?'

'I'd believe dirty stop out more. What is the world coming to?' she mutters, biting back a smile as she turns her attention back to her screen.

'Editing?'

'Hmm. I need to finish this, then load it to the website later this evening. I'm going to take a break soon,' she says, stretching her arms high above her head.

'Gimme a few minutes to shower—'

'To dispose of the evidence?'

'I was going to offer to put the kettle on, but if you're going to tease . . .'

'Tea!' she says, baring her teeth. 'I would shag you for tea, and I don't even swing that way.'

'No shagging necessary. Just give me a few.'

When I get to the kitchen, scrubbed clean and still smiling in yoga pants with wet hair, Chastity is already at the tastefully scrubbed and whitewashed table.

'I fancied gin instead,' she says, holding a lime in her hand. Two bowl-like glasses sit in front, half filled with clear liquid and ice. 'Lime?'

'Yes, please.'

'Ah, yes. Fruit in alcohol works for you.'

I begin to giggle, my mind slipping back unbidden to this afternoon.

'What's so funny?' she asks, dropping a slice in each. Without waiting for an answer, she carries on. 'Troy must've been some man is all I can say.'

Ah, hell. Why didn't I realise she'd jump to that conclusion? 'Actually, I wasn't with Troy. I was with Keir.'

'You were?' Chas looks back at me, her expression a little crestfallen. 'I thought for sure you and Troy would hit it off.' She slumps onto the bench like the wind has dropped out of her sails.

'What have you got against Keir?' I ask, pulling out the chair at the head of the table and seating myself.

'Against him? Nothing. Nothing at all. How could I have anything against someone I've never met?'

'But you aren't happy . . . happy that I'm still seeing him.'

She blows out a breath, folding her arms and leaning her weight against the table. 'It's just . . . I feel sort of responsible for encouraging you in the first place. And a one-night stand with someone who's emotionally unavailable is one thing. But continuing to see him? On his terms? I worry, sweets. How could I not?'

'One thing,' I say, leaning across the table to grasp her hand. 'You are the best woman I know, but my choices are mine only. My mistakes are my own. And if we'd had this conversation yesterday, I would've said the risk was worth it. That I was having such a good time with Keir, the potential fallout would have been worth the risk.'

'Would've? Was? Has something happened.'

'Well, I met his daughter today.'

I can't keep the smile from my face. In fact, I feel giddy about the whole afternoon. Sorcha has such spirit, and she certainly keeps Keir on his toes. When we'd made it back into the kitchen from the laundry room, Agnes pretended not to notice our lack of clothing. We'd excused ourselves, dashing upstairs to Keir's bedroom like teenagers who had been caught making out. We'd taken a minute shower each, dressed quickly, laughing and kissing the whole time, before returning downstairs for formal introductions.

Agnes. Sorcha. Princess, the kitten.

His house, in upscale Notting Hill, is more home than house. He's clearly quite wealthy, but then I could tell that from the cut of his clothes. Not that this kind of thing is super impressive to me. After all, I was almost married to Robin Reed. The thought of *what might have been* makes me shiver. I had a lucky escape, for sure.

'Let's just say that I'm pretty sure our relationship has turned a corner.' Even if I'm not sure which direction it's going in. 'Also, today is Saturday.'

'Honestly,' Chas says, holding her hand in front of her mouth as she laughs. 'Anyone would think you're auditioning for a job on the theatre production of *Rain Man* or something. I'm well aware what day it is. I just hated the thought you were being compartmentalised. Because you, my odd American friend, should be revered, not pigeonholed.'

'Are they really making a theatre show out of *Rain Man*?'

'Yeah, a musical. No, of course they're not. But we can do a Fast Girl version if you'd like?'

'I can't even imagine.' I open my mouth, then close it again. 'Nope, not one thing to voice.'

'So we'll toast,' she answers, raising her glass. 'But I need you to promise you'll introduce Keir to me.'

'Yeah, sure. Definitely.' I raise my own glass. 'Like you're the queen.'

'Here's to those who love us.'

'I can drink to that, though I'm not saying he—'

'And to those who don't,' she says, cutting me off, 'may God turn their hearts.'

'Okay, but—'

'And if he doesn't turn their hearts, may he give them cankles, so we will know them by the sight of their fat ankles.'

'Oh, that's harsh!' We giggle, glasses are raised and clinked before we proceed to inhale half a bottle of Islay gin over the evening.

The next day, I do something I haven't done for months; I pull out my running shoes and pants and go for a jog. The sun is shining, the air is crisp, and I feel a bit like skipping along the route I've chosen, high on the scent of not love, but maybe the possibility of that illusive thing.

It's true that I have felt like I might be in love with Keir, though never allowed myself to give even the smallest of space in my head to even consider this. I told myself this had to be the result of the dozens of mood-altering orgasms I'd received at the hand of the man. *And tongue. And penis.*

I'd even thought about mentioning the idea to one or two of the girls on set last week. After all, if orgasms could be connected to mood, then adult entertainers must be the happiest people in the world! But then we'd had a couple of off days. Shots that weren't a breeze to film. Bodily parts that required buckets of lube. Sort of stop-start, *ow-he-jizzed-in-my-eye* kinds of days where it became more than apparent that not every porn star had fun, or even orgasms, during their work day.

Anyway, it all became a bit of a moot point following the weekend.

But I'm trying not to get too carried away. Too ahead of myself. That's not to say I'm not hopeful that our tentative relationship won't blossom into something deeper.

Because I want it to. Because I definitely feel those first flutterings of l . . . No, I'm not going to go there. Even if I feel it might be possible that Keir feels the same.

As my phone begins to vibrate against my thigh, I slow down, pulling it out from my pocket.

'Oh, thank God,' I mutter. An excuse to stop.

'Hello?'

'Is someone chasing you?' Chastity's cut-glass accent enquires.

'No. Why?' I hold my hand to my chest as I try to get my breath.

'Why on earth are you running?' she asks as though genuinely perplexed.

'Because it seemed like a nice day for a run.'

'Yes, you looked like you were having fun as you passed. Personally, if I'm going to make my hair stand on end, get sweaty, and need Chanel mattifying paper for my red shiny face, there had better be an orgasm at the end of it.'

'Where are you?' I look around, answering my own question as I spot her in the garden of a café I just passed.

'I'm sitting in a beautiful patch of sunshine, soaking up its rays like a cat, while drinking tea and eating *cake*.'

'You had me at cake,' I answer, making my way to her. Walking, not jogging. And before I can even say so, she says it for me.

'Chocolate, not fruit.'

'That's why I love you.'

'I ordered you an extra-large piece with cream, seeing as how you will have burned thousands of calories.'

'Hardly,' I say, sliding out a green painted chair from under the table. As I sit, the cold metal chills my butt. 'I think I've been running for under ten minutes.'

'But think of all the sex calories you've burned recently.'

'Sex calories?'

'Yes, I think there's an online calculator. At least, Tianka seemed to think so. She uses it a little bit like a FitBit for work."

'I'm not so interested in calories. Just taking care of myself. I've got an interview. *Wild Women* on BBC.'

'That's the midmorning chat show, isn't it?'

'Yep. No four a.m. starts for me if I get it.'

'When, not if. Congratulations, sweets! Someone to take care of you in the bedroom department *and* a job interview! When are you seeing Keir next?'

'Wednesday. I've been invited to dinner with his daughter.'

'His daughter?' Her eyebrows are in her hairline as she bites back a smile.

'Yep, and he's mentioned having me meet his friends, too.'

'Oh, I see how it is,' she says, folding her arms with a huff. 'You're meeting *his* friends before I get to meet *him*. Keep the scary porn lady out of the loop.'

'Really? Do you think I'd really let that happen? Of course, you come first, crazy porn magnate or not.' Chas smiles a little slyly as I begin to lay it on thick. 'Friday night, he's coming to pick me up.' No meeting him at a hotel this week. 'I thought we might have predinner drinks.'

'Acceptable,' she replies, hiding her smile behind her tea cup. 'Where are you meeting his friends on Sunday? Purely out of interest.'

'Of course, we're just making small talk. Not comparing friendship terms.'

'I knew you'd understand.'

The waitress arrives with my espresso, a fresh pot of oolong for Chas, and a large wedge of chocolate cake for me.

'If you hadn't given me the right answer, I'd have sent that back for apple cake.'

'Good thing I know you're the best friend in the world then, isn't it?'

'And so easily bought. I'm beginning to wonder if Keir is taking you to The Savoy for high tea to meet his friends and that's why you're avoiding the question.'

'Ha! As if. We aren't going anywhere fancy. A pub lunch, I think he said. Oh, and a casual invitation to watch Keir and his friends roll around a muddy rugby field.'

'Oh, God!' she groans, throwing her head back suddenly.

I look left and right, wondering how much attention we might have attracted while Chas mini orgasmed in the chair opposite me.

'I'm the one with the chocolate cake. Why are you moaning in ecstasy?'

'Thighs,' she says, fanning her face with her hand. 'Rugby thighs are so rucking hot.'

'Am I supposed to get that reference? Because I so don't.'

'The ruck. It's a thing. We'll watch some,' she says, suddenly sitting up straight. 'When we get home. I can explain a few of the finer points.'

'About the game?'

'No, about the men, silly. I love a man with rugby thighs. Rugger buggers are just so . . . '

'Whole body shiver eliciting?'

'Exactly.'

'So it looks like I'm learning about rugby today.'

Only, when we get home, the afternoon doesn't play out that way.

Chapter Twenty-Three

KEIR

Sitting in my home office, I find myself typing a note. *A note to Paisley*. It's not a love letter exactly. Though I will admit to feeling the first stirrings of something. Not in the letter, of course, or even out loud; it's still early days. But I will say that I can't ever recall feeling like this for a long time. *Maybe even ever?* And it's fucking scary. Can a heart grow to accommodate more? Adapt? And if it is possible, why didn't my ex feel the same when Sorcha was born?

Why do my thoughts always come back to her? Love to hate. Hate to love. They say lightning doesn't strike twice in the same place, but I've seen the YouTube videos.

So I type. It's not exactly loving or cathartic. More like filth.

I'm not sure if I'll ever send it, but I type it all the same.

Paisley, I can't get the image of you yesterday out of my head. The white shirt I could see the lace of your bra through. The dark skirt hugging your curves. Do you know, I sometimes think your arse deserves a frame? It's like a work of art.

I have a request, too. For our next date, can you wear the little black belt—the one with the gold buckle? Does it make you think of being tied as much as it makes me think of tying you? Wear it for me if it does.

No pressure, love.

Love? Is this love or an obsession? It's hard to tell now that I've cracked the seal; now that I'm allowing myself to think. Allowing my thoughts of Paisley to breathe.

I want to watch you cross the room in those heels you love so much, letting your swaying curves torture me. I want you. Always. But I also want to look after you. I want to be the wall that protects you from all harm. Your home and your sustenance. Yes, that's right; I want to feed you more than just my cock. And I want to cook for you. Don't worry—it won't be fruit.

I'll sit you at the table with a glass of wine, then drop the napkin across your thighs while pretending not to look down the neck of your blouse. And as we eat, I'll imagine all the things I want to do to you, waiting for a sign that you want those things, too.

I'll wait for you to climb on my lap.

Wait for you to wrap your fingers in my hair.

Wait for the kiss that tells me what you need.

I'll make you crawl to the bedroom. Watch your arse as you make your way there. I want to strip you. Take my time peeling you from your clothes, unravelling you like the treasure you are. I want to love you with my body. Mark my possession of

*you with my teeth. Hold you in my arms. Love
you all night long. Love you all my l—*

My fingers are frozen above the keyboard as I
realise with a jolt of panic where my thoughts are
heading. But then my phone begins to ring. *Saved
by the bell.*

Or Mac.

'Was I supposed to pick you up?' I turn my wrist
to check the time, his next words not really
computing. Not quite making sense.

'No, listen. This might be a wee bit of an odd
thing to say, but that girl you were talkin' about.
Did you say you met her at that wedding you went
to?'

'Aye. Why?' This isn't like Mac. He doesn't fish
for information, and he rarely sounds spooked. If
he's got a question, he'll ask it. If he has a
grievance, he'll probably get satisfaction on the
rugby field. *A grab of the balls. A punch in the
ribs.*

He sighs, clearly uncomfortable. 'I'm no'
bothered if you're getting your end away or as
celibate as a monk. Your business. Not mine. Not
Will's. But we had the kids out for breakfast in
Covent Garden, and I read something in the
newspaper while we were there.'

'Mac, whatever it is, just say it. I've got nothing to
hide.' Not anymore, at least. He'll meet Paisley
soon enough. They all will.

'Aye, so. This girl you're seeing. She doesn't
happen to be engaged, does she?'

'No.' My answer is immediate and partly a growl. 'Why d'you ask?'

'That poncy singer Ella's so fond of—the ginger bawheid? He's had an accident. Wrapped his Aston Martin around a lamppost while off his face.'

Oh, fuck. How many singing ginger bawheid's can there be? So it sounds like Paisley's ex-fiancé, but why is Mac calling me?

'I remember Ella saying you'd mentioned he sang for the bride and groom that day?'

'He did, but I'm not sure what you're getting at.'

'Just that he was there. And you met *her* there.' He pauses, letting the implication settle before he begins again. 'Just do yourself a favour and have a look at one of the Sunday papers online. Maybe stay away from the tabloids, aye?'

Before he's even finished his sentence, I've closed my email and brought up one of the Sunday rags, greeted by a paparazzi shot of a very bedraggled ginger singer being bundled into the back of a police car.

I start to read the article, blood beginning to boil in my veins.

Exclusive!
Robin Reed Looks "Devastated" Following Car Accident
Said to be "distraught" from the recent split with his fiancée.

Everyone's favourite Brit Boy, the crooner Robin Reed, has been ordered to rehab by his management after a car crash involving three vehicles during the early hours of this morning.

Robin, allegedly under the influence of an illegal substance, was seen being placed in the back of a police vehicle to be taken to Wembley Station for further questioning.

According to management sources, Robin has been suffering from stress and anxiety after recently splitting with his American fiancée of two years, Paisley Byrne. In a further twist to the story, it's understood Byrne reportedly had an affair with London property magnate, Keir McLain, which allegedly led to the breakdown of their engagement.

As I scroll down, there's a photograph—a photograph of me taken at Sorcha's school, which is bad enough. But I'm not the only one in the frame; Sorcha is, too. I'm helping her out of the car, and though her face is distorted, it'd be easy enough to tell what school she attends given she's in her uniform. *A distinctive, private school uniform.* The thought makes me feel ill. Some fucker has been following me—following me while I was with my child. And this image predates the ginger bastard wrapping his car around a lamppost yesterday, so what's it all about?

Sources close to the pair are said to be "saddened" and "dismayed" that the bubbly twenty-five-year-old makeup artist has begun to work in the adult entertainment industry since the split.

Fuck off. Now they're trying to paint Paisley as someone working in porn? What the fuck! The back of my office chair creaks as I scrub my hands through my hair. How did I not know her surname? It's a strange thought, a little abstract even, as I struggle to get a fucking handle on the rest. I know a lot about her, I remind myself. Small things. Personal and ridiculous things. I know she has an aversion to fruit. Loses her shoes. That she's kind and caring and great with kittens and little girls

I don't read anymore. Because it's bullshit—pure and simple. What I do instead is pull up the online edition of each Sunday newspaper's front page. The story is on every. Fucking. One. What's worse, the tale seems to get more lurid and phony with each telling. It's like a game of Chinese fucking whispers.

She wasn't still with him when he grabbed her that night—she couldn't have been. *Could she?* He wouldn't have given up because I threatened him. . . no. *Think, Keir. The rest is bullshit.* So she works for a porn company, but the bastards made it sound like she was selling her arse—that she was having sex on screen.

I'm not the reason for their breakup—that was because the twat couldn't keep his dick in his pants. I run my hands through my hair, pulling at the ends. None of this is right or sane. But what must she be feeling, having her character torn apart like this? I don't have long to wait before I find out. As I pick up my phone to call her, the thing starts to buzz in my hand, her name flashing up on screen.

'Paisley, where are you?'

I don't hear her voice immediately. Instead, there's static and a lot of swearing coming from a woman who isn't her.

'Fuck off! Get away from my front door! You bastards are trespassing! I shall call the police.'

I hear Paisley cry out, my heart tightening like a fist. I push up from my chair and start to pace around the room.

'Paisley? Paisley, darlin'? Are you okay?' A lot more scuffling and shuffling follows, indistinct questions being shouted over the noise.

'Paisley! Over 'ere!'

'Have you heard from Robin, Paisley?'

'Is he an addict?'

'Have you sent your apologies to the inhabitants of the other cars?'

'Paisley, who's your favourite co-star in porn?'

'Is it true you'll be starring in the remake of *Taken Hard Two*?'

I'm literally pulling out all of my hair here when the call cuts out.

'Fuck!' I bounce my phone off the palm of my free hand. 'Fuck! Fuck!' Then I hit her number again, whispering a small prayer as the call connects.

'No, give it to me,' Paisley calls out. 'It's Keir. I can see his name!'

A man grumbles, and a minute later, I hear her voice.

'Keir? Are you there?'

The fist around my heart eases immediately. 'Aye, it's me. Are you okay? Who was that?'

'Who? Oh, Max, Chastity's brother. But the tabloids, they're outside like a pack of rabid dogs out for blood.' Her breath hitches. Is it a sob? 'We were just out for coffee, and then on our way home, they pounced! They said something about Robin having an accident. Do you know anything about it?'

'I've just read about it. He's okay.' The absolute fucker. 'But . . . ' I don't know how to say it. How to tell her. 'They're not saying very nice things about you.'

'Me?' She sounds shocked, pained, incredulous. 'What have I got to do with his accident?'

'They're saying you left him.'

'Hell yeah, I did!'

'That he was under the influence of drugs because he's depressed.'

'And that . . . that it's my fault?'

'Darlin', they're making it sound like you're starring in Chastity's shoots.'

'That I star in porn?' She sounds saddened, her voice small. And I have neither the heart nor the balls to tell her it's worse than that. To tell her that one paper in particular made it sound like she's a high-class prostitute.

'Oh, my Lord. What am I going to do?'

Already, my mind is working in overdrive. 'Do you have a solicitor . . . a lawyer, I mean?'

'No, I . . . wait.' There's conversation on the other side of the phone, words I don't quite catch before she's back. 'Chas says she can consult her family guy.'

'I feel like I should come over there.' My heart does, at least. My head, not so much.

'No, don't,' she advises softly. 'It's not necessary. Besides, this isn't your problem.'

'I might not be the root cause, but I can see how I can't have helped. I smashed his nose, for a start.'

'Bones and cartilage heal, Keir. Hearts, too.' I don't know what she means by that, but I don't get a chance to protest or question as she carries on. 'Look, you have your own reputation to protect. A child to think about.'

She's right, of course, and when I look up, said child is at the door to my office, the ball of calico kitten cradled in her arms. My head immediately swings to the window behind me as though I could sense the black presence of the press lurking there. Loitering in the hedgerows, hiding in the flowerbeds, just waiting to spring out and embroil my child in this mess. *Ridiculous.*

'Are you still there?'

'Aye. I am.'

'Look, give it a few days. Let things cool down.'

'That sounds . . . ' Like a relief. A huge relief. And a copout and everything in between. I want to be there for her, hold her in my arms, protect her with my being. I'm a big lad—I can take care of myself—but can I protect Paisley and Sorcha at the same time? Probably not.

Which makes me feel like a total shit.

'You're sure you don't want me to come over? Or maybe you could pack a bag and come stay here?' As much as the thought appeals to me— all the people I want to take care of, safe and under one roof—I'm not sure it would be for the best. But I want to do something—I want to help.

'This isn't your fight,' she says with a sigh. 'I know this is hard for you to hear, but you said it yourself; I'm trouble, Keir. You can't fix this.'

Chapter Twenty-Four

KEIR

'You're not dressed for work? Turning from the pantry with a loaf of bread in hand, Agnes looks a little startled when I appear in the kitchen. She frowns as she takes in my appearance; my running shoes, shorts, and t-shirt, sweat causing the fabric of the latter to stick my skin. 'You'll be late to take the bairn to school.'

'Flynn's coming to take her. I've got a few calls I need to make.' I keep my expression impassive despite experiencing what it must feel like to be a volcano internally. I thought the run would help. Thought I might be able to run off the steam, or maybe exhaust myself, especially as I've barely slept all night.

'Can you go with them and walk her to class?' I feel a bit of a shit for asking because I've made the school run my thing. I might not always be here to tuck Sorcha into bed, but if I can, I'll always be there to take her to school. If I'm ever travelling, Flynn and Agnes step in. I do have a car service I can rely on, but I prefer to trust the people closest to me if I can.

'Speak of the devil and he shall appear,' Agnes says as Flynn enters the kitchen.

'Agnes, babe,' he says, clutching his heart. 'You wound me.' He swipes a shiny red apple from the large fruit bowl on the breakfast bar, polishing it on the lapel of his blue suit.

'Not yet, I haven't,' she answers, taking the apple out of his hand and depositing it back. 'But it can be arranged, y'ken.'

'He promised not to curse at the traffic this morning. Didn't you, Flynn?'

'That's right, Scorcher,' he answers using his silly nickname for her, picking her up and spinning her in his arms. 'I'll try my very best.'

'It's Sorcha,' my daughter answers, giggling as she pulls on his arm.

'And I'll believe it when I see it,' Agnes grumbles, but I barely hear as I turn my attention to my daughter.

'What have I told you about opening the front door without telling Agnes or me first?' Despite trying to keep a tight rein on my temper, both adults in the room look surprised by my tone. In contrast, my daughter, it appears, couldn't be less concerned.

'It was just Flynn, Daddy,' she answers with an unconcerned flip of her hand. 'I checked before I opened it.'

'That's not the point. When I ask you not to do something, I expect you to pay attention. Do you hear me?' With each word, my tone becomes louder. Fiercer. 'You don't know who could be lurking on the other side of the door. There are bad people out there!' Like newspaper reporters and her nut of a mother.

I don't often yell, and when I do so, Sorcha's expression fills me with remorse immediately. Her wee eyes brim with tears, her bottom lip quivering.

'Come on now, chicken hen,' Agnes says softly, providing us all with something else to focus on. 'Let's get a wriggle on, or we'll be late for school.'

Flynn adds his own brand of specialness to the moment, exaggeratedly wiggling his arse as he leaves the kitchen. 'I'll be wriggling on out this way. See you in the car, Princess Scorcher.'

Grabbing Sorcha's school branded bag from the worktop, Agnes levels me with a look full of censure before she follows, leaving Sorcha and I alone.

'I promise I'll try to remember next time,' my daughter says, directing her words to her black shiny Mary Janes.

'I know you will. I'm sorry I'm in such a bad mood.' My words are rough as I bend to place a kiss on her head. It's been a mindfuck of a night, but she doesn't deserve to bear the brunt of my worries and fears. I fucking hate telling her off at the best of times, though I do so, for her own good mostly. But this is different. This is me lashing out because of my fear she'll be taken away from me. Before I realise I've even done it, I've pulled her wee body up against me, my arms wrapped around her so tight.

'Ew, Daddy! You're all wet,' she complains, struggling against me. 'Wet and icky.'

'Sorry, darlin'.' I set her back on her feet again. 'And sorry I can't take you to school this mornin'.'

'Are you okay?' Her blue eyes stare up at me as though trying to decipher my thoughts. 'You're not sick or anything, are you? Because—'

'I'm fine,' I answer, cutting her off. 'I'm just very busy this morning. Lots to do. Sorry I can't take you to school.'

'That's okay,' she says, swinging on her wee heel before skipping out of the kitchen. The rest of her words are chucked over her shoulder, her thoughts already on other things. 'Flynn says he'll stop and get me a hot chocolate before school.'

'Only if Agnes says,' I call back as the door to the garage slams shut. Then I realise I haven't braided her hair.

I grab a glass, filling it with water from the dispenser on the fridge, then pull open the fridge door to contemplate the contents. Close it again. Drink the water. Then do the thing I've been avoiding all morning. I open my phone and answer the message I'd received late last night.

Arriving at Gatwick on the 10:50 from LA. Pick me up, or shall I go straight to the offices of the Daily Mail?

In answer, I type out, ***I'll be there.***

Chapter Twenty-Five

KEIR

She arrives in a cloud of perfume and animosity. It's unsettling to see her walk towards me, almost like going back in time. From a distance, she looks like the same woman I fell in love with all those years ago, yet she's also the same woman who walked away. There are so many memories, and the bad far outweigh the good. Yet as she draws nearer, I can't help but acknowledge she's still beautiful, and she draws attention to herself like she could be on film. *And likely is, though not the way she feels she deserves to be.*

I imagine she's seen a few casting couches in her time. That's why she left, supposedly. She decided she was too young to be a mother and a wife.

Her impulsiveness once endeared her to me. She was fun and spontaneous in the beginning, but she's as ruthless as she is charming. Reckless and immoral. She thinks of no one but herself.

'Darling.' Her nails are pink talons she rests on my shoulder as she leans in to kiss my cheek. And I let her, while hating myself. But we're playing a game here. It's been two years since I saw her last. Two years since she walked into my office, trying to sweet-talk money out of me while threatening me with court. Today, I hate to say it, but she has the upper hand.

'Jayne.' I feel nothing in her embrace—feel nothing but her countenance stiffen with displeasure as she pulls away. *Plain Jayne.* She hates her name and changed it to Gianna years ago, shortly after she left for the US, I think. And though I can see the changes in her now that she's in front of me, she's still anything but plain. She certainly doesn't look thirty-two years old, let alone old enough to have borne a child Sorcha age.

She's tall and lithe. Dressed from head to toe in high fashion, she carries a designer purse in hand. These things remain a constant in her life. Appearances mean everything, and she is always flawless. But all the same, I hate myself for noticing the differences in her. Her long hair, an expensively tended-to shade of blonde, is a little darker, her mouth a little fuller. Her tits a little larger. She makes me think of one of those wee dolls Sorcha played with for about five minutes. She's never been a doll kind of girl. She likes animals. Games. A wee bit of science.

'Shall we?'

Before I turn to make my way to the exit, I take the handle of her case from her grip, and after a slight incline of her head, she follows me to the car. We don't speak until we're at the hotel. *Centrally located, five stars.* I usually find myself footing the bill, but this time, she asks me to wait while she checks herself in.

A new boyfriend? Maybe a wealthy or jealous one. Maybe both. It's a novel experience for her not to expect me to pick up the bill. I often feel like I'm the one getting fucked, but instead, it looks like she's screwing some other idiot for a change.

A liveried member of the concierge team walks by the coffee shop with her luggage. *Her Louis Vuitton trolley case.* Small enough for her to take herself. A case that indicates she doesn't intend to stay in London long. *Thankfully.*

'Are you coming up?' She's suddenly standing in front of me, all but batting her lashes, her voice a sultry purr.

I almost laugh in answer. If she wants me in her hotel room, it's not because she has plans for my body or my cock. She's definitely planning to fuck me, but I doubt it's in the physical sense.

'We can discuss what it is you want here, Jayne.'

'It's Gianna.' She narrows her eyes, and I decide not to point out the tiny crow's feet her Botox nurse seems to have missed. 'How many times do I have to tell you, Keir? It's Gianna. And this is too public a venue for what I have to say.'

'Not for me, it isn't,' I retort.

'Trust me, Keir, it is.'

I don't trust her, not one bit, but something in her tone has the hairs on the back of my neck sticking up. So I take her advice but not for my sake. I do it for the daughter she has yet to ask about.

We don't speak in the lift, nor in the corridor. And I don't look at her as we reach her room. Instead, I stare at the green light on the door.

'Come in, sweetie.' Says the spider to the fly. But the fly isn't buying what she's selling today. And the spider? She's got herself a hotel suite, not a room. *Maybe a sugar daddy to boot.*

'What is it you want, Jayne? I've got other shit to do today. How much?' Because it always boils down to cash—money to fund her lifestyle. She left to become an actress, and though I've yet to see her in anything of note, I think she must live like Hollywood royalty. She received a hefty settlement when we split and has since been back for more. Several times.

'Who said anything about money, Keir? Why do you have to be like this?' she whimpers, looking for the world like she's about to cry.

'Call it a sixth sense. Or better still, experience.' Because this is what it always comes down to. 'I'm not in the mood for your games, and I'm too busy to bend over for you today. How much do you want?'

'Oh, you wish you could get rid of me that easily,' she taunts. 'No, Keir. This is much better. Perfect, in fact. A friend sent me a links to the articles. So of course, I got on the next flight home. Who would've thought the mighty Keir—Keir, the upstanding; Keir, the moral; the man I'd entrusted my baby's care to—could be fucking Robin Reed's fiancée?'

'She's not his fiancée,' I reply in a bored tone. I sit in the seat by the window. 'They weren't even together when we met.'

'But darlin',' she says, laying on the transatlantic twang. 'It's better than that. The newspapers say she's now doing porn. Of course, I think, especially after seeing pictures of her, it's probably the homemade stuff. You always were a little kinky, though, right?'

'You're boring me,' I reply, straightening my shirt cuffs as I cross my legs.

'Boring? How about we try it the other way? Maybe I don't want you to bend over for me,' she says, her narrow hips swaying closer. Her hand lifts between us, her pink painted fingernails raking through my hair. 'You used to like it when I bent over for you, as I recall. You liked it when I grabbed my ankles . . . spread myself wide.'

She's not beyond using our past as a weapon, and the memories flash through my mind, each swiping like a rapier. *Rapid and poisonous tipped*.

Jumping up, I grab her hand, pulling it from my head and pushing it away. 'You must be desperate.' Or delusional. It's been a while since she's used sex as a bargaining chip.

'I'm not desperate. I think in the eyes of any court, you'd be the desperate case. Maybe I'm feeling benevolent. Have you thought of that? You look a little hard up, baby.' Her hand reaches for the front of my pants, though I catch her wrist before contact. 'You must be desperate if you've resorted to fucking small-time porn stars.' She *tsks*, a playful click of teeth and tongue.

'Funny, I don't remember fucking you.' Not in some time, at least. Not since a weak moment when Sorcha was small.

Her expression tells me I've hit a raw nerve. Maybe it's worse than casting couch recordings she's stared in. I might feel sorry for her . . . if it wasn't for the fact that she tore out my heart. Not when she left me, but when she abandoned our little girl. We might not have been perfect together, but the little girl we made was that very thing. Pure and innocent and in need of our love and protection. But she left. And I'm the wicked fuck who paid her to.

'Wait. I know,' she says. 'Maybe your deviancies have driven you to fucking cam girls now. Because nice girls don't like the things you like, Keir. The ropes. The pain. The degradation.'

Her barb is well aimed and hits me hard. I've keep my sex life on a tight leash all these years. Tamped down to nothingness. Even the couple of times I tried to date—tried to fuck casually—I held it all back. But with Paisley, I can feel it leaking out. The letter I wrote. The things I want to do with her and to her—it's all true. I want to see her crawl on her hands and knees to me. See her tied and at my mercy. But I also want more nights falling asleep with my arms around her curves. Wake to her messy hair and goofy smile. But I'm not a deviant, no matter what *Gianna* suggests, unless a little rope and dominance extends to that. In which case, I guess I'm a deviant to a good portion of the world.

'That's strange.' I fold my arms as though considering something. 'Because I remember you used to like it when I fucked *you* like that. But . . .

wait.' I snap my fingers as though remembering some point. 'I forgot you're not a nice girl.'

'I used to be a nice girl,' she retorts, her eyes flaring as I step towards her. The look she slides me isn't one of fear but of excitement. And my siren's call.

I slide both my hands into her hair, grasping tight at the base of her skull to pull her head back. 'I know a nice girl when I see one, Gianna.' I drag her name out with disdain, tilting her farther still to examine her face, her flushed neck and chest, her hard breasts pushed up against my chest. Her darkened eyes. 'And I know I'm not looking at one right now. You're anything but a nice girl.'

My words are harsh in her ear, though she whispers a rasping, 'Yes!'

In a fit of confusion and annoyance, I push her down on the bed. It takes me everything in my power not to follow her. To place my knees against the mattress. To slide my hands around her throat. I don't want to fuck her but maybe fuck her over. Fuck her up. Torture her a little as payback.

'Want to know why you're not a nice girl?' I ask, towering over her.

Her reaction is unexpected as she spreads her long legs, running her hands over her chest. And if her reaction is unexpected, her words are even more so.

'Because nice girls don't take it up the ass.'

'You're not a nice girl. Not even a nice human, in fact. You haven't once asked how your daughter is.'

My jaw aches from the tension in it as I pull open my jacket and lift out the bundle of notes I'd taken from the safe in my bedroom before leaving this morning.

'There's about twenty grand there,' I growl, staring down at her shocked face. 'Don't even bother coming to look for me. We've moved, and the new house has security. You won't even get past the gates before I call the police.' I stalk to the edge of the room, then turn before I pull open the door. 'Your dad said not to bother them, either. Not after last time. You're on your fucking own.'

I'm not ashamed to say my whole body is shaking as I leave.

Chapter Twenty-Six

KEIR

I text Flynn to tell him I won't be coming into the office. I also suggest he go home, to which he replies that he's coming over to the house as he witters something about me having a brain tumour. I decide, as he's coming over, to ask him to pick up Sorcha. Which, in turn, allows me to pull out a bottle of Talisker I've been saving for a special occasion. This might not be a special occasion, per se, but it is monumental in a kind of fucked-up way. And six shots in, this is where Agnes finds me an hour later. I'm in the dining room. The whisky was here, so I haven't moved much farther since pulling it from the drinks cabinet.

'Whatever is the matter?' she asks, placing her string shopping basket down on the dining table. She's been using string bags since I was wee. I've no idea where she gets them from. They're like something out of the annals of history.

'Did you buy a job lot of these in the seventies?' I ask, pulling out a packet of sausages and some milk and putting them on the oak table before wrapping my finger in the string.

'What?' Only, in her annoyance, her accent becomes a bit stronger, rendering the word *whit*?

'These bags. Where do you get them?'

'Out of a wee catalogue that comes out every year at Christmastide.' She slaps my hand away before grabbing the bag, the sausages, and then milk, before bustling out of the dining room, returning almost immediately. 'Why? Are you wanting a wee string baggy, too?' she asks ridiculously.

I chuckle and take another slug of my drink. 'No, hen. I was just reminiscing.'

'Thinkin' of the past is all well and good, but that's not what's bothering you,' she asserts, swiping the whisky bottle from my reach.

'Aye, you're right. But I think I've fu—buggered everything up.'

'Is this about the nice lassie you brought home the other day? The American one?'

'Yes and no.' I sigh protractedly.

'I like her. And the bairn did, too. You can't fool children into thinking you're nice if you're no'. Especially if they're intuitive about such things, like Sorcha is.'

'Better not introduce her to her mother then.'

'What?'

'I'm glad you liked Paisley. I'm sad because I liked her, too.' Probably a bit too much.

'Liking her made you sad? What's with you today, and what's with the mention of Jayne?'

'*She who shall not be named*, mainly because she no longer goes by that name, is back in the country. And, sadly, I think Paisley and I have had our time in the sun.'

'Has this got something to do with the stuff in the newspaper?' she asks, pulling up a seat and sitting next to me.

'You still like her after reading all that?'

Agnes harrumphs. 'Anyone who believes what they read is a bampot—a daftie. Newspapers print a load of rubbish, and Paisley's a nice lassie. Even if her parents must be a wee bit simple in the head,' she says, touching her own head, 'for naming such a bonny girl after a Scottish town.'

'Paisley.' I huff out a laugh.

'Sure, there are nicer things to call your child, but it could've been worse, I suppose. They might've called her Auchtermuchty. Or Dull. I have a cousin who lives in Dull,' she adds, ignoring my slightly shaking shoulders. 'It's no' such a bad place, but it would make a stupid name.'

'So,' she then says, folding her arms under her cardigan-covered bosoms—bosoms, because women of Agnes's ilk and measure have bosoms. Not breasts. If she had breasts, I wouldn't be thinking about them, so it's just as well she has this sort of battleship kind of shelf. Which is what I think bosoms are.

'Keir.' She raps on the French oak to gain my attention. 'How much whisky have you drank?'

'*Ocht*, I'm fine.' *Mostly*. I shake my head, coming away from the contents of Agnes's cardigan.

'So the newspaper,' she prompts.

'It's bullshit.' Mostly.

'Watch your language,' she warns, then affirms, 'but I thought as much myself. And most people will. What's the problem? Not the singer, surely? Yon man couldn't shout coal up a passage, by the way.' Which is Agnes's way of saying, *He couldn't carry a tune in a bucket.* 'And his songs?' She tightens her arms across her chest, pursing her lips and shaking her head. 'I've seen more exciting blancmange.'

'He's part of the problem.' I don't really feel like rehashing it all for Agnes's benefit, but I know there's no avoiding it. 'He's not really the reason I've taken to drink.'

'I should hope not. The man seems as weak as his chin.'

'But he's still got me in the newspapers. And Sorcha, too,' I add darkly. 'And brought her mother back.'

'Jayne's in London?' she yells. *Fuck me, rolling pins at dawn. I wouldn't like to be on the wrong side of this woman.* 'Don't you worry. She'll no' get past me. And I'll be callin' her ma and tellin' her so.'

'Agnes, her parents don't want anything to do with her. Not after last time.'

When Sorcha was four years old, Jayne fooled her parents into thinking she wanted to be in her daughter's life. So they gave her a place to stay and money to take me back to court. I suppose they wanted to think the best of her. Regardless, there isn't a court in the land that would change the current order we have. Jayne gave up all parental rights, even had counselling before doing so. That year, she took their money and more of mine, before pissing off back to the States without so much as a word of legal advice.

It took her parents and me a while to get back on good terms. But they're Sorcha's family, and I wouldn't keep her away from them . . . even though I paid her mother to do exactly that. It was for the best even though I never thought in a million years she'd choose cash over her own flesh.

'You'll not be giving her money this time, though, surely?'

'I already have,' I reply, leaning back in my chair and rubbing both hands through my hair until it's standing on end. 'I gave her nearly twenty grand, yet I know she'll have sold her story, such as it is, to the newspapers. It's just a case of when it goes to print.'

It wasn't until after I left the hotel that it had made sense. She didn't want me to pay for the room because one of the tabloids will pay for it as part of the deal. Her story and its tenuous and probably twisted connection to Robin Reed, who appears to have disappeared into a treatment facility until the possibility of an investigation into a conviction for driving while off his face disappears.

'Well, what's there to tell.' It's not a question, though not quite the assurance she means it to be. 'Who'd be interested in what she has to say? And what's with all the sighing? This isn't like you.' Agnes's frown is full of disapproval.

'There are things Jayne will say that I rather she didn't. Things that might or might not be true, but I don't want Sorcha to hear them anyway.'

'I'm no' so green as I'm cabbage looking, lad.' A burst of deep laughter breaks free from my chest at her words. 'I wasn't always old, you know.'

'You're not old now.'

'Not too old,' she says, 'but once, I was young. And bonny. And in love. And I 'ken things that go on in a marriage bed are supposed to stay there.'

'Exactly. But I guarantee that Jayne will have sold shi—stories to the newspapers. Sorcha doesn't need that.' *I* don't need that.

'No, true,' she agrees, 'but life isn't ever perfect.'

'You don't need to tell me that.' If my tone is harsh, she doesn't bite. 'For years, I've put my child first. And the first time I think of myself— think with my dick—I turn into my mother.' I'm angry and embarrassed to be voicing the parts of my life I keep to myself, the things I only think of alone and in the darkness. I push back my chair and begin pacing the long room. 'I sometimes think if it hadn't been for you, I'd have probably gone the same way as her.' *Addiction, selfishness, and bad choices.* 'This just confirms it all. And fuck, if that doesn't hurt.'

'How so, lad? Tell me where you see the parallels.'

'I came second to the blokes my mother was screwing. Second to drugs and to booze. I won't— *won't*—let the same happen to Sorcha.'

Agnes sighs. It sounds like disappointment and stops me in my tracks. I'm right—I've known all along. My mother didn't love me like she should. I just couldn't voice it aloud.

'Your mother didn't choose to make you second choice. That's not how addiction goes. She loved you.'

Sliding my hands into my pant pockets, I snort derisively. How can she say that—say that to me? I was there. My psyche still bears the scars.

'I know she did,' she adds vehemently, ignoring my scorn. 'When you were a wee lad, before we took you in, Alf used to say you had buckets of determination. That you would go far. And look around you—you have. You're a good man, Keir. But you're sometimes a hard one. Oh, you're good to me, and you're good to that wee girl. A good father and a grand friend. You even give that terror of an ex-wife far more than she deserves. But you're not kind to yourself, and you're not kind to the memory of your mother. You'd do well to remember that there are those in this world who aren't as strong as you. And your mother was one of them.'

Agnes's words strike me immediately, painfully, almost bringing my knees out from under me.

'You think she loved me?' I say, my palms hitting the table. 'Maybe you're right. Maybe she did love me, but not enough. I wasn't her priority. Her drive. Her reason to live.'

Agnes stands, taking my face in her hands. 'She did love you, and you've just proved my point with your own words. You are not your mother, and

Sorcha will never live your life, but you must live it, son. Live it for you. You know, you didn't get to be a child when you were wee, and you were barely twenty-five when you became a dad. You've grown so much. Learned so much. But you've denied yourself, too. Whatever the papers say, we'll hold our heads high. We know what's true, so bugger everyone else. But if you want that lovely girl to be a part of your life, you'd best move quick. Those kinds of women aren't on the market too long. Just ask Alf,' she says, her eyes glistening with tears.

'I don't know. I mean, can I?' I collapse into the chair, my thoughts scattered but my heart hopeful. 'You think I should give her a call?'

'No!' she says, frowning and slapping both of my cheeks. *Twice at the same time.* 'I think you should get off your bahoochie and go see the girl!'

In the kitchen, I grab my wallet and keys from the worktop as the door into the house from the garage bangs shut.

'Agnes,' I say, turning to her. 'I expect journalists will start to call.'

'*Ocht*, they already have. I told the first one who called to go take a running shag at a rolling donut.' I'd laugh if she wasn't so blasé in her delivery. That has got to be the best—or worst, depending on the perspective—thing I've ever heard Agnes say. 'Since then, I've had the house phone switched on silent. And I instructed the school to only contact us on our mobiles and explained why.'

'What did the journalists have to say?

Agnes sniffs, her expression full of scorn. 'I did'nae care to listen to them past their introduction. I just told them you weren't available to speak.'

'Good. Good idea.'

'I sometimes have them,' she answers wryly.

'Listen, Keir.' Without his usual and universal greeting of *G'day*, Flynn strides into the kitchen. 'I had a thought on the way home. I reckon you're worried about kids teasing Sorcha at school—you know—what with the shiii . . .' His gaze slides to Agnes, and he moderates his language accordingly as he grabs an apple from the fruit bowl. 'What with the shizz printed in the newspaper. But listening to what Sorch said in the car? The scandal in your life is nothing, mate. Do you know her little friend's dad has both her mum and her nanny up the duff?'

'Would you stop shortening her name,' Agnes chastises, taking the apple out of his hand.

'Where is Sorcha anyway?' I ask.

'She's gone to pet the furball.' My expression must be confused as he adds, 'Mate, you're person-non-what's-it compared to the new kitten.'

'*Persona non grata*,' I correct.

'Whatevs, man. We're all second-class citizens next to the thing with four legs.'

Shit, I forgot about the cat. 'This MBA I'm paying you to study . . . '

Flynn's head turns slowly, his expression suspicious. 'What about it? It's tax deductable, isn't it?' he answers defensively.

'I feel the need to protect my investment, and I think you need a few days at home. For study purposes.'

'What's your game?'

'And for cat sitting.'

'No way. No way, man.'

'*I'm* at home,' Agnes says. By her tone, she might as well have said, *I wouldn't leave him to look after the kippers I have stored in the freezer,* especially with the look she's giving him. But he's not so bad, really. Just a bit overly familiar with the old girl sometimes.

'Agnes. I need you to pack Sorcha a few things. And while you're on, pack a few things for yourself.' It's a perfect plan. We'll be away when whatever Jayne has to say goes to print. Plus, there's something else I'd like to do. Like get Paisley naked. See her tan without lines. Live with her—have her live with us. Enjoy her in our alone time. Give her so many orgasms she can't help but promise to move in permanently.

It's mad and it's out of character, sure, but I think it's a fucking fantastic plan.

'What? What are you talking about?' Agnes demands.

'We're going on holiday,' I announce, suddenly feeling incredibly light. Or maybe insane. 'You'd better dig out your passport.'

'Where are we going?' She sounds aggrieved, but she can't hide the accompanying smile.

'Wherever he books for us,' I say, pointing at Flynn as I walk backwards out of the room.'

'I'm not looking after the cat,' he calls back.

'Yes, you are. And you're staying here. In the guest room.' When he smiles, I see exactly where his thoughts are going. '*Alone.*' I fill the words with so much meaning, his expression falls. 'And if you book us somewhere shitty, I'll have your balls.'

'And they said working for you would be an opportunity.'

'It is. Ask Agnes,' I crow.

'Where are we going?' asks Sorcha as I reach the hallway. 'And can Princess come?'

'Ah. No. She can't.' Before she begins to give me a hard time, I add, 'Flynn's going to stay here, plus you're getting time off school.'

She seems to have decided that's a fair trade-off as I open the door into the garage.

Chapter Twenty-Seven

PAISLEY

I spend most of Monday in bed in a bad mood and heavy funk.

According to Max, the photographers have gone, and the calls requesting interviews have stopped mainly because the world has moved on. Apparently, today the trolls are hounding a member of the British Parliament who got caught with his pecker in a glory hole in some Amsterdam sleaze pit. *It puts a new slant on European relations, I suppose.*

While I sort of feel sorry for the man—*and his wife*—I'm also glad I'm no longer a source of scrutiny. One man's misery is another girl's . . . well, not exactly pleasure. Freedom, maybe? Whatever. Either way, it is nice to be able to switch my phone back on. I'd used it exactly once yesterday to speak to someone from Robin's management team, who'd basically blew me off. He'd said he'd get back to me once Robin had been released from rehab, and that was that. He wasn't interested in the slightest that Robin might've been stalking me. And of course, they couldn't trace the source of the lies the press had been told.

Or sold. I guess I'll never know. The official line is that it's all hearsay, and they can't do anything about it.

So I switch my phone on and delete the million alerts and the voice messages requesting interviews. There's nothing from Keir. Not a text. Not a missed call. Not a voicemail.

I know I told him he couldn't fix this yesterday, but I didn't expect him to drop me like a hot stone. Being painted to the world as the woman who tore apart Robin's heart is bad enough—a whore and a cheat—but I can cope with it. It smarts, sure. It makes the blood sizzle in my veins with maximum rage. *Set against an inherent kind of impotency.* But not hearing from Keir for over twenty-four hours? It does sting. Quite a bit actually. Maybe even more than the stuff on the internet.

I swing my legs out of bed while listening to the last two voicemails. The second to last one is a bit of a given—I didn't get the job with the midmorning TV show. No one wants a makeup girl who stars in porn, even allegedly. It's with a sigh of resignation that I listen to the final call. And when the beep sounds at the end, I find myself bursting into a flood of tears.

It's another hour before I make it downstairs. Still in my old robe. Still with a tear-stained face.

'Where's Chas?' I ask Max as I slide two slices of white toast into Chas's space-age toaster.

Sitting at the kitchen table, he barely looks up before answering. 'In her office, I think. Probably editing.'

A dark chuckle sounds from my chest as I open the silverware drawer. 'I'm sad, not suicidal,' I mutter.

'What?'

'There are no knives in the silverware drawer,' I announce a little louder, gesturing at the drawer. 'How am I supposed to butter my toast?' Is that a touch of hysteria I hear?

'What are you talking about?' Max asks, his expression clouded with confusion as he finally looks up from his iPad. The fact that he's looking makes matters worse as I pull open the dishwasher and find the cutlery basket jam-packed.

'Obviously, I'm losing my mind.'

'Oh, sweets,' Max says. 'I hate to tell you, but you've always been a little crazy But you know what would make you feel better right now?'

'If you say sex, I will disembowel you with this melon baller,' I say, grasping the thing in my fist.

'But sex makes everything better.'

'Chickenpox?' I sort of screech. 'Can it cure chickenpox?' And now I want to cry again as I think of Sorcha. And then Keir. And what might've been if not for, 'Robin fucking Reed!' I launch one of the recently popped slices of toast across the room. Max ducks as it sails past his head, and I continue my rant. 'He's a bastard, and I'm going to kill him before drugs ever get the chance!'

'Okay!' Max calls back, holding his hands up in surrender. 'Want to hear some good news?'

'Yes!' I fold my arms and throw my ass against the deep butler's sink. 'Good news would be welcome right about now.'

'The portal for Fast Girl Media almost crashed with the sheer volume of new subscriptions yesterday.'

'Oh, that's good.'

'And Chas thought it might, so she cancelled all weekly and monthly options, meaning anyone looking for you has to pay for a year's membership.'

'Oh. Ew. People are looking for me? Searching for me on the internet?'

'Yeah, why wouldn't they? You're hot. I keep telling you—'

'Don't.' I hold my hand up, palm out. 'Just don't.'

'Would it make you feel better if I said people are probably looking for a connection to Robin Reed?'

'The Robin Reed experience?' I giggle at the thought of someone doing him on screen. It's not a pleasant sight, as I recall. And not the best of experiences. 'They'd all want their money back.'

'Think of it this way,' he says, pushing back his chair. 'People are looking for whatever, but being exposed to amazing, tasteful pornography. They're not being duped, but maybe educated. They might spend a little while looking for you but will eventually find something else they like. And all the while? Chas is raking in the subscription coin.' He deposits my abandoned toast in the garbage.

'You really ought to try to go back to being a venture capitalist.' He'd gotten a job with a big city company, leaving after only a few weeks. 'You could probably sell snow to the Eskimos.'

'Venture capitalists invest in ideas, not sell them,' he says with an air of benevolent patience, patting my head as he passes. 'We'll both find our way. I'm sure of that.'

'Yeah,' I say to the empty room. 'But mine is a one-way ticket back to the States.'

The doorbell rings, shortly followed by Max's voice as he makes his way up the stairs. 'You'll get it!' he sings.

'Sure,' I grumble. 'Why not? It's not like I have a new job or anything.'

I trudge up to the front door, making sure to look through the peephole.

'You have no business to react like that,' I whisper to my heart, placing my hand over it to stop it from dancing. Then I pull open the door to Keir.

'Hey.' I paint on a smile that feels all wrong. 'How are you?'

'About as well as you feel,' he replies, smiling as he looks my stained robe up and down.

'It's not dirty, just old.'

'It's . . . unexpected,' he answers, still smiling. *Like a total loon.*

'We can't all be pulled together every minute of every day,' I snipe, regretting my tone immediately as his smile falls.

'No, of course not,' he says, his expression sobering. 'How are you?' His throat moves as he swallows, his hands sort of fidgety by his sides before he slides them into the pockets of his slacks.

'I've been better,' I answer honestly, folding my arms across my chest and giving a one-shoulder shrug. 'And you?'

'Well, I spent an hour or so with my ex-wife, so I'm sure you can guess exactly how I'm feeling.'

'How could I guess, given that you've barely mentioned her?'

'I imagine most people don't enjoy spending time with their ex,' he says, slightly annoyed. 'Are you going to invite me inside?'

'Nope.' I pop the *p* loudly. 'Unless you do a better job of explaining.'

'Seeing her was about as pleasant as I expected, but it has complicated matters somewhat. And I'd really prefer not to stand at the front door telling you about it.' The end of his sentence ends a little loudly. A little commanding. And I like it. Like that he's a little fiery. A little pissed off. And I'd keep him at the door for a little longer if it wasn't for Chastity's sudden appearance.

'So this is Keir,' she says, bumping me with her hip, like that's some secret signal of approval.

'And you must be Chastity.' Chas doesn't answer, though she eyes him critically. 'I imagine this is what it must feel like to be a horse on a stud farm,' he says.

'Sorry,' she replies, looking anything but sorry. 'It's a professional hazard. Plus, Paisley didn't mention you were funny. Come on in.'

'Something tells me you like them best when they don't talk.' We follow her and her tinkling laughter to the kitchen. But this isn't fair; flirty Keir is winning over the toughest woman I know.

I take a seat at the head of the kitchen table. 'Right, so,' I begin sharply, 'you saw your ex?'

Suddenly, Chas's expression could sour milk.

'Yeah, she lives in the States. But I suppose I'm here to say a couple of things to say. One good, or at least I think so. And one not so good.'

I open my mouth to complain—to say something like, *and here I was thinking you'd come to see how I am.* But I don't get a chance as Chas cuts me off.

'The bad first?' she asks, mistaking my inhalation of breath as an indication I'm about to choose. But what the hell; I shrug in acquiesce.

'The bad news is she's in the UK at the invitation of a tabloid newspaper. She's come to add fuel to the Robin Reed fire.'

'How is that bad news for me?'

'Well, it's not me the public is interested in, except maybe as the Joker to his Batman. Same with you, I expect. We're both just a means to an end where there's news of the ginger git—pawns in the media game. And I know—I could do without it just the same as you. Which brings me to my second, happier point.'

'Which is?' Chas asks, just a curious as me, it seems.

'We're going on holiday.' He looks very pleased with himself while I'm equal amounts pissed off.

So much so, that I don't quite hear what he says next. It's all right for some, I think, all right for those who can just . . . 'And I'd like you to come.'

'What? Why do you want me to come?' I place my clasped hands on the table.

'Have you heard the saying, *today's news is tomorrow's chip wrappings*?'

Fish and chips are traditionally wrapped in newspaper in the UK, I recall. Today's new is tomorrow's garbage.

'I get the reference,' I say, 'but I'm not sure it's possible.' After my complaints and my anger, now I'm just plain disappointed. Because I'd go with him, wouldn't I? If he'd asked me yesterday to go away with him for a few days, I'd have jumped at the chance.

'You don't want to?' he asks carefully. 'Or is it something else?'

'Does it matter?'

'To me, it does. Look, Paisley,' he says, engulfing my clasped hands with his larger ones. 'I know it's early days, and I know you've just gotten out of a relationship, but I can really see this working.'

My heart misses a beat as my mouth speaks without the permission of my brain. 'Why? Why can you?'

The intensity in his answer almost knocks me from my chair. 'Because I've never felt this way about anyone.'

I'm slayed. Just slayed. Suddenly destroyed by what could've been as I pull one hand from his and reach into the pocket of my grubby robe. I place my phone on the table between us and play back the message I'd received earlier for all to hear.

'Miss Byrne, my name is Elaine Crosby. I'm ringing from Immigration and Border Control in respect of your application for a spousal visa. I've scheduled an appointment for you to speak with a colleague and myself on Thursday of this week at two o'clock. If this appointment is inconvenient, could you contact me on—'

I hit *end*.

'They're going to send me home,' I say simply as tears begin running down my face.

'Can they do that?' Keir is out of his chair in an instant. Kneeling before me, he rubs one hand over my cold fingers, his thumb swiping away the wetness from my cheeks as his gaze, greener than usual, never leaves mine.

'I guess so. My visa was conditional on being in a relationship with him. As that's no longer the case . . . '

'Then I guess we'll have to find you a new fiancé.'

From the other side of the kitchen, Chas gasps. Meanwhile, I try to pull my hands from his. 'Don't be ridiculous,' I begin. 'I'm almost certain you can go to jail for faking a fiancée. And they don't wear makeup in jail.' I shiver at the thought of that horrific indignity. 'I couldn't do it. I'd be better off in *bumfuck-nowheres-ville.*' Marginally. There's no Sephora near my hometown, and the nearest thing to a department store is more likely to stock equine fly repellent than Chanel.

'Who said anything about—'

'Seriously, Keir. I'm *so* not getting engaged to Flynn or any of your employees just so we can . . . ' *do the things we do so well. Just so I can fall a little more for you.* 'Just so we can—'

'Woman, *hauld yer whesht*!' he almost yells. 'Jesus wept. Is she always like this?' he asks, turning to Chastity.

'She's had a trying couple of days.' He nods just once, as though suddenly understanding or empathising. But he can't—not really.

'Keir, I'm serious—' I begin.

'Sweets!' Chas interrupts loudly. 'For goodness' sakes. The man on his *knees in front of you* is trying to propose.'

My head swings from Chastity to the gorgeous man on is kn—on his knees! I jump up from the chair, my hands suddenly on my cheeks.

'No. No, no, no, *noooo*.' I back away from him, finding my spine pressed up against the fridge. 'No. You don't mean it. B-because you can't fix this.'

'You're right,' he says, rising and stalking towards me. 'I can't fix it because it's not broken. It's lovely, and it's new, and it's special; so special. But darlin', it's also real.'

And then he kisses me, my face in his hands, his body curved around mine.

He kisses me like he's trying to kiss some sense into me—like he'd kiss me into submission, if he could. And I imagine he could, especially as his hands fall to my hips where he pulls me against him. Against his hardness. My knees almost give way, and I moan into his mouth. But I can't do this, can I? Not even I'm that gullible.

'Say yes,' he growls. 'And I'll make you the happiest woman alive.'

For a moment, I don't doubt it. He could keep me on my back each day, and I expect I'd be happy—compliant, even—for the rest of my life.

'But . . . what's that?' From somewhere beyond the kitchen, Chastity's voice gets a little posher, if that's possible.

'If you don't move away from that door, I'm going to knee you in your balls. Shortly following, I expect a doctor in the emergency room will tell you that you'll never father children. On account of said testicles being lodged next to your tonsils.'

'Come one step closer and these balls will be in your face. And not in a good way.'

'Is that Flynn?' I whisper. 'She must think he's the press.'

Keir nods, ducking his head to my ear. 'I hate to say it, but she sounds like his kind of foreplay.'

'Oh, please,' Chastity calls back, her cut glass accent sharp enough to draw blood. 'I spend my day with men, not little boys like you. In fact, I expect I eat balls bigger than yours for breakfast.'

'Lady, I don't give a flying fuck who you eat, or who eats you, or what you do to get your rocks off, I need to speak to Keir—'

'If you're a journalist, I swear, I'll stick this very expensive Burberry umbrella up your backside and wave you around like a Guy Fawkes toffee apple!'

'You sound like you've done that before.' There's a distinct change in Flynn's tone. Less angry and more amused. 'And enjoyed it.'

'See?' Keir whispers, his lips travelling down my neck as his hands gripping my butt.

'Perhaps not an umbrella,' Chas says.

'Is this little anecdote going to make me puke?'

'I don't know,' she replies evenly. 'Are you homophobic, or can you enjoy a little gay porn?'

'I know it's early,' Keir whispers, 'and you might not feel the same way as I do, but come away with me, darlin'.'

'Just you and me?'

He tilts his head to the side as though weighing his words. 'Sorcha and Agnes, too.'

'You want me to marry into the family?'

'We're sort of a package deal.'

'I will . . . come away with you on vacation, but that's all.' He looks like he doesn't believe me—like I've already said yes—but we'll see who wins in the end. 'Where are we going?'

'No idea. Somewhere hot. Pack light. I don't expect you'll need much more than shorts and a couple of bikinis.'

'How do you know I own a bikini?'

'Don't you?' he asks, pausing in thought as though this might be a possibility.

'Excuse me,' I say as he takes a step backwards. I don't like the space between us, so I step into him. 'Have you met me?'

'I have,' he answers, smiling down at me. 'You're trouble, and I like you just fine.'

Chapter Twenty-Eight

PAISLEY

'Flynn chose well.' Keir sighs with contentment. Balancing his pineapple cocktail on the palm of one of his large hands, he digs his toes deeper into the sand. He's quite a sight, not that he at all notices other woman as they check him out. *All those muscles on display. That golden tan and tussled hair.*

He's right. Flynn did choose well—epically so. The Seychelles has been a wonderful escape in more ways than one. Endless blue skies, golden sands, and blue ocean as far as the eye can see. I haven't hooked up to the internet once since arriving four days ago, other than to talk briefly with Chastity who, thankfully, had nothing to say about the newspapers, photographers, or exes.

'I hope Flynn is looking after Princess well,' Sorcha says, looking up from her white sandcastle next to our pillow-festooned daybed. It's hard to take her slight frown seriously when looking at the painted blue strip of zinc plastered across her nose. She made friends with a family of Australians staying in the same resort, promptly adopting their method of UV protection, which includes a liberal application of multicoloured zinc war paint every day.

'She spoke with you yesterday.'

'Cat's don't speak, silly.' Sorcha sighs. 'And she was more interested in playing with Flynn and that mouse on a piece of string.'

'True, cats aren't big on FaceTime,' I say, hoping to reassure her. 'And Flynn is just entertaining her until you get back. You're her person, Sorcha. Flynn is just the cat sitter. She won't forget you.'

Somewhat placated, she returns to her bucket and spade.

'It's almost time for an afternoon siesta.' Keir peers over the top of his pineapple, his eyes green and full of mischief in the light.

'Any more of those,' I reply, peering over my sunglasses balanced on the end of my nose, 'and sleeping is all you'll be doing.'

'Wanna bet?'

'Why? What else have you been doing?' asks Sorcha, her head popping up over the bed again. I need to remember to engage my brain before my mouth when she's around. She really doesn't miss a thing, which has made for some interesting conversations. 'Because Agnes says siesta is sleeping time, and if I don't sleep, I can't stay up late.'

'Agnes is right.' Keir leans back against the pillows, his eyes falling closed as though that's the end of the matter. Or maybe it's just his version of playing dead.

'Yes, but what have you been *doing*?' she persists. 'If Paisley says you'll go to sleep after too many pineapple rums, that must mean you *haven't* been sleeping when I go for a nap.'

'I've been busy,' Keir replies, opening his eyes again. 'I've got trouble to take care of . . . while Paisley's in bed. Take yesterday, for example. She lay very, very still . . . ' Mainly because I was tied to the bed, arms above my head and my ankles secured to the edges. 'While I worked hard. Very, very hard, trying not to make any noise.'

His gaze slides to mine, and I shiver, a whole body kind of affair as I recall the silken feel of the rope strapping me down. The feather-light touches of his fingers and mouth. As for a lack of noise, that's true. He promised to make me come until I couldn't breathe. And he did. Though I'm pretty sure I screamed my release when he eventually slid into me.

It's definitely a good thing Sorcha and Agnes are staying in the hotel. Meanwhile, Keir and I have a villa at the edge of the resort. A beautiful place—all teak wood, thatched roofing, and billowing white cotton. Best of all, there are views of the Indian Ocean from three sides of the building. *The infinity pool, the bathtub, and the veranda*. And we've made love on them all. Because even when we're fucking, Keir makes love to me. *With his eyes. With his hands*. It seems so much more since our vacation began.

But I can't get carried away. This isn't reality, but a break from it. Besides, he hasn't mentioned marriage again. *And why would he?* whispers a voice in my head.

'Daddy, why are you looking at Paisley like you're trying to steal the thoughts from her head?'

'Am I?' He immediately adopts a blank expression. Meanwhile, I grasp my own cocktail to snigger behind. 'I was just thinking of all the hard work I'll be doing when you're sleeping this afternoon. That's the problem with trouble, you see,' he says, all rumbly and sexual. 'It needs managing.'

'Are you sure you're not just having sex?'

I inhale, choke a little, and sneeze a little mai tai from my nose. 'Oh, that burns,' I complain, holding the cocktail napkin to my nostrils.

'I-I beg your pardon, young lady,' Keir splutters, adopting the tone of someone's elderly maiden aunt. Back in 1870, maybe.

'S-E-X,' she returns, spelling it out oh-so helpfully. 'Toby says you can only have sex when you're married, but I told him that Tiger Blossom's daddy has had sex with both her mummy and her nanny. That's why she's getting two baby brothers next year. And a divorce.' She taps her finger to her lip, considering something for a moment. 'But maybe Toby is right because, technically, Tiger's daddy *is* married. What do you think, Daddy?'

'What?' His word hits the air quite aggressively, sounding more like *whit?* 'I think you shouldn't be thinking about sex,' he answers decisively. 'And I think I might need to go have a wee talk to Tiger Blossom's dad.'

'You'll have to wait until he comes back from rehab,' she says, sifting sugar-like sand through her fingers. Meanwhile, Keir looks like his temper is about to eject his head.

'Sorcha, do you know what rehab is?' I ask, keeping my tone even.

'Tiger's mummy says it's currently a means of keeping him from being served.' *I'll bet.*

'And what about sex?' I ask, evenly. 'Do you know what sex is?'

'Well, *duh,*' she answers, suddenly looking back at me as though I've grown another head. And a dumb one at that. 'It's what makes *b-a-b-i-e-s,*' she says, spelling it out helpfully. 'The mummy and daddy do some round kisses like they do on TV.' She turns her back to us both, crossing her hands over her chest, her fingers appearing at her shoulders as she mimes cuddling. Then she begins tilting her head side to side like a cat watching a washing machine, adding kissy noises for effect.

'See,' she says, turning back. 'Then two years later, a baby comes along.'

'I must be doing something wrong,' Keir mumbles.

I slide him a confused look; doing something wrong with regards to his parenting, or his virility?

'Of course, you're doing something wrong,' she replies, jumping up and placing her hands on her hips. 'You're not married, so you can't have any babies.'

'Aye, but I've got you,' he answers reasonably.

'And who have I got? Princess kitty, that's who. Come on, Dad, I need some sliblings.' I try not to laugh and don't correct her. *That would be wrong*. 'Someone I can teach ballet to,' she continues, pirouetting and kicking up sand onto my legs.

'Oh, Agnes is coming!' Sorcha suddenly begins jumping and waving, trying to catch the older woman's attention, and in doing so, she kicks up even more sand. 'She promised to take me to book a trip on the glass bottomed boat to see the fish.'

'Come on, hen. Watch what you're doing,' Keir says, holding up his drink to protect it from the spray.

'See what I mean,' she answers, her words filled with the pique of a teen. 'I need someone else for him to pick on. He's only got me. I think you should marry him,' she says, throwing the words at me as an afterthought—as though her father is some issue to take off her hands. She goes to run off in the direction of Agnes when Keir catches her wrist.

'Hang on a minute. Are you trying to get rid of me?'

'No, silly.' She rolls her eyes. 'I'm trying to get some baby brothers. And I like Paisley.' Her gaze slides to mine. 'She's nice, and she's pretty, and she can teach me to do makeup when I'm big. So I think you should marry her,' she says, nodding her head. 'And then have sex with her without any condoms so I can get those baby brothers!'

She scampers off, leaving us both stunned and mute. We don't speak—not for minutes, at least. *How awkward.*

Then Keir turns to me with a sly sort of smile. 'How about we go back to the villa and get a head start on that?'

'Which that? The marriage or the babies?' I purposely leave sex off the table. *Or something.*

'We could practise the baby making bit. I'm not ready for babies right now. But I'd be up for plenty of baby making practise.'

I'm suddenly and irrationally annoyed. Why? Probably because he said he'd marry me and then never mentioned it again. And I know how ridiculous my anger sounds, especially as he was already on his knees at that point in Chas's kitchen. His offer was well meant but ridiculous—a reaction to my call from the immigration department, that's all. *Because Keir is a good man. A kind man.*

Which all just serves to remind me how ridiculous my anger is. I'll probably return to London from this vacation to an angry immigration official who'll confiscate my passport. I'll be lucky if I'm given time to pack before being escorted to a flight to the States—probably with a guard and a prison jumpsuit.

And these hips weren't built for stripes.

As Keir reaches out and strokes my arm with the backs of his fingers, tears prick behind my sunglasses. I love him. I think I knew before we even arrived on Mahé Island. I just couldn't admit it to myself.

'What would you say to a little afternoon delight?' he asks, his tone dripping with innuendo and suggestion, unaware of the knots my insides are currently tying themselves in.

On instinct, I decide to stay in the moment. We no longer have an infinite number of those ahead of us.

'To a little afternoon delight, I might say *he-llooo*.'

He chuckles at my answer—part sexy, part silly, but all yes.

'Oh, trouble,' he says, smiling as he stands. He holds out his hand, helping me to my feet. But what I don't anticipate is when he throws me over his shoulder.

'Oh, don't! Put me down, Keir!' I begin pummelling his back, giggling like a schoolgirl as the blood rushes to my head.

'You know,' he says, jogging away as I bounce upside down, 'I don't think I will.'

But when I begin to pull down his shorts, he does.

The drapes blow in the afternoon breeze as Keir wraps his arm around my waist, kicking the door to the villa closed. He gathers my hair and pushes it over my shoulder, his fingers teasing the skin as he slips my beach cover-up from one shoulder, then the next.

'Keir,' I whisper, pulling free from his arm. The villa is set high in the bay, but the whole place is open right now—the shutters pulled wide— exposing the interior to the elements. And to potential eyes.

I step from the pool of gauzy fabric, placing my sunglasses on the table, then make my way to the shutters with the intent of closing them.

'Leave them.' His voice is one of absolute authority as, from behind, his fingers stroke my spine as he toys with the string tie of my orange bikini, before pulling the knot loose.

'People will see.' I turn my head over my shoulder, even as I let my bikini top fall. As it drops to the floor, I cover my breasts with my hands as I turn.

'You are so fucking sexy.' Keir draws the words and his compliment out, his body so tanned and so strong, his gaze igniting my skin. Electricity pulses between us in short bursts, like an understanding or an acceptance of what this moment means.

Because these moments mean everything.

My breath hitches as he steps towards me, hooking his thumbs in the sides of my bikini bottoms and dragging them down my legs until I'm standing before him bare and shivering, every inch of my body aching with need. His hand begins to stroke and touch, to squeeze and hold like he doesn't believe I'm here—that I'm real. *Like he can't quite get enough.* His eyes intent on mine, he splays my fingers farther, exposing my nipples to the warm air. He looks unholy, wicked, and all kinds of delicious and wrong as he begins to tease between the *V* with the point of his tongue. My nipple stiffens, and I throw my head back, the echo of the sensation beating between my legs.

'I want you,' he whispers. 'All the time and everywhere. But right now, I want you on your knees because I'm going to eat you out.'

This man owns me—owns me with his dirty promises. Owns me with his body. In less than a moment, I'm there, on the bed, my hair splayed out against the comforter, the embroidery tantalising my nipples as he spreads my thighs farther apart.

'Fuck, what a sight. I love this arse,' he growls, his hands kneading and touching my flesh roughly. He slaps each cheek—once, twice—an absolute first, causing my breath to catch in my throat with a gasp that's electrified.

'You like that, darlin'.' It's not a question, but a proclamation as I push myself up on my palms. *Push myself farther into his hands.*

His fingers stroke my cheeks, slipping to where I'm wet. When he pushes two fingers inside, I cry out, arching my back and impaling myself on his hand. In seconds, I'm writhing and whimpering as his fingers work me into a frenzy. And I'm glad— glad for the distraction. Glad of the release building in intensity inside me. I'm not thinking about the window. I'm not thinking about what awaits us back at home. There is only this. Keir and me. And our ecstasy. Our unspoken love.

His fingers slide from my pussy, his voice part groan, part wonder. 'You're so slippery, darlin'.' Covering my body with his, he rubs the evidence between his glistening fingers and thumb in front of my face. 'So wet. Just for me.'

'*Yes!*' Just for him. And only for him.

He pulls back, and with a rustle of fabric, he hooks his forearm under me, adjusting my position at the edge of the bed. Then, with a groan of pure masculine appreciation, his tongue slips between my legs. I cry out, the sensation of this one swipe enough to turn my legs to Jell-O. *To make my entire body ache for him.* One lick and I'm done for, sobbing as my fingertips ball in the bedding, but I'm unprepared for the sensation as he buries his face between my legs.

As he works me with his tongue—with his fingers—as he savours me like I'm a banquet and he's a starving man, he murmurs to me.

He tells me how much he wants me.

How beautiful I am.

How delicious I taste on his tongue.

How he could drown in me.

His words and his body drive me to the brink of insanity. I'm so desperate to touch him, my hands grasping and groping blindly for him. I want him— all of him. Harder, faster—I want him more than I can remember ever wanting anything.

'Keir, please,' I pant, '*please.*'

'You want somethin', darlin'?' His words are puffs of air against my skin, mere wisps swallowed by his seeking tongue.

'*I need, need, need you.*' I chant a litany of pleasure as the sensation builds between my legs, white hot and blinding but just beyond my reach.

In a spark of realisation, I slide my hands between my legs to touch my clit. Or at least, I would, if Keir didn't grab my wrists—first one, then the other—pulling them to the small of my back.

'That's cheating.' He chuckles, wrapping my wrists in his hand.

'You didn't think so last night,' I retort. Turning my head, I attempt to blow the hair away that's covering my mouth.

'Last night I asked you to—for both our pleasure. Today, I'm telling you *not to*. For mine.'

If I had a response, its stolen from my tongue as he suddenly slicks the head of his cock between my legs. My breath hitches and my body stills, filled with the anticipation in the moment.

'And I own this body.' He slides himself along my wet seam, bumping my swollen clit. I whimper or cry, I'm not sure which. 'That sounded like an agreement,' he purrs, his tone full of satisfaction, but with an edge of something that sounds like desperation. A desperation I understand.

The flickering of my orgasm is quick to rise again, my mind woolly, my skin hot and tight as I rock back against him, as though the desire to have him fill me is enough to make the sensation reality. But as is often the way with Keir, he anticipates my actions.

'Greedy girl.' His hot skin covers me as he kisses my cheek. Bites the soft skin of my neck. My wrists still in hand, we're pressed skin to skin, his cock rubs and tantalises, just a fraction from where I need him to be.

'Greedy because you make me.'

'And I love to hear you beg,' he agrees. 'Come on, darlin'. Do it . . . for me. Tell me what you need.' He pulls back, kissing his way down my spine, decorating my back and sides with licks and sucking bites. And as he reaches my hands, he sucks my fingers, bites the knuckles. Flicks his tongue between the flesh of the soft *V*.

Before Keir, I would never have thought of these things as sexy, but as he tongues between my fingers, all I can see is his wicked gaze between my thighs. And as he sucks and bites, I can only revel in the possession of the moment. *His possession of me*. I don't realise I'm speaking—chanting—until he pulls away, balancing the head of his cock right where I need him.

'That's it, trouble. I know it. I know you need me. I just need to hear how much.'

'God, Keir.' My whimper sounds desperately but I just don't care. 'I need you so much. I need you inside me more than I need air.' And right now, it's true. I can barely breathe for the anticipation of the feel of him.

'I own you. Say it,' he demands. I twist my head back to look at him. The sun streaming through the drapes casts his hard body in bronze. But this is no statue. His body was made to fit mine and for as long as I can have him, I will.

'You own me,' I whisper, my voice hoarse with longing and love.

'And you own *me*.' His tone is so dark and so seductive, my heart beats hard, my insides along with it. 'Say it,' he whispers hoarsely. 'Tell me I'm yours.'

'You are—' my voice catches, tears stinging my eyes '—you are mine.'

Mine. Mine. Mine.

My insides pound to the beat of my longing and love as he loosens his hold on my wrists. I twist my head to meet his mouth and he kisses me again and again, his lips a mixture of command and gentleness, our tongues entangled in a slow, passionate dance. 'Mine forever.'

Keir's eyes are dark as he pulls away, not trusting my body's answers. One hand suddenly tight on my hips, the other holds his cock as he balances it between my lips.

'Fuck.' It's not a curse but a prayer as he casts his eyes heavenwards. 'You will be the ending of me.' And with his final appeal, he slides himself inside. Everything falls away. There is nothing more. Not him. Not me. Just us. Just pleasure. Just the feel of him inside me. 'And I will die a very happy man.' With an undulation of his body and a grunt to counter my cry, he starts to move. His hands on my hips steady me and stop me from floating away, as he fucks me so solidly it's like he'd touch my heart if he could.

'I'll spend my life worshiping you with my body.'

'*Yes!*' I cry out in my pleasure. I cry out his name.

'I'll endow you with my cock.'

'*Yes!*' My hands ball the sheets as his tempo changes, deep thrusts now shallow bursts.

'Endow you with my worldly goods.'

As my orgasm is drawn from every inch of my skin, I arch my back, grinding into him, crying out.

Everything blurs around the edges—the window in front of me, the wet sounds of our pleasure, our breathing—everything. Everything but the most intense, writhing kind of pleasure that detonates deep inside.

Behind me, he pulses once, twice. And the sound he makes? I'd bottle it if I could.

Limp and boneless, Keir slides his arms around me, his harsh breath blowing against my damp skin.

'I'm so fucking happy.' His words are part whisper, part groan as he pulls me into his body, somehow rolling us across the bed. Propped on his elbow, he brushes the tangles of hair from my face. 'So fucking happy.' And boy does he look it, staring down at me with this post orgasm grin

'Orgasms.' It's all I can say, though I add a limp wave of my hand.

'Aye, and plenty of them.' My eyes closed, I feel him take my hand, pressing both to my heart. 'For the rest of your life.'

My eyes spring open. More than the tease in his tone, I realise what he's just said.

'What?' he asks amused. 'You didn't think I meant it when I got down on my knees, so I thought I'd try it another way.'

'Ano—That was a proposal? And you thought you'd fuck a yes out of me?'

'I think I fucked a few of them out of you,' he replies with a sexy smirk.

'You haven't even told me you love me yet!'

A beat later, I'm sitting at the end of the bed, Keir on his knees in front of me—no, that's not right. He's in front of me on *one* knee.'

'Paisley,' he begins. 'Let me tell you how ardently I covet your body.' I open my mouth to protest—to tell him I'm still not taking him seriously when he grasps my hand. 'How ardently I love your heart and your soul. If you'd so me the honour of becoming my wife, I promise to spend the rest of my life making you happy. And making you come.'

'This is *not* the kind of proposal story we can tell our grandchildren—or your daughter.'

'We'll keep the good bits to ourselves. Come on, trouble. What do you say? It's not so hard. Just say yes.'

Chapter Twenty-Nine

KEIR

Of course, she did say yes.

So it might have taken me crawling up her body, placing kisses as I'd travelled—it might have taken an afternoon of worshiping her pussy while whispering promises of my everlasting love. But none of that was any great hardship. Because this woman. My trouble. She's everything.

I don't think I could put a point or time to it, or tell you the exact instant that I knew I was in love. I'd spent years promising myself I wouldn't put go through it again—I wasn't going to risk my heart and my sanity. I kept telling myself I don't need companionship or sex. Until a chance meeting at a wedding I didn't even want to attend brought me to this point.

My own wedding.

Four days have passed since I proposed to her, my knees against the hard wooden floor, stark bollock naked, and still desperate for her. And I don't care what she says, it's an excellent story to tell our grandkids. I can see it now . . .

Well, it was like this, little Jimmy. Your Grandma was on her knees after the best orgasm of her life, when I looked down at her beautiful pink pussy and I knew—I just knew—that I'd be the luckiest man alive to get be the one to pound it for the rest of her life.

It'll be an awkward conversation for the dinner table, sure, but one they won't forget. I only hope I don't live long enough to lose the memory of her smile to dementia—her smile as she'd watched me open the tiny velvet box to her ring. Yep, I'd bought it before our flight and had it couriered to the hotel. And it wasn't a last-minute panic buy, but something I saw and just knew she'd love . . . if I could only get her to take me seriously.

It's Art Deco in style, to remind her of the Claridge's and our first night. Sapphires for the colour of her eyes. A teardrop shaped diamond of several carats, that reminded me of a certain part of her anatomy. Or rather, *two* shapes of her anatomy.

'What's the smile for? Will suddenly appears in front of me, dressed in a white linen shirt and pale pants. Pinned to his chest is the smallest, most pale pink rose I've ever seen, and he has another in his hand. 'Actually, I recognise that kind of look. I'm just not used to seeing it on *your* face. And on second thoughts, keep it to yourself, whatever depravity you're imagining, yeah?'

'It's not like that,' I reply. 'I was just thinking about getting old.'

'What kind of lunatic thinks about losing his hair and getting saggy balls on the day of his wedding,' he asks, pinning the flower to my chest. Then he slaps both hands against my cheeks.

'Ignore him,' Sadie says, coming up behind her husband, beaming the widest smile I've ever seen her face wear. 'You look so handsome, Keir. And just wait until you see your gorgeous bride. Oh, and Sorcha, too.'

Handsome and dressed almost identical to Will. White shirt, pale pants, a pale pink tie, and a waistcoat vest. *And pink because Paisley said Sorcha should choose the accents.*

What is it about weddings that makes everyone cry? Sadie's eyes are glistening and I'm fighting the same effect.

'You did good,' she tells me. 'The venue is perfect, Sorcha is on cloud nine, and your bride . . . ' her words trail off as her eyes begin to further well. 'She's beautiful, on the inside as well as out.'

'Like me you mean,' interjects Will.

'Yes, but not quite so modest,' Sadie replies, giggling as Will wraps her in his arms. Pulling her back to his chest, he places his hands wide on the slight swelling under her dress.

What's in front of me is exactly what I've found in Paisley. Love. Acceptance. A place to call home.

'What are you smiling about now?' Will asks, his tone tinged with humour. 'You know, they lock people up for grinning into empty space.'

'You're meant to smile on your wedding day,' Sadie responds, digging him with her elbow.

'Oh, yes. I forgot. The misery and nagging doesn't come until much later.' He makes a yakking motion with his hand, his expression one of extreme mischievousness.

'You know, for a complete dick,' I tell him, 'I can't tell you what it means to have you here.'

Paisley doesn't have any family, just Chastity, so she says. And I'd always considered Sorcha and Agnes as mine, but I've come to realise my family is bigger than that and they've always been there for me. My family is Mac and Will, and by extension, Sadie, Ella, and their kids. *Current and future.*

And my family holds me up and challenges me. Tells me when I'm wrong. Looks out for me when times are tough. And tells me what being invited to my wedding means to them.

'Thanks for the free holiday.' His chin balanced on his wife's head, Will shoots me a wink.

'I'd like to say you're welcome, but I won't. But thanks for helping us out with the immigration thing.' Will and his envoy, aka Flynn, have been liaising with the immigration people to try to smooth the issue with Paisley's currently sticky visa status.

'It's my pleasure. I think I might need to get myself an assistant as smooth talking as Flynn.'

'Try to poach him and I'll cut off your balls,' I retort.

Because Flynn is invaluable. While I've been sunning myself and relaxing for the first time in years, he's started the ball rolling on our several pronged legal attacks. Firstly, I'm suing Robin Reed and his team for slander—and anything else I can think of. Second, I'm going after a couple of the tabloids. They're already saying they'll print a retraction along with an apology for blackening both our names. Time will tell. Third, I'm taking Joe to the cleaners for ruining my deal with the convent. Seems he took them news of my debauched nature himself. He might be laughing now but we'll see if he's still happy when I tie him and *his* deal in legal knots.

But I'm not thinking about business today.

'Will couldn't afford to keep him—he certainly couldn't afford to treat him to vacations in the Seychelles!' Sadie laughs as she teases Will. 'Besides, Paisley's friend—the one with the accent like the queen?'

'Chastity?'

'Yes, that's her. She might make him unavailable to you both. She's got this very dangerous looking parasol which she's already threatened to part Flynn from a certain part of his anatomy. I doubt Will would like to add himself to the castration list. Oh, before I forget.' She says, stepping free from Will's embrace, she pushes a cream envelope into my hands.

'How many applications for immigration have been supported by members of the aristocracy?' I wonder aloud, assuming that's what she handed me. Before leaving for the Seychelles I'd tasked Flynn and Will with helping me keep Paisley in the country. 'It must pay to have friends in high places.'

'In high places with low minds,' Sadie corrects.

'Well,' I reply, tapping my palm with the envelope. 'My thanks to the eighty-ninth Lord Travers, then.'

'There haven't been eighty-nine Lord Travers,' Will pipes up, slinging his arm around Sadie.

'Just as well,' Sadie replies. 'The world couldn't take that many. Come on, Doctor P,' she adds, which is a name that makes no sense to me—and I know better than to ask. 'You go and protect Flynn from the perils of an angry lady with a pointy umbrella, while I get cuddles from Louis and Juno.'

As the pair walk away, I open the envelope in my hand, expecting to find some affidavit or paperwork relating to Paisley's visa. Instead, I find a note in a feminine hand. It's not a penmanship I recognise, but one I know, given time, I will. There's much we don't know about each other, but we've a lifetime to learn it all. *And I look forward to every moment of it.*

Darling Keir,

If you were a woman, they'd say you are a nurturer. And I suppose my love would make me a lesbian. (lol jks) I just wanted to say, thank you for taking me into your stable of nurturing. I see you and I see what you do for those you love.

I just wanted to say that this marriage means I get to cherish you, too.

And in case I forget to tell you later, thank you for loving me, and thank you for taking me into your family.

All my love, Paisley.

P.S. I'll be the one in the knock-out white dress . . . the white dress I can't wait for you to peel me out of later.

'Fuck me, trouble,' I whisper to the empty space. 'You bring me to my fuckin' knees.'

After a few deep breaths, and a swift shot of rum, I make my way down to the private beach where we've chosen to hold the ceremony. Our friends and family are already there, seated on lace tied chairs. Our aisle is sand and rose petals, our altar a white flower festooned pagoda.

I take my place beside the smiling celebrant, his hibiscus pink shirt pulled tight across his barrel of a stomach. The sun is setting, bleeding gold into the horizon as the strains of a guitar nearby begins to accompany the soft susurrus of the waves. As I turn, it suddenly occurs to me we haven't asked anyone to walk my bride to me.

As Paisley steps onto the beach, I realise I don't have to worry as she's holding the hand of my daughter. *The two halves of my whole heart.*

White dresses with a simple Grecian air, bare feet and pink painted toenails, matching milkmaid braided hairstyles, woven with tiny white flowers. With each step the golden pair take, my heart swells. *Can a heart grow to accommodate more? To adapt?* These are questions I've asked myself. The answer is in how I feel when I look at her. When I look at my family.

And then they're here, standing before me. Everything I'll ever need but didn't understand I wanted. I kiss my daughter's head as she places my bride's hand in mine. We're so close, Paisley and I, almost sharing breath. With the proximity, I can't resist the temptation, so slide my lips against hers in a glancing touch. Because I will never be as full as I am right now.

New love. New life. New beginning.

The End

Acknowledgements

Thanks to my family. I know, I'm getting worse, but it's the werdz, not dementia—I promise! Thanks to M for picking up the familial slack. Didn't I tell you they were a cactus bunch?!

To Natasha Harvey, the Queen of OCD, thanks for listening, OCD-ing, keeping me right, and listening to me panic and flap. And thank you for ringing me and sharing your very visceral reaction to the ending. I hope it hits everyone else in the feelz, too.

To Aimee Bowyer, or Aimee *Boo-yaah!* Thanks for stepping in at the last minute and de-englishing Paisley. It was an arduous job and I'm stoked you stepped in to the fray. You're fab, lady.

And thanks to the Lambs for putting up with my general lack of timing and surprise releases. And thanks to the people who pick up my books. I have no words.

About the Author

Donna writes about exotic locations and the men you aren't married to but might sometimes wish you were. Escapism reads with heart, humour, and plenty of steam.

Hailing from the North of England, she's a nomad at heart moving houses and continents more times than she cares to recall. She once worked at a school like the one described in her Pretty Series, where the wheels of her imagination began to turn.

When not bashing away at a keyboard, Donna can usually be found, good book in hand, hiding from her family and responsibilities. She likes her wine and humour dry, and her mojitos sweet, and language salty.